The Osterlund Saga

Two generations taking twentieth-century America by storm!

It's 1933 and the great depression has left heiress Jolie Cramer's family in ruin. A convenient marriage to wealthy Randal Osterlund is her only hope. Could this practical partnership actually be a perfect match?

Find out in

Marriage or Ruin for the Heiress

Twenty-three years later... It's 1956 and Jolie and Randal's daughter, Randi, is all grown up! When she's reunited with her high school enemy, sparks fly! But their fiery encounter has unexpected consequences...

Look out for

The Heiress and the Baby Boom

Coming next month!

Author Note

Thank you for picking up a copy of *Marriage or Ruin for the Heiress*. The crash of the stock market in 1929 brought on the great depression that impacted the world and lasted for over the next decade. It was a devastating and crippling time, and people sought for possible ways to provide for their families.

Yet life went on, as did love, and that was what I enjoyed most about writing this story. Jolie and Randal had a lot on their minds and shoulders when it came to providing for their families, but they refused to give up on their dreams. Because of that, their dedication and resiliency, they also find their happily-ever-after.

I hope you enjoy their journey from an arranged marriage to everlasting love.

LAURI
ROBINSON

Marriage or Ruin
for the Heiress

HARLEQUIN®
HISTORICAL™

PLEASE RECYCLE • **THIS PRODUCT IS RECYCLABLE**

Recycling programs
for this product may
not exist in your area.

ISBN-13: 978-1-335-40760-3

Marriage or Ruin for the Heiress

Copyright © 2021 by Lauri Robinson

This edition published by arrangement with Harlequin Books S.A.

For questions and comments about the quality of this book,
please contact us at CustomerService@Harlequin.com.

Harlequin Enterprises ULC
22 Adelaide St. West, 41st Floor
Toronto, Ontario M5H 4E3, Canada
www.Harlequin.com

Printed in U.S.A.

A lover of fairy tales and history, **Lauri Robinson** can't imagine a better profession than penning happily-ever-after stories about men and women in days gone past. Her favorite settings include World War II, the Roaring Twenties and the Old West. Lauri and her husband raised three sons in their rural Minnesota home and are now getting their just rewards by spoiling their grandchildren. Visit her at laurirobinson.blogspot.com, Facebook.com/lauri.robinson1 or Twitter.com/laurir.

Books by Lauri Robinson

Harlequin Historical

Diary of a War Bride
A Family for the Titanic Survivor

The Osterlund Saga

Marriage or Ruin for the Heiress

Twins of the Twenties

Scandal at the Speakeasy
A Proposal for the Unwed Mother

Sisters of the Roaring Twenties

The Flapper's Fake Fiancé
The Flapper's Baby Scandal
The Flapper's Scandalous Elopement

Brides of the Roaring Twenties

Baby on His Hollywood Doorstep
Stolen Kiss with the Hollywood Starlet

Visit the Author Profile page
at Harlequin.com for more titles.

Dedicated to Ivadelle Salmon for
being such a wonderful fan.

Chapter One

Chicago, 1933

Disbelief rendered Jolie Cramer speechless. How could it not? She'd never expected her life would come to this. Being sold. Like she was a dress hanging in a store window. There was more to a dress than thread and material. There were hours of designing, sewing, pressing. And there was more to her. She had feelings, goals, dreams.

Staring out her bedroom window that overlooked the massive backyard of their prestigious downtown home, made with brick and mortar generations ago, she shook her head, trying to dispel the disbelief still holding her mind hostage like a mob victim. The bright sunshine of the warm summer day was out of place compared to the iciness filling her. "You can't be serious."

"He's a very wealthy and prominent young man. Not to mention handsome. You should be happy he agreed."

A peculiar burning sensation spread over Jolie as she spun around to face her mother. Disbelief was replaced with anger boiling hot enough to cook a three-minute egg in less than a minute. Everyone knew Randal Osterlund was wealthy and prominent, and every woman under the age of forty in all of Chicago knew he was handsome. His silver-blue eyes were so unique, in such contrast with his dark hair, that they caught and held attention. Like many others, she'd found him attractive, until the last time she'd seen Randal. She'd been mortified with embarrassment that day and hoped to never set eyes on him again. "Happy?"

"Yes. I myself was flattered." Mother stood and patted the short brown curls at the nape of her neck, and then ran a hand over the finger waves that flattened the hair on the crown of her head. She'd worn her hair that way for a decade, despite the fact the short hairstyles of the twenties were now in the past. With an exaggerated sigh, her mother said, "I would consider remarrying myself, but as you know, your father is the only man I will ever love. There's not another one out there like him. I will never get over his death. Never. I still cry myself to sleep each and every night."

Jolie rubbed her forehead at the woe-is-me tale she'd heard a thousand times over. It wasn't that she didn't sympathize with her mother. They'd all loved her father dearly—he had been a wonderful man—but her mother just didn't seem to realize there were other people in this family who were still alive. Who might need her to do her job as their mother.

"There's no reason to act so shocked. We discussed this, Jolie."

"Discussed is not the same as agreeing, Mother," Jolie insisted. She had in no way agreed to anything. In fact, when her mother had brought up the subject of marrying to *save* the family last week, Jolie had voiced that marriage was not the answer and that there were other ways to *save* the family.

Her mother smoothed the floral bedspread on the corner of the bed where she had been sitting. "The taxes are due by the end of the month. If they aren't paid, this house will be sold by the city. If that happens, we will have no choice but to move to Kansas and live with Uncle LeRoy. Is that what you want for your brother and sister? For me? For you?"

No, it wasn't what she wanted. Jolie closed her eyes at the overwhelming despair that overshadowed all of the other emotions running rampant inside her. Uncle LeRoy, her mother's brother and their only living relative, lived in Kansas, where they were not only experiencing the great depression blanketing the nation, they also had dust storms that were burying entire towns. She'd heard stories on the radio, read about them in the newspaper as well as the firsthand accounts Uncle LeRoy penned in his letters.

The dust storms that were plaguing the central plains is why people were calling it the *Dirty Thirties*.

Damn the stock market crash of 1929. That's what had started it all. It had wreaked havoc on the country and her family. Three months after that crash her father died of a heart attack, and for the four years since then, her family had barely survived on the small amounts of holdings and cash her father hadn't had invested in the markets. Hers wasn't the only family affected, but unlike others, who'd openly admitted their dire straits and did something, or at least attempted to do something constructive, her mother had kept their poverty hidden. And continued to. Very few people knew the

Cramers were surviving on bread crumbs bought with the pennies they'd managed to scrape out of the bottom of the washing machine and beneath the sofa cushions.

"We've sold everything worth selling," Mother said. "This house is all we have left. All we have left of your father. This is our only choice."

"No, it's not," Jolie argued. "We could get jobs. You and me and Silas. Even Chloe could—"

"I won't hear of such a thing! Your father must be rolling over in his grave to hear you say that! He did not believe in women working!" Mother spun around and marched to the door. "Silas has two more years of college. Once he graduates, he'll take over providing for this family. Until then, it's up to me. And you." She pulled open the bedroom door. "I suggest you change. Randal will be here in half an hour."

"Change into what?" Jolie threw her hands in the air as her mother shut the door as if she hadn't heard the question. "Everything I own has been made over so many times the material is worn out," she muttered and walked over to the bed, plopped onto the mattress.

She wasn't one to pitch a fit, but she was contemplating doing so on this occasion.

Randal Osterlund.

Huffing out a breath, she flipped onto her back and stared at the ceiling. Of all the men in Chicago, why him?

Jolie sat up as her heart began to beat like it had the wings of a hummingbird. Or is that exactly why? He knew how destitute her family had become. She'd hoped he'd forgotten about their encounter at the grocer, but obviously, he hadn't.

It had been so embarrassing. There had been money

in the bank to cover the check. She'd just made a deposit the day before, after getting paid for altering a dress for Mrs. Rivard—unknown to Mother, of course, because heaven forbid a female Cramer would work for a living. Jolie had done that often enough, altered clothing and sewn underclothes for Mrs. Rivard and her elderly friends, and put the money in the bank so when they needed groceries, anyone in her family could pick them up and pay with a check. No one in her family had ever written a bad check, and she was certain that Amy Casswell had put her name on *the list* on purpose—for no reason other than spite. Amy had hated her for years.

Why had she stopped at the Casswell store? Why? She knew better!

Randal had just so happened to be the next customer, and the cashier had just so happened to sweetly explain to him that the Cramer family's name was on *the list*—the list of people who couldn't pay with checks. The depression was felt by many, and no-credit lists, along with lists of people who were known to write bad checks, were commonplace. The Cramer name was not on any other list, just the one at Casswell's.

It had only been a few items, and Randal had offered to pay. Fully humiliated, she had refused his offer, told the clerk she'd never shop there again and left the store.

That had been two months ago, and Jolie had informed her entire family they were not allowed to shop at Casswell's. Amy had started a feud between the two of them in elementary school. One that had never ended. Last she'd heard, Amy had gone to Europe or Asia, or some such place, but that hadn't stopped her childhood enemy from embarrassing Jolie from afar. With her father owning the largest grocery store chain in the state, the stock market crash hadn't crushed the Casswells' business like it had others, and therefore had never affected Amy. Her clothes had always been the most stylish, and her attitude the haughtiest.

With all that circling in her mind, Jolie couldn't even begin to grasp at hairs as to why Randal Osterlund would consider marrying her instead of Amy, let alone agree to it.

It didn't make sense.

Amy Casswell was the type of woman a man like him would marry.

Jolie leaped to her feet. That was it! Amy had accused her of *eyeing* Randal last year at Marie Beyer's— now Marie Gains's—wedding. She hadn't been eyeing him, even though he had looked extremely handsome in his tuxedo. That had to be it. He and Amy must still be dating, corresponding while Amy was abroad—or had been abroad—and now Amy was attempting to humiliate her. Again.

That had to be it. He must be trying to embarrass her—for Amy. Get her family's hopes up and then expose their dire financial straits without marrying her.

That wasn't about to happen on Jolie's watch. Amy wouldn't win this time.

With all the determination of a bee finding the perfect flower, Jolie flew across the room, opened her closet door and homed in on the one and only dress she could wear for her meeting with Randal.

It was actually a skirt and blouse, but she'd used two old dresses to make the ensemble. The blouse, white with tiny blue polka dots, had gathered, flouncy sleeves that fell just short of her elbows, and the skirt, blue with tiny white polka dots, had a tight-fitting waist, with two tiny strips of the white material around the knee-length hem. It was one of her favorites, mainly because it was in the current popular style.

That would give her confidence in facing down Randal. Her family might be broke, but she wasn't broken.

Randal Osterlund stared at the door of the brick home in one of the older, downtown neighborhoods, where many shipping and railroad magnates had built homes during the previous century. Old money—and lots of it—had once filled these neighborhoods.

His family's home, just as big and just as expensive, was on the other side of town, where new money had created their own neighborhoods within the last couple of decades, as a way of distinguishing between the two.

Old and new money. He knew all about that, and the stories, trials and tribulations that went along with it. He also knew that there were empty houses in both old and new money neighborhoods due to the market crash.

It was his job to make sure his family home remained as is, and that his family maintained their status of being one of the wealthiest in Chicago. That had been driven into him since the day he'd been born.

His grandfather had arrived in America with little more than two coins to rub together in his pockets and had used them to create a family fortune. He'd struck oil in Pennsylvania and eventually sold his oil fields to Rockefeller and his Standard Oil company, before moving west, to Chicago. There, Randal's father had increased the family fortune in the stock market, and that's what Randal had inherited when his father had died seven years ago.

Stock market investments.

The crash had affected the family's finances, just as it had nearly every other family in the nation, but he'd taken steps before the crash had happened and diversified his holdings far more than other investors had. The trouble was, that diversification wasn't enough to continue to bring in the money needed to hold their status, and his grandfather was breathing fire down his neck to do something about that, to make his own footprint in the financial world.

One that would keep the Osterlunds on the top.

Money, that's what makes a man. That had been the motto he'd grown up on.

Randal had discovered the way to make that happen— airplanes—but he had one hurdle in his way.

Marriage.

He didn't like the idea. Marriage did little more than make it harder for a man to focus on his plans and goals, to be his own man. And love…that was dangerous.

He'd seen men go down that rabbit hole. Good men. Men who'd thought they'd found love, the perfect wife, only to have said perfect wife leave them for another and take the contents of their bank account with her.

That wouldn't happen to him.

He might need a marriage, but he would never need love. Never be broken by it.

At the click of the knob turning, Randal straightened his stance and planted his best false smile on his face. Never one to give in to nerves, he was surprised at his own reaction to the idea of facing Jolie Cramer. He'd seen her at a wedding last year and had been struck by her beauty. That image had been the first one that had come to him when he'd considered his need to marry.

"Mr. Randal, I'm sorry, I didn't hear your knock."

Amelia Cramer was middle-aged, with short brown hair, and appeared soft and small, but there was an undeniable shrewdness about her. He wondered if Jolie had that same shrewdness hidden beneath her quiet and meek exterior. Her family was about to lose their home and their only hope was for her to marry someone who could pay the taxes owed on it.

That was him.

The fact that Jolie was also very attractive was simply an added benefit.

"I do hope you haven't been waiting long," Amelia said.

"I just arrived and had yet to knock, Mrs. Cramer," Randal replied.

"Oh, please, call me Amelia." With a sly smile, she tugged on her earlobe. "After all, we will soon be family."

Randal lifted a brow. "Jolie agreed?"

"Yes, of course she agreed," Amelia responded with another coy smile. "Do come in. She will be down in a moment. Chloe, her sister, just went upstairs to tell her you've arrived."

Which told him that Amelia had been watching out the window for him. The woman was desperate. He had questioned Amy's tales that the Cramer family had lost all they'd had in the stock market crash and that the shock of it had caused the death of Joseph Cramer, because Amy talked like that about everyone. It wasn't until a couple of months ago, when he'd made a quick stop at the store and encountered Jolie, that he'd begun to wonder if Amy might have been telling the truth.

That unexpected encounter had planted Jolie on the

top of his list for possible partners. Quite unexpectedly, the opportunity to investigate if Jolie, and her family, might be open to his plan, had appeared today, when he'd bumped into Amelia Cramer at the courthouse this morning.

"Would you care for a drink?" Amelia asked as she led him into the front room of the home.

He instantly noticed the empty spots on the walls where paintings had obviously once hung, bare spots on the floors where rugs had once lain, and the minimalist furniture and accessories in the room.

Amelia Cramer made no excuses for the missing pieces as she stopped near a small wooden credenza. "I have wine or brandy."

"No, thank you, I'm fine," Randal replied as his attention was drawn toward the stairway that swept upward along the elegant curve of the dark wooden banister until it disappeared beyond the ceiling of the front room. A pair of white heels, gracefully stepping from stair to stair, came into view, followed by a very stylish amount of stockinged legs. A white-and-blue dress that highlighted her slender figure appeared next, and then he got his first full look of Jolie.

Both at that wedding and the store that wouldn't take her check, he'd acknowledged her beauty, but this evening, he was viewing it in a different light.

If he deemed that she was right for the position, and if she agreed, they would marry. That was a sobering thought. He'd sworn off marriage and love for years, and had done so again, vehemently, a few months ago, when Amy had laid down an ultimatum. Either he married her, or she would find someone else to marry.

He'd wished her well.

No woman would ever rule him.

Less than a week later, he'd questioned if he should have married her when he'd discovered that Carl Jansen was considering selling his airplane business—but only to a married man. Amy had been gone for months now, and though he'd fleetingly considered contacting her, he'd chosen alternatives instead. If he had to get married, he wanted it to be with someone he could live with. That wasn't Amy.

The only thing Amy was faithful to was money. He'd had people breathing down his neck to make more money his entire life, and didn't need a wife doing that to him.

What he wanted was someone quiet and kind, who would be happy simply running his household.

Watching Jolie stop shy of stepping off the final step of the stairs, he stepped forward. "Hello, Miss Cramer."

She gave a slight nod. "Mr. Osterlund."

He held out a hand, and when she took it, he lifted it to kiss the back of it while watching her closely. "You look very lovely this evening." Her light brown hair was parted in the middle, with both sides rolled and pinned back, exposing delicate ears with tiny pearl earrings dangling from each lobe, but it was her eyes that had snagged his full attention. They were dark brown, and full of hostility. In that moment, he questioned if she should be on his list. Let alone topping it.

She took the final step off the stairs and with the clear intent of letting him know he'd held her hand long enough, pulled it from his grasp.

"I've made reservations for us at the Congress Hotel Restaurant," he informed her, attempting to take the upper hand. As much as her mother may have suggested

Jolie was agreeable with his proposition, Jolie clearly wasn't impressed with the idea.

"Oh, my, that is the finest dining site in the city," Amelia said. "The chef worked at the Waldorf Astoria Hotel in New York before moving here."

Jolie provided no response to her mother, but the hostility in her eyes gleamed a shade darker.

Taking full note of that, Randal said, "We can leave whenever you're ready."

With her elegant chin lifted high, Jolie stepped toward the door. "I'm ready."

He wasn't thrilled with the idea of marriage any more than she appeared to be, but he liked challenges, and the idea of winning Jolie over was one he couldn't deny thrilled him. He stepped around her, opened the door and bid farewell to her mother as he followed Jolie outside.

His new, dark blue Cadillac was parked in the driveway, and he kept his hands to himself as she walked directly to the passenger door. Though the sides of her hair were rolled and pinned up, the back was left hanging loose, well past her shoulders, and shimmered in the evening sunlight. The fit of her dress said it had been tailor-made, which made him wonder if they were as impoverished as he'd been led to believe. If not, his plan may not work. Unless there was something else that Jolie wanted out of the deal…

He opened the door, waited as she sat and swung in her feet, then he closed the door and walked around the hood of the car. As well-known as Jolie was amongst the younger crowd, she'd never had a steady boyfriend, and that intrigued him. Amy had declared that it was because Jolie was as homely as a wet dog, which was another flat-out lie.

He'd barely started the car after climbing in when she said, "When did Amy return?"

It took a moment of thoughtful concentration for Randal to release the clutch and back out of the driveway, because he'd had to search his mind for the latest news that might have included Amy. He'd never paid any attention to rumors and had to wonder if he'd missed news of Amy's return. Although, it wouldn't have interested him anyway. "I wasn't aware that she had returned."

Jolie twisted and leveled those dark brown eyes, full of scorn, on him. "Don't the two of you correspond?"

"No."

"Why?"

He shrugged. "Why would I correspond with her? She left the country to find a rich husband, and I hope she does."

Her frown knit her brows together. "Weren't you rich enough for her?"

"Perhaps, but I had no interest in becoming her husband."

Her frown turned into a look of disbelief. "That's not what I heard."

"Perhaps you were listening to the wrong people."

She huffed out a tiny breath. "Perhaps, but I doubt it."

"I don't." He shrugged. "I have no idea where Amy is, nor do I care."

"But the two of you dated for some time."

"We attended events together, but that doesn't mean I was interested in marrying her." Sensing more than fully knowing, he asked, "Why didn't the two of you ever get along?"

"Who says we didn't?"

He glanced at her and grinned, letting her know that she wasn't hiding her dislike of Amy any more than Amy had hidden hers of Jolie.

She pinched her lips together as if hiding her own grin. "I'm assuming she told you about the ink episode."

"No, I don't know about any ink episode." But he was certainly curious now, given the tone in her voice.

She grew thoughtful for a moment, then asked, "She didn't tell you?"

"No."

After another moment of silence, she asked, "Is this about the episode at her father's store? Because I had money in the bank that day."

In his opinion, the store clerk should have been ashamed of her behavior. He'd wanted to catch up with Jolie after she'd left the store, and tell her so, but had figured she'd be too embarrassed to appreciate his thoughts.

"And," she continued, "I know, this…arrangement… between us has something to do with Amy."

He focused on steering the car along the curving road that led out of the neighborhood and into downtown. "This isn't about that day, and it doesn't have anything to do with Amy."

She waited until he pulled the car to a stop at an intersection, then leveled a steady, brown-eyed glare on him that he couldn't ignore. Turning, he waited, because she was clearly about to say something.

"Then, what is it about? And be aware, I can pick out a lie as easily as I can pick out a con man."

He withheld the want to grin and turned his gaze back on the traffic. There was more to Jolie Cramer than he'd imagined, and that didn't disappoint him. In fact, he appreciated her bluntness. "I thought you knew." He pulled the car onto the main road. "I need a wife, and it's my understanding that you need a husband."

Chapter Two

"I don't need a husband," Jolie insisted, irate that he wouldn't admit the truth behind his reasons. "I don't need anything."

"Except to have the taxes on your home paid. Or do you like the idea of moving to Kansas?"

That charged her ire even more. "Is there anything my mother didn't mention?" Because there was obviously plenty her mother hadn't mentioned to her.

"Such as?"

The list of things her mother could have said was longer than she was willing to discuss. Her mother was disillusioned and believed life could go back to what it had been before the market crash. Jolie knew that wasn't possible. "Why do you need a wife?" With his looks and status, nearly any woman in Illinois would fall at his feet, agreeing to marry him in a heartbeat. She wasn't one of them, and there was no reason for him to believe she might be such a woman.

"For the same reason you do." He glanced her way, flashing a smile. "Money."

Her insides shivered at the same time her heart skipped a beat. "You want money from me?"

He chuckled. "No."

"Good, because you'd be out of luck if that was your goal." She hadn't said that to make him laugh, but his chuckle didn't irritate her. It was the truth. A laughable one at that.

"I'm in need of a wife in order to complete a business deal that I'm interested in making," he said. "My plan is designed to benefit you, too. And your family."

Jolie held her opinion of that while he pulled the car into the hotel parking lot. She needed time to consider if there truly was any way she could benefit. Her family—possibly. Her—none that she could think of. That wasn't likely to change, either, no matter how long she thought about it.

"We can discuss it in more length over dinner." He turned off the car. "If you are still in agreement?"

She met him eyeball for eyeball. "I was never in agreement."

"I am beginning to understand that, although your mother led me to believe otherwise." He removed the key from the ignition without pulling his gaze off her. "But I have a sense that you might be interested."

A hint of her ire withdrew. She couldn't say why, other than he was right. Partially. She *might* be interested, only because the taxes did need to be paid, and because she was interested in what type of a business deal he was interested in making. She didn't want to become her mother, sitting at home crocheting doilies and being the perfect housewife, and then taking to bed, weeping and sobbing for months on end after her husband had died. Giving someone that type of power in the name of love was ridiculous.

It was 1933! Women had jobs, made their own money and didn't *need* husbands.

"Am I right?" He opened his door, but was looking at her, waiting for an answer.

"Possibly," she admitted. "I'll need to know more."

All she truly had left was her pride, and at times, it was a stubborn pride at that. Currently, it was telling her that nothing he could say would justify marrying him and giving up on what she wanted. However, her conscience was chiming in louder. More than just the taxes needed to be paid. Other bills, as well as Silas's tuition, were past due. There were no pennies left to be found in the washing machine or under the sofa cushions, and unless she was willing to move her entire family to Kansas—and have them all blame her for that the rest of her life—she needed to listen to what he had to say.

Agreeing would go against the grain, it would entail agreeing that she was willing to give over control of her life, and she wasn't willing to do that. Using the time it took him to walk around the car to open her door, she worked on convincing herself that she would listen to what he had to say only for the benefit of her family.

She stepped out of the car and walked beside him to the hotel. For all of her outer bravery, her insides were quaking as if she was about to face a judge and jury for a crime she hadn't committed.

Or maybe it was for one she was about to commit.

The murder of her hopes and dreams.

"We can go someplace else if you prefer," Randal said.

Swallowing some of her damnable pride that could be her downfall if she wasn't careful, she shook her head. "No. This is fine." There truly was no reason to pretend she wasn't nervous. About everything. She was; there was so much at stake. However, she could pretend that her last nerve was about to snap for other reasons. Lifting her chin, she said, "It's been a long time since I've eaten in a restaurant."

"I hope you will enjoy it."

She wouldn't, but to be fair, that wasn't his fault. In all reality, for reasons she couldn't understand, she was finding it difficult to dislike him.

Within minutes they were seated at table in a corner that allowed privacy, in the large and somewhat crowded dining room. The single flickering candle on each table was meant to add ambience, elegance to the already sophisticated atmosphere. So did the soft music being played by the quartet on a triangular stage near a small dance area where several couples were gracefully sashaying around the floor. It seemed prohibition had been all but forgotten. Dining clubs, such as this, were now as popular as speakeasies had once been. The one thing neither prohibition nor the depression could stop was people wanting to drink, dance and have fun, to go on living despite the obstacles. Maybe she could learn to do that, too.

"Would you care for a cocktail?" Randal asked.

"No, thank you." They were here, so might as well get down to business. "Exactly what will you get out of marrying me?"

He leaned back in his chair, and gave a slight shake of his head, as if he'd thought of something to say, but chose not to. "A wife."

Her teeth clenched every time the word was mentioned. She didn't want to be a wife. She wanted to be in charge of her own life. "Why do you need a wife?" She held up a hand for him to wait before answering. "And don't tell me it's for a business deal."

"That's the truth."

A great sense of frustration filled her. No one needed a wife in order to make a business deal. She withheld her response as the waiter arrived at their table and made small talk while filling their water glasses from a silver pitcher and providing them with two menus. When he took his leave, she idly opened the folded menu. "What is the rest of the truth?" Already frustrated, she added, "And please, don't make this more difficult by skirting the truth."

"I'm not skirting the truth, nor am I attempting to make it difficult." He set his menu aside. "My father, like yours, invested heavily in the stock market, and it was good to him. When he died seven years ago, I took over his investments and diversified them, which proved to work in my favor when the market crashed. I fared better than most and am now looking to increase my wealth by purchasing a business of my own, one where I'm in charge of the growth and success." He took a drink off his water glass. "The man who owns the business that I'm interested in purchasing will only sell to a married man."

Like the teeth on a zipper, things came together in her mind in one swift movement. As ridiculous as his reason sounded, Jolie believed him, because she knew the business and she knew the man. "You're interested in buying Dad Jansen's airplane company?"

Randal took another drink off his water. He couldn't deny he was impressed by her straightforwardness, and by her astuteness, but was a bit shocked by her knowledge and the fact she called Carl Jansen "Dad." Many people knew Carl, but only those very close to him called him Dad and, as far as he knew, Carl hadn't made it public that he was interested in selling his airplane business. Carl had two sons—married sons—that he'd turned his other businesses over to on their marriages years ago.

"That's why you chose me, isn't it?" she asked. "Because Dad's my godfather."

Through his research, Randal was aware that Carl Jansen and her father had been friends, but he had not known they'd been that close. However, that made her an even more perfect choice. He'd spent his life so far investing in other people's companies, and he was ready for that to change. He wanted to invest in his own company. Build it into something great rather than merely pushing numbers, and Carl's company had the potential of doing just that. "I did not know that he was your godfather."

She nodded her head slowly as the hint of a grin formed. "You didn't mention that you were interested in buying Dad's business to my mother, did you?"

"No. There was no reason."

She let out a huff. "If you had, we wouldn't be sitting here right now. She doesn't like Dad. Never has. If she did, she would have accepted his assistance after my father died, and my family wouldn't be in the situation we are now."

A plethora of questions filled his head, but Randal refrained from making any further comment as the waiter approached their table. Nodding toward her menu, he asked, "Do you have a preference of what to order or need more time? If not, I'll order the special for both of us."

Like him, she had barely glanced at the menu, and when she nodded while shrugging, he ordered the chef's evening special for both of them. The waiter explained the meal included braised pork chops and sweet potatoes, and after a few additional questions concerning options pertaining to the meal, left.

Randal took a moment before returning to their conversation about Carl Jansen. He wanted that company more than he'd wanted anything before, but if her mother hated Carl, that could be a real bump in the road.

Her mouth twitched slightly as she let out a loud sigh. "It'll never work."

"Why?"

"Because if Dad figures out you married me just to buy his company, he'll never sell it to you."

Randal had already considered that, and wasn't going to let it deter him. "He might, but I have to take that risk. I'm not looking for a loving wife, Jolie. I'm looking for a partner. One who will benefit from our union as much as I will, which is why I'm considering you."

A hint of something—he wasn't sure what—flashed in her eyes, but she remained silent, waiting for him to say more.

He chose his words carefully. "I'll pay the taxes on your family's home, pay your brother's tuition and other outstanding bills, as well as provide your family with a monthly allowance, and not demand anything from you, other than you perform the social duties of being my wife."

"Social duties?"

"Yes, attend functions, dinner dates, parties, those types of things, as needed."

"For how long?"

Interesting. He hadn't considered a timeline or end date. To him, marriage didn't have one. "I have no intention of going into this just for the short term and then seeking a divorce. No need to worry about that."

Brows lifted, she asked, "Do I look worried?"

"No, you don't, but I do recognize that your family would be back in the same position as they are now if that was to happen."

She opened her mouth as if she was going to speak, but then closed it and looked around the room.

"You don't have to decide tonight," he said, fully aware of just how life-changing this would be for both of them. "You can think about it for a few days."

"Is that what you are going to do?" She met his gaze squarely. "Think about it? Take the other women you are *considering* out for dinner?"

"If you were to say yes tonight, I would be ready to set the wedding date with you."

"And if I say no?"

"I would review my list of other potential wives."

She tried hard to not smile, but it eventually came through, along with an adorable dimple in one cheek. "I have to say, you do appear to be an honest man."

He gave her a nod. "And you appear to be an honest woman. Lying to each other right from the start wouldn't set a very good foundation for us."

"No, it wouldn't." She took a sip of water off her glass. "Will you tell me more about Dad's airplane company?"

"Yes." He leaned closer to the table. "Will you tell me about the ink episode?"

Her cheeks pinkened. "Why would you want to know about that?"

He shrugged. "Because it must be important to you, otherwise you wouldn't have brought it up." Watching the influx of emotions that crossed her face, he added, "And, for the record, I think that clerk at Casswell's should have been ashamed for the way she treated you that day. I was impressed by the way you handled it."

"By refusing your offer to pay for my items and walking out?"

"Yes. That took pride, dignity."

She shook her head. "I should have known better than to go in that store."

"Why?"

"Because Amy has hated me forever."

He'd never put much credence in what Amy said about others because she'd never had a good thing to say about anyone—man or woman. "Since the ink episode?"

"Before then. That just increased her hatred."

"What happened?"

"We were in elementary school and the teacher asked me to fill the ink pens for penmanship, and that made Amy mad. She always called me the teacher's pet. Anyway, she acted like she was going to the pencil sharpener and along the way, tried to knock over a bottle of ink, but I caught it." With what appeared to be a regretful expression, she sighed. "And then let it fall from my hand. It hit the edge of the desk, shattered and splattered her with ink. She had blue freckles for weeks."

It sounded simple, but he'd seen the wrath of Amy

come out when a waitress had accidentally spilled a glass of water on their table once. He'd been embarrassed by her behavior, and after insisting to the owner that the waitress did not need to be fired, had left a hefty tip for the young woman.

"It was mean of me to do," Jolie said. "But I had still been mad over her cutting my hair."

"Amy cut your hair?"

Jolie nodded, picked up her napkin and placed it on her lap due to the approaching waiter. "Yes. A year before that. My desk had been in front of hers, and she'd cut one of my braids off right at the back of my neck." She pointed to a spot on the nape of her neck and grimaced. "I'd thought she'd just been pulling my hair, and ignored her, until she handed me the braid."

He picked up his napkin, and as the waiter set their plates on the table, asked, "Handed you the braid?" It wasn't a laughing matter, but her expression was so adorable, he truly wanted to smile.

"Yes, she flopped it over my shoulder. The rest of my hair had to be cut short, it was awful. It took a year of growing out before I could braid it again, and it's never been that long again since."

He thanked the waiter, and assured him they didn't need anything else, before he cleared a chuckle from his throat and said, "How long had it been when she cut it?"

"Down to my waist. I'd never had it cut before then."

"That sounds awful for you."

"You ought to tell that to your face."

"Tell what?"

"How awful it was, because you look like you're trying extremely hard not to laugh."

He met her gaze, and as her smile broke through, so did his. "So are you."

"It was awful, but like a lot of things, I can laugh about it now." She scooped up a forkful of mashed sweet potatoes. "Including the ink episode."

"That's very mature of you," he said.

"Maybe. Or maybe I'm just imagining her with all those blue freckles."

Chuckling, he cut a slice off his pork chop. He couldn't remember a time when he'd found a woman more likable in a shorter amount of time.

"Your turn," she said. "Tell me about Dad's airplane business."

As Carl's goddaughter, she might know more about it than him. "Do you know when he's putting it on the market?" he asked.

"No, I wasn't aware that he was selling it, but I do know that neither of his sons want it. He bought it four years ago, and they'd thought he'd been crazy to buy it at his age. It's just when you said the company you wanted to buy would only be sold to a married man, I knew you were talking about Dad. He always said that he was successful because of Anna. His wife."

"I've heard that," Randal replied. "And that he believes a man without a woman behind him will never amount to anything. Which is why I'm interested in getting married. With the right man at the helm, his airplane company could become the largest in the world."

"And you want to be that man?"

"I do." He looked directly at her and asked, "But the real question is, do you want to be the woman behind that man?"

Chapter Three

Jolie stared at the mail in her hand. Overdue bills. It had been four days since she had gone out for dinner with Randal and during that time, the turmoil inside her had grown. It had grown within the household, too. Her mother was barely speaking to her, and just this morning, before leaving for school, Chloe informed her that she'd run away before moving to Kansas.

Her sister was fifteen, and headstrong, making Jolie believe they could wake up one morning to discover Chloe had disappeared during the night. Chloe was also afraid. Afraid that if Jolie refused, she was next. Unfortunately, that was a real possibility.

Silas was the only one who appeared slightly understanding, stating—in private because Mother would have a fit if she heard him—that he'd quit college and get a job.

Jolie couldn't let that happen any more than she could let Chloe run away or marry some man their mother forced on her, and ultimately was leaning toward accepting Randal's proposition, despite how frustrating it was to think of giving up her own dreams. All she'd ever wanted was to design and sew clothes. She'd been doing that for her dolls and herself for years, and wanted to build a business out of it. Getting married could change all that.

In spite of her frustration, a grin formed at the memory of eating dinner with Randal. They hadn't left the restaurant for hours after finishing. They'd shared childhood stories, and he'd told her more about how he'd taken over his father's business activities but was dedicated to creating his own. She didn't know much about airplanes, but he certainly did, and it had been interesting hearing him talk about them.

She hadn't met someone that easy to talk to for a long time, and most certainly, never a man.

But none of that, the laughing and talking, made her ready to jump in and marry him. She'd loved her father, deeply, and missed him, but when he'd died, she hadn't wanted to die, too. Not like her mother. Her mother still had days when she didn't get out of bed, claiming she missed him too much to do anything. That was no way to live and not a fate Jolie wanted for herself.

Her mother had also been jealous. Embarrassingly jealous at times. Jolie wouldn't live like that.

Even now, four years later, her mother was fully dedicated to his memory—and in keeping everything just how father would have wanted it.

The house.

Silas's education.

Women not working.

Both of her parents had thought it was cute that she sewed clothes for her dolls, but as she got older, and sewed her own, they'd refused to let her wear them. They had considered home-sewn clothing a sign of poverty.

Her mother still did, and Jolie was concerned that Randal might feel the same way.

That, however, was only one issue.

The other one was her fear of not knowing exactly what Dad would expect from Randal's wife. If it was to merely be a housewife, she didn't think she could do it. She'd dreamed of doing more for too many years.

She wished Anna was still alive... Jolie paused as a thought formed and twisted about in her mind. Anna wasn't, but Dad was. She didn't want to jeopardize Randal's chances at buying Dad's business, but talking to Dad could be exactly what she needed. If she could find out exactly what he meant about a man having a woman behind him, she might be able to figure out if it would be worth it or not.

Before she had a chance to change her mind, she dropped the mail on the desk in the study and pulled open the drawer that held the keys to her father's automobile. The gasoline in the car was highly rationed for emergency use only. To her, this was an emergency.

She hurried upstairs, changed into a more fashionable dress—another makeover from old clothes—and collected her purse. Mother was nowhere in sight, and Jolie hoped she wouldn't hear the sound of the car starting and try to stop her.

Half an hour later, she pulled the older model Cadillac, which was not nearly as nice or elegant as Randal's, onto the long, tree-lined driveway leading up to Dad Jansen's stately home. Painted white, with black shutters and tall white pillars framing the double set of mahogany front doors, the house sat on a tree-filled, five-acre lot that she'd played on many times as a child, while her father had visited with Dad.

What had seemed like a simple enough act, as well as a smart one, at home, was now making her stomach burn. She hadn't seen Dad for a long time, too long, and hoped he wouldn't hold that against her.

She parked the car on the paved driveway that looped around the front of the house, and took a moment to appease the nerves flapping about in her stomach by drawing a deep breath before climbing out of the car.

The front door was opened by the same dark-haired and brushy-browed butler as years before.

"Miss Cramer," he said. "It's good to see you."

"Hello, Mr. Blocker, is Dad home?"

"Of course, miss, right this way."

She followed him through the entranceway of tall, dark wood-stained walls, and down a long hallway to a closed door.

Without a word, Mr. Blocker spun about, opened the door with one hand and gave her a slight bow.

"Jolie, Jolie." Smiling, Dad walked toward her, arms wide. "You gave my old heart a start just pulling in the driveway, but look at you! As beautiful as ever. More beautiful than ever!"

She didn't expect the emotions that struck at seeing his smiling, wrinkled face and shimmering bald head, and had to press a hand to her mouth to cover the sob that bubbled in the back of her throat.

"Now, now, none of that," Dad said, pulling her into an embrace. "I've thought of you so often, Joey-girl. So often."

He was the only one who had ever called her that. Resting her head against the front of his shoulder, she closed her eyes against the tears slipping out. "I'm sorry, Dad. Sorry I haven't been over sooner. Sorry I wasn't at the funeral." She truly felt awful about that, and had been very angry at her mother for months for not allowing her to go to Anna's funeral. She'd considered going anyway, but knew her mother would never have forgiven her if she had.

"That's all right, sweetheart." He kissed the top of her head, then gripped her shoulders and took a step back, smiling. "You're here now, and I'm very happy about that."

She wished she could say the only reason she was here was to see him, because she should have been here long before now for just that purpose, but couldn't lie to him. "I need some advice, Dad."

He gave her shoulders a squeeze. "I'm glad you thought of me. Come, let's sit down."

She walked beside him into the depths of the massive library and took a seat on the navy-blue velvet-covered sofa, setting her purse on the floor by her ankle.

Dad sat down next to her. "How is everyone doing? Your mother? Brother? Sister?"

"Everyone is fine. Silas is doing well in college, and Chloe is now in high school."

"How are the finances?"

Dad had never been one to beat around the bush. "We're managing," she replied.

"Managing?" He shook his head and huffed out a breath that was full of frustration. "I do wish your mother wasn't so stubborn. As you know, I've offered assistance."

"I know. She believes…" Jolie let out a long sigh and shook her head. "I don't know what she believes. Maybe that the few stocks we still own are going to miraculously make us wealthy again."

The tight grimace on his face said what he thought about that, but he was too kind to voice it. Instead, he asked, "Do you need money? Just tell me how much."

Her heart softened. She'd always known that she could ask him for money, but not only would that upset her mother beyond all else, it wouldn't solve anything. "Thank you for the offer, but I'm not here for money. Just advice."

"All right, about what?"

She was still feeling unsettled, and wasn't quite ready to broach that subject. "First tell me how you are doing. I was truly sorry to hear of Anna's passing."

His dark blue eyes shimmered with moisture. "She was tired, Joey-girl, ready to go be with the Lord, but I surely do miss her, every day." He patted her hand. "The card you sent meant a lot to me."

"I wanted to attend the funeral, but—" She stopped because of the way he was shaking his head at her.

Rather than pat her hand again, he picked it up and sandwiched it between both of his. "Your mother loved your father with all of her heart, and I'll never hold that against her. That's how it should be. A man should love his wife just as strongly, and your father did. He loved her, and his children, above all else." He glanced at the bookshelves lining the walls. "True love is a rare commodity, Jolie. When you find it, you have to hang on to it tighter than anything else, because it is the one thing that can both make and break a person."

His hands shook slightly, and she cupped her other one over his. Her heart ached for the pain she saw in his profile, but words escaped her.

He turned back to her, smiled. "Your mother just didn't like your father and I being such good friends. She was jealous, that's all it was. Joseph was as close to me as any brother would have ever been, and for some reason, that made her feel threatened."

He was right, but it hadn't been just him. Her mother had been jealous over all of her father's friends and business associates. "It never threatened me, Dad, and I've missed you."

"I've missed you, too, Joey-girl." He lifted their clasped hands, kissed the back of hers that was on top and then released his hold. "Now, tell me, what sort of advice is it that you need?"

She smoothed the material of her skirt covering her thighs, knowing she couldn't put it off any longer. "Fatherly advice." Drawing in a deep breath, she stared straight ahead at the bookshelves. "I'm thinking about getting married."

"Well, now, that is a big decision. Do I know the young man?"

Not daring to look his way, she said, "His name is Randal Osterlund."

"Do you love him?" Dad asked.

"Do you know him?" she asked in response, glancing his way.

"I know of him," Dad answered. "I knew his father, and I know his grandfather, although Ness Osterlund doesn't get out much these days. Arthritis, I hear."

She had no idea if Randal's grandfather had arthritis or not, but felt inclined to nod.

"From what I hear, Randal is an upstanding young man. Took over for his father at a young age, when his father passed away in an automobile accident, and did well when the collapse hit. I'd say he's someone your father would approve of." He paused for a length of time. "But, the important thing is, do you love him?"

Love Randal? She barely knew him, furthermore, she wasn't interested in loving him or any other man. Unable to come up with a response, she looked at Dad.

He was looking at Anna's portrait hanging over the fireplace. "Did you know that my first job was at a saddle shop?"

"No," she replied, thankful to be off the love subject.

"I was twelve, big for my age and strong. The man who owned the shop had hurt his hand and couldn't drive an awl in the leather for the stitching. He hired me to do that and there was a girl who sewed the leather together."

"Anna?" she asked.

He nodded. "She was two years older than me. Fourteen. And the most beautiful girl I'd ever seen. I still remember that first saddle, and I remember looking at it, thinking how we'd created it together. That neither one of us could have done it alone." He let out a long sigh. "We worked at that shop together for the next six years, until I was eighteen and she was twenty. Then we got married, bought the shop a year later, and, well, from there we went on to buy more businesses, build them up, sell them and buy others, all the while building a family, a couple of houses and a damn good life together, all because of true love."

Perplexed, she asked, "You and Anna found true love when you were twelve and fourteen?"

"It found us," he said.

Even more perplexed, she stared at him.

"Sit back, Joey-girl, and let me tell you about true love."

* * *

Jolie had been on Randal's mind nonstop. Sometimes he'd thought of her long and hard, and other times, just a fleeting thought would make him smile. But he hadn't expected to see her, not at his office. They'd left the restaurant the other night with the understanding that they would both think about the venture for a time, and that he'd call her in a few days. Dismissing the shock of seeing her with a mental head shake, he stood. "Come in," he said to Jolie and nodded at his secretary. "Thank you, Mrs. Adams."

He walked around his desk, held the back of the chair as Jolie practically sank into it, and then made sure the door was tightly closed before he walked around her chair. The desire to touch her shoulder in comfort was hard to withhold, but he wasn't sure she'd welcome his touch. "Is something the matter?"

Clutching onto the handle of the white purse on her lap with both hands, she looked up at him as if the world was about to end. "I'm sorry."

A good amount of hope that she would agree with his plan disappeared. He leaned back against the edge of his desk. "There's nothing to be sorry about. You agreed to think about it, and I appreciate that you took the time to do that."

She blinked and stared at him blankly for a brief moment. "No." Shaking her head, she said, "I mean, yes. My answer is yes to marrying you."

The hope didn't return. In fact, it sank even lower at the sadness that still filled her eyes. After their dinner the other night, he'd come to believe she was the perfect woman to marry. She'd agreed that she wasn't looking for love, either, and had suggested that a partnership that could benefit both of them was something she would seriously consider. "And you're sorry about that?"

"Yes. I mean, no." She stood up, set her purse on the chair and pressed both hands to her temples as she turned and walked across the room.

"Which is it?" he asked.

She was wearing a red-and-white-striped dress, with a fitted waistline, and puffed sleeves. A red scarf was wrapped around her head and tied at the nape of her neck, beneath the long hair flowing in waves across her shoulders and down her back.

She reached the wall before she turned to face him. "I honestly don't know."

He folded his arms across his chest. "You can take more time to think about it."

"No, I can't." Shaking her head, she walked toward him. "And that's what I'm sorry about. The date is set."

Shocked for the second time in about as many minutes, he took a moment to check his hearing before asking, "The date is set?"

Grabbing the back of her chair so hard the purse almost tittered off it, she sighed loudly. "Yes. The date of our wedding has been set. Two weeks from tomorrow."

He planted both hands on the desk behind him as a shiver zipped up his spine. Maybe he wasn't as prepared for this as he'd thought.

"I hope that date works for you."

"It'll have to," he answered, trying to get his head around what she'd said.

"It's a Saturday, so…"

"I realize it's a Saturday, so my office will be closed." He took another moment to absorb it all. "Two weeks?"

She nodded. "My mother will take care of most of the planning, if that, too, is all right with you?"

Although he'd paid for both of his sisters' weddings, he had no idea what went into planning for them. He'd steered clear of his sisters during that time, doing little more than writing checks. "That's fine." Things still weren't adding up in his head. "But you can still take time to think about it. We can change the date."

"No, we can't. I've agreed, and we need to go ahead as planned."

"Why?"

She threw her hands in the air. "Because if we don't, Dad will never sell you his airplane business."

"How do you know that?"

"Because he's paying for the wedding."

That struck and sank in instantly. "I see."

"Yes," she said heavily. "And that's why I'm sorry. I didn't expect—"

"Of course you didn't." He truly believed she was sorry. Her mother was the one who wanted the marriage and would have pulled any strings possible to make it happen. He'd wanted it, too, and despite the idea that it would be nice to have a fraction of time to get used to the idea, it was too late for that. Her mother must have contacted Carl. There was no backing out now. Not if he wanted the airplane company. Which he did.

However, there was one final stipulation he did need to let her know. "There will be no infidelity. On either of our parts."

She shook her head as if disgusted. "You don't have to worry about that. I promise."

Satisfied with her answer, he pushed off the desk and picked up her purse, handed it to her. "Shall we?"

Frowning, she took the purse. "Shall we what?"

He stepped around her chair. "Go buy you an engagement ring."

"I don't need—" She stopped upon noticing the look he gave her.

"We need to make this look as real as possible," he said.

She turned to walk to the door. "You can say that again."

"Don't worry. It's just while we are in public. In private, there will be no expectations whatsoever."

"Where will that be?" she asked. "Where will we live?"

He grasped ahold of the doorknob, but didn't open it, fully aware that Mrs. Adams would be able to hear once the door was opened. "At my house. My grandfather and sister Danielle, and her husband, James, live there as well, but the house is large enough to accommodate us all."

"How many siblings do you have?"

"Two sisters. Danielle and Willa. Willa, her husband, Dan, and their two children live in their own home a short distance from mine."

She nodded, but had yet to look up at him since they'd stopped near the door. Fully understanding her hesitancy, he offered, "We could live with your family, if you'd prefer." It wouldn't be ideal, or acceptable to his grandfather, but he'd do it for a time if it would ease her worries.

She shook her head. "No."

"Or we could look for an apartment if you'd prefer."

"It's fine, Randal. Your house is fine."

He didn't want to admit he was having second

thoughts, because this was his plan and it was all falling into place. He'd done his research, and Carl's company had the best potential of him making his own footprint.

Even while knowing all that, he couldn't help but feel guilty about pulling her into all of it. He might have thought he was made of stone, but he wasn't. She was proving that to him. "Do you want to call it off?"

She looked up at him, searched his face as if hesitant to say her true feelings. Then, a faint smile formed as she quietly said, "No, but thank you for asking."

That was her answer, and he had to abide by it. "All right then, let's go buy you a ring."

Chapter Four

Jittery, fraught with nerves, Jolie pressed a hand against her stomach and closed her eyes, blocking the image reflected in the floor-length mirror. She'd spent hours designing and sewing the dress, working into the wee hours of the morning, diligently making this her absolute best work.

That had greatly irritated her mother. Nearly every day for the past two weeks Mother had found errands they'd had to run or another wedding detail that had needed to be seen to immediately—all excuses to keep her from working on her dress. Despite Mother's refusal to accept financial help from him before, she had readily accepted the funds from Dad for the wedding, and continuously insisted that there was more than enough money to purchase a dress from one of the many department stores.

Jolie understood that purchasing ready-made clothing was the style and that many of the stores had some beautiful dresses. She'd even conceded and bought a few day dresses so she had a more stylish wardrobe for once she became Randal's wife. However, she'd also decided that if this was her fate, she was going to find a way to make it work for her.

She hadn't received the answers she'd sought from Dad, because she'd never got around to asking exactly what he felt a wife needed to do in order to propel her husband forward. Dad had talked about love, and assuming she wasn't sure what that was, he'd spent the better part of an hour explaining it to her. He'd said that love changes a person, makes them want different things, feel differently about things.

She'd seen what else love does last night, after the rehearsal, when her mother spent hours sobbing, wishing Jolie's father was here to walk her down the aisle.

But if her father was still alive, she wouldn't be walking down the aisle today.

Jolie huffed out a breath.

Randal was nice, and Dad was convinced that marrying Randal would be exactly what her father would have wanted.

She wasn't so sure. She had looked forward to hearing from Randal each day, and had enjoyed going out to dinner with him some evenings, but that could be because it had given her reprieve from her mother.

Last night hadn't been the only time her mother had shed tears over her father not being here.

Jolie sighed, wondering how she'd managed to add an entirely new dimension to this whole predicament.

Neither she or Randal expected love from their union, they'd discussed that, and it was a major reason that she'd agreed. She just wished she knew what was expected of her. She didn't like the unknown. Never had.

Slowly, she opened her eyes, and once again scanned her reflection in the mirror.

The gown she'd worked so hard on designing and sewing had turned out exceptionally well. It was made of snow-white silk and satin, with a fitted bodice, long, flowing skirt, a high neckline and long sleeves. It was the epitome of a high-fashion wedding dress, yet had been made on a depression budget. As was the long tulle veil attached to the pearl-encrusted tiara head-dress pinned into her hair.

It truly was her best work. She'd taken what was in style and added her own little twists and turns. The money from Dad had given her the ability to purchase the materials and notions needed to make her wedding dress become as much talk of the town as her wedding.

At least that was her hope. She hoped once her dress became the talk of the town, others would ask her to design clothes for them. The public outings she'd partake in as Randal's wife could then continue to provide her the opportunities to show off her design work, and hopefully gain even more clients. That was a possibility because Randal had a chef, a maid and a butler, so she wasn't expected to just be a housewife.

She truly was putting all of her eggs in one basket, but it was the only basket she had, and ultimately, she couldn't give up her dream of designing clothes.

Just couldn't.

When mother had pitched a fit over not buying a ready-made dress, Randal had put a stop to it by saying that if she wanted to sew her wedding dress, then she could sew it.

She had appreciated his support, because no one, not even her father, had ever supported her love of designing and sewing.

A sigh escaped her chest and she stared down at the

diamond engagement ring on her finger. It was a beautiful art deco, white gold, ring, with engraved foliate and orange blossom detail. There was a matching wedding band that he would slide on her finger during the service. He'd seemed to know how much she'd liked the ring the moment the clerk at the store had set it on the counter. The ring was extremely lovely, but she'd liked it so much because although intricate, it was also simple enough to be unpretentious.

That's what she wanted. Things to be simple.

But none of this was simple. She couldn't even pretend that Randal had roped her into this marriage. It was the other way around. She'd thought going to Dad would give her insight. Instead, it had been the catalyst that catapulted her into marrying Randal today.

Today.

Her heart beat so hard she had to part her lips to suck in air.

Dad, with his assumption that she'd fallen in love—that they, she and Randal, had fallen in love—had insisted the wedding take place as soon as possible. That true love shouldn't have to wait, and had set the date himself.

She hadn't been able to say no, and she still hadn't told Randal that she'd gone to see Dad. For a reason that wasn't crystal clear, but sat heavy inside her, she didn't want him to know.

But he was sure to find out today, and Dad was sure to question him about his love for her.

A knock on her bedroom door shattered her thoughts and increased the dancing of her nerves.

"The car is here." Wearing a pale blue, floor-length

dress, a store-bought one, Chloe entered into the room. "Oh, Jolie, you look beautiful!"

Jolie drew in another deep breath. "Thank you. So do you."

"I mean really, really beautiful." Chloe hurried across the room and circled Jolie. "Your dress! I saw it while you were sewing, but it's gorgeous!"

"Thank you, but let me look at you." Jolie took ahold of her sister's hands. "Do you like your dress?" Like her, Chloe hadn't had new clothes for ages, and her younger sister looked adorable with her hair pinned up beneath the tiny veiled pill hat the same shade of blue as her dress.

"I love it, and like you said, I'll be able to shorten the hem and wear it over and over." Chloe stepped closer and hugged Jolie. "Actually, I'll have you hem it." Her sister's hug became tighter. "Oh, Jolie, I'm going to miss you."

"I'm going to miss you, too." Although Randal's money would help financially, she didn't believe that would secure a future for her family. That took more than money, and she was sincerely worried about leaving Chloe and Silas.

"And I'm so grateful for what you are doing for all of us." Stepping back, Chloe shook her head. "I'm truly sorry for saying that I'd run away, but I just couldn't imagine moving and living with Uncle LeRoy."

"I couldn't, either," Jolie admitted.

"You saved our entire family," Chloe said.

Jolie couldn't help but question if she was saving anyone. She gave her sister's hands a final squeeze and then released them. "Well, we don't want to keep the car waiting." A car had been arranged to take her to the church. Her mother and brother had already left in the family car.

"Do you need me to carry anything?" Chloe asked.

Jolie looked around the room. Most all of her belongings had been sent over to Randal's house yesterday. It was surreal that this was the last time she'd be in this room. Once again, she pressed a hand to the somersaults in her stomach. "No. All I have to carry is my purse."

Chloe lifted the white purse off the edge of the bed. "I'll carry it for you."

In less than an hour from the time she'd left her bedroom, Jolie was walking down the aisle of the church, on Dad Jansen's arm, toward the altar where Randal stood.

Though sheer, the veil still hindered her sight, but not enough that her heart didn't skip a beat at how handsome Randal looked in his tuxedo. He was watching her, and smiling, and his silver-blue eyes were shimmering brightly.

She was glad the veil hid her face, because her lips trembled.

Her entire being trembled.

Right up to the point where Randal took hold of her hand. The warmth of his touch raced up her arm and spread through her body, chasing aside her shivers. There was something about him that grounded her. Perhaps because they were in this together. She wasn't the only one that was having to pretend. Neither one of them wanted love, just a partnership.

"Your exceptional beauty takes my breath away," he whispered.

The huskiness of his voice took her breath away, leaving her unable to do more than nod slightly. She truly could find no fault in him. He'd not only been patient and understanding throughout the past three weeks, he'd been supportive and kind.

That thought played over and over again in her mind throughout the service, as they repeated vows and slid rings on each other's fingers, but when Randal lifted her veil, her thoughts shifted. She'd known this moment would happen. That he would have to kiss her during the service. Her heart stopped at the shimmer in his eyes, the smile on his lips, as his face drew closer to hers.

She'd thought of this moment, more than once, with curiosity. She had no intention of falling in love with him or any other man, but that had made her wonder if their partnership included other wifely duties. She assumed it would. People slept together without being in love all the time.

At the first touch of his lips against hers, her eyes fluttered shut and a great wave of warmth washed over her, all the way to her toes, making them curl inside her shoes.

The sensation, the feel of his warm lips pressing against hers was so appealing, she cupped his face and stretched to keep their lips connected. His hands, on her waist, slid around her back and pulled her closer, sending another thrill through her system.

She'd been curious about kissing him, but hadn't expected this overwhelming feeling of complete surrender. She had never surrendered to anything in her life, but there wasn't a single part of her that wanted any of this to end.

Feeling, more than hearing, Randal's slight chuckle, she forced her mind to search for what he found humorous. Until she heard someone clear their throat.

Randal pulled his lips from hers at the same time her eyes snapped open. Winking at her, he glanced toward the minister.

Heat filled her cheeks, as she fully understood the minister had been the one clearing his throat as a sign to stop their kissing.

Randal caught her hands as they slipped off his face and then kissed her forehead before he turned his attention to the minister.

She closed her eyes in hopes of gathering her wits, which really wasn't possible with the way her lips were still tingling, her heart still thudding. She opened her eyes when the minster instructed her and Randal to face the guests.

Another wave of heat filled her cheeks, knowing well over a hundred people had just witnessed her and Randal kissing. He released one of her hands, but held on to the other and gave it a squeeze as they both turned toward the rows upon rows of people.

"Allow me to present Mr. and Mrs. Randal Osterlund," the minister said.

Looking out over the sea of people who stood up, clapping and smiling, Jolie's embarrassment grew, once again remembering the deceit she and Randal were committing.

As if he'd read her mind, he whispered, "It's going to be fine, get your bouquet."

It was a moment before she realized that Chloe was handing her the bouquet of red roses that she'd carried up the aisle earlier. She took the flowers and held on tighter to Randal's hand as they began to walk past the guests. Holding a smile on her face, she accepted congratulations from both people she knew and those she didn't. The guest lists had grown large, which had thrilled her mother.

Between her mother and Dad, keeping things simple, as Jolie had wanted, hadn't been in the cards.

At least it would soon all be over.

Randal turned to her. "Ready to get pelted with rice?"

The kiss they'd shared a few moments ago still had Randal's blood pounding through his veins. Never had a kiss nearly knocked his socks off, but that one certainly had. She'd melded against him as if their bodies had been made to fit together. He hadn't been prepared for that, nor for how gorgeous she'd looked walking down the aisle. The dress she'd sewn was spectacular, but her wearing it was the reason. He wasn't a guy that had read fairy tales, but he had two sisters, and if he'd had to describe how Jolie looked, it would be like a princess.

"I guess we don't have a choice," she said with a grimace.

Needing the space to breathe, he loosened his tie, and flashed her a smile. "No, we don't, but if we hurry, we can beat them to the hotel and have some quiet time before the reception starts."

"I'm game for that."

Her smile didn't say as much as the gleam in her eyes. He laid a hand on the small of her back and guided her toward the front door, where people were already lined up down the steps and along the sidewalk.

He needed more than some quiet time. It was going to take a whole lot more than quiet for him to come to grips with the fact that he'd married a woman who once again had proven he wasn't made of stone.

Furthermore, they needed to do more than hurry. As soon as the rice was thrown, they needed to run for his car and drive like bootleggers outrunning a posse of bulls in order to make it to the hotel without getting caught.

The moment the doors opened, he wrapped an arm around her, pulled her close and ducked his head over her, trying to take the brunt of the rice being tossed at them. Luckily, his car was parked at the curb, covered with crepe paper, with strings of empty cans tied to the back bumper and *Just Married* painted on the back window with white shoe polish. He'd expected all that. He'd helped others do the same to some of his buddies' cars when they'd gotten married, and he expected what would happen next.

Once they reached the end of the sidewalk, people shouted for her to toss her bouquet. He stepped aside as she whipped her flowers over her head. With little more than a backward glance, she said, "Let's go!"

"You've got that right!" Glad she understood the urgency, he grabbed her hand and they ran to the car.

"Look what they did to your car!"

"Doesn't matter! Jump in!"

She jumped in as soon as he'd opened her door. Closing it, he ran around the car and noted his friends making mad dashes to their cars.

He wasn't about to lose his bride to any of them. "Hold on!" he told Jolie as he started the car.

"Hold on? Why?"

He put the car in gear and laid his foot on the gas, squealing his tires as he pulled away from the curb. "Because we have to beat them to our hotel room."

"Beat who?"

The cans tied to his bumper clinked and clanged against the street, and bounced high enough he could see them in the rearview mirror, along with several cars pulling away from the curbs and blowing their horns. "Everyone who follows us."

"Why?"

"Haven't you ever been in a wedding chase before?"

"No."

"But you've seen them? Heard about them?"

"Yes, I've seen them. Heard the horns honking. Isn't it just for fun?"

"Yes, but there is a goal, too."

"What's the goal?"

He took the corner so fast the car felt as if it was on two wheels instead of four. "To steal the bride!"

"What? Steal me? What for?"

He wasn't going to let that happen. "Whatever they have planned to do!"

"Like what?"

"Whatever they decide. Joyriding, cocktails." He took another corner, then another fast right into an alley. "Jerry Hansen's bride was put on a bus for Springfield."

"What! Why?"

"It's all for fun, but Jerry had to get the police to pull the bus over to get his bride back." In hindsight, Jerry would have been better off if he'd let her stay on that bus.

"Jerry was one of your groomsmen!"

"Yes, he was!"

"Were you part of the group that put his bride on the bus?"

He took a moment to flash her a grin. "It was all in good fun."

"It's all fun and games until someone loses an eye!"

He glanced at her again, and laughed at the merriment on her face.

"I'm not going to lose an eye! I'm not going to lose you, either! Hang on!"

She twisted in her seat to look out the back window. "Drive faster! I don't see anyone, but I can hear horns honking!"

There was an excited urgency in her voice, and it was zipping through him. "So do I!" He took a left at the end of the alley and had to do some quick steering, weaving around cars to keep from hitting any of them. "But I know a shortcut to the hotel. And I anticipated this."

"Did you anticipate the cans hanging from the bumper? We're leaving a trail that even a blind man could follow!"

"Keep an eye out for Jerry's red-and-black Buick," he told her while weaving through more cars and running a stop sign. Used to seeing such antics, people on the sidewalks and in cars were cheering, clapping, honking and pulling over for him to pass. "That Buick of his has more horsepower under that hood than a Kentucky horse track!"

"I don't see a red-and-black car, but there's a green one coming up fast behind us."

"Leslie Graham. We have to lose him!" He shot around a bread truck and then hit the brakes and turned into another alleyway.

She let out a squeal at how bumpy the ride became, even as she shouted, "Don't slow down!"

"Hold on!"

"I am!" A second later, she shouted, "Red and black! It just flew past the end of the alley!"

He slammed on the brakes again to make a fast turn into a parking lot off the alley and then sped past the parked cars. "The hotel is only two blocks. Hold on, we are going to jump the curb!"

"I told you, I am holding on!" She laughed. "It's like we are bootleggers or something! Oh, no! Look! It's the red-and-black car again! He's coming up behind us!"

"I see him in the mirror!" He wrenched the wheel, making the car turn a complete U-turn, and then laid on the horn as they drove past Jerry, who was grinning and waving a fist out his window.

"He's flipping a U-turn, too!" she shouted.

He'd seen that in the mirror and shot between two cars in the other lane to enter another parking lot. "That's the back of the hotel. Right up there. Get ready to run for the back door. They're expecting us!"

"Expecting us? You had this all planned?"

"I had to. I'm not about to let them put you on a bus to Springfield, or anywhere else, but it's not over until we reach our room."

He kept his foot on the gas all the way to the back door of the hotel, then hit the brakes and killed the engine while wrenching open his door. Jolie leaped out of her side of the car and they met near the door, which a hotel worker opened and then slammed shut behind them.

"The service elevator is right over there!" the man said.

Holding hands, they ran for the elevator. An attendant quickly closed the metal gate and pulled the cord to send the elevator upward.

Laughing, Jolie said, "We made it! We won!"

Envisioning his buddies catching the elevator in the hotel's lobby, or running up the six flights of stairs, he warned, "Don't count your chickens before they're hatched. We still have to get to our room."

"It's unlocked, Mr. Osterlund," the elevator attendant said. "Like you requested."

Keeping his eye on the little level ticking past the floor numbers, he nodded. "Thanks, I appreciate it."

"You really thought this out." A slight frown formed between her eyes. "How many brides have you been a part of stealing?"

"Several," he admitted, and their grooms were all now working in tandem for payback.

The elevator came to a stop and he tugged Jolie closer to the door. "Our room is straight ahead, but the lobby elevator is on the other end of the hallway. We have to run."

As soon as the door opened, he pulled her forward, but was stopped by her screech.

"My heel! It's caught!"

Before he had time to react, she pulled her foot out of her shoe, and took off running. "Which room is it?"

She was running, but it was off kilter because she only had one shoe. He caught her around the waist, lifted her into his arms and ran toward their room just as the lobby elevator clanged to a stop at the other end of the hallway. Several of his groomsmen shot out of the gate, gleefully shouting.

"Room 612!" he shouted. "Get ready to grab the door-knob!"

As soon as he found the door, she grabbed the knob with one hand and pushed it open. He shot inside, kicked the door shut and leaned back against it. Within a millisecond, pounding and laughter from the hallway penetrated the wood.

Jolie's laughter echoed in the room. His did, too.

"We did it!" she exclaimed. "We won!"

"I never had any doubt," he said, still breathing hard from the mad dash down the hall.

The desire that struck as he looked at the excitement on her face drowned out the noise in the hallway. One of her arms was still around his neck, and her face was so close, he'd barely have to move in order to capture her lips. He couldn't do that, though, because he'd told her that he wouldn't expect anything from her in private. He'd never explained exactly what he'd meant by that, but he'd known. At the time, he'd thought it would be simple, that he'd never have desires for her, or if and when he did, it would be sometime in the future. Not on their wedding day.

If he scared her away by going back on his word this soon, it would all have been for naught.

Gathering his senses, he started to lower her, but stopped when she let out a little yelp and grabbed the tiara on her head.

"My veil is caught in the door," she said.

Laughter, shouts and knocking still emitted through the door, and he wasn't sure what to do. Knowing his buddies, this wasn't over.

She reached up, plucked two pins from her hair and removed the tiara.

"I promise you'll get it back," he said.

She frowned.

He slowly released her, lowering her until she stood beside him. The veil was stuck in the door and he took the tiara from her hands. "If we give them this as a consolation prize, they'll go away."

She laughed. "Then by all means, give it to them."

He nodded at the table. "Get the key and lock the door as soon I shut it again."

She grabbed the key and held it ready as he kept as much weight on the door as possible while cracking it open enough to toss the tiara into the hallway. Cheers echoed into the room as he slammed the door shut and she locked it.

Holding up the key, she said, "Now we've won."

He laughed. "Yes, we have!"

She dropped the key on the table and held on to her stomach. "Oh, my, I haven't had that much fun in ages and ages."

Although he was glad that she'd enjoyed the wedding chase, a part of him was sad for her. She had friends—several of them had been a part of the wedding—but he'd witnessed how controlling her mother had been over every part of the occasion, of her life.

His thoughts turned into concern as she turned about to walk farther into the room. "You're limping. What's wrong?"

"I only have one shoe."

The grimace on her face told him it was more than

that. "I'll get your shoe back, but did you hurt your foot?"

"I just twisted my ankle when my heel caught on the edge of the elevator track. It's fine."

He stepped forward and once again swept her up into his arms.

Chapter Five

The pain that had shot up her ankle a moment ago was completely forgotten as Jolie once again wrapped an arm around his neck as he carried her toward the cream-colored sofa in the center of the room.

"How bad does it hurt?" he asked.

She heard him, but at the moment, was remembering how he'd kissed her at the altar. A large part of her was hoping he would do that again. Until her senses returned. That kiss had been for show. Pretend.

"It—it doesn't hurt at all," she said.

"I don't believe you."

He really was a handsome man, and always smelled so good, fresh and a little bit spicy. She was feeling light-headed being so close to him. "Put me down. I'm fine."

"I will, and I will look at your ankle."

When he'd picked her up in the hallway, she'd thought the racing in her heart had been because of being chased, the fun and wild, crazy drive to the hotel, but her heart was racing all over again now. No one was chasing them. His shoulders and chest were firm, muscular, and being in his arms affected more than her heart. Every part of her was tingling, like when he'd kissed her. It was all a bit overwhelming.

He set her down on the sofa, knelt before her and planted her shoeless foot on his thigh, and for the life of her, the only thing she could think of was Cinderella and Prince Charming. She hadn't read that story for years and years, and it was a foolish comparison, but it was there, front and center in her mind.

"It doesn't appear to be swollen," he said.

He was softly caressing her ankle, and that was sending heat waves up her leg, as if the entire leg was on fire. Not a painful fire, rather an unusually exciting one. If there had been any lingering pain in her ankle, it was long gone, and she attempted to pull her foot off his thigh. "I just twisted it. It's fine now."

His fingers tightened around her ankle, keeping it put. "You're sure?"

"Yes, I'm sure."

A knock sounded on the door and Jolie tried harder to pull her foot off his thigh, but he still didn't release it. Instead, with a grin, he lifted her foot and gingerly set it down on the floor before he rose and walked to the door.

"Who is it?" he asked.

"The elevator attendant, sir. I have your wife's shoe. I waited until the hallway emptied to deliver it."

As Randal picked the key off the table, Jolie leaned back and pushed out the air that had been locked in her lungs. What had she gotten herself into? She'd already determined that she thought Randal was nice, and handsome, but this—the way her body had reacted, now and at the church—was ridiculous. From today forward, she'd be living with him, and couldn't go breathless every time he was near like some senseless ninny.

With her shoe in hand, he closed the door and walked back toward her.

Sure as the sun would rise tomorrow, her heart skipped a beat, stealing her ability to breathe all over again when he knelt down in front of her.

He lifted her foot off the floor and slipped her shoe back on. "Perfect fit."

Struggling to breathe as something inside her, deep and somewhat hidden, grew soft and warm in the most unusual manner, she managed to nod.

He set her foot back down on the floor. "Are you sure it's okay?"

Her foot, yes, the rest of her, no. Knowing she couldn't say that, she forced herself to stand. "Yes. See. It doesn't hurt at all." To prove that, she took a few steps away from the sofa.

"All right." He stood. "But if it starts hurting later, let me know and we'll leave the reception."

The reception. Dear Lord, would today ever end?

And what would happen after the reception? The thought hit her like a bucket of ice water. He'd said she wouldn't be expected to do anything in private, yet he'd rented the bridal suite for them. She knew this was the bridal suite because she'd seen the sign next to the door as she'd opened it. They were married. And married people sleep together. Why did she have to keep reminding herself of that?

"I'm sorry about the wedding chase. I knew my friends would do that, and I should have warned you."

"I have seen chases following wedding ceremonies, but never participated in one before. It was fun." That was somewhat of an understatement. Her heart had been racing as fast as he'd been driving. Mostly from excitement, with a touch of fear at being stolen mingled in. "Thank you for not letting them steal me."

"I couldn't let that happen." He stood near a round table and was holding a bottle in one hand and a glass in the other, which he held out toward her.

Recognizing the bottle was champagne, she crossed the room and took the glass.

The bottle made a popping sound when he uncorked it and fizzed as he poured it first into her glass, and then into the second glass on the table. "Can you imagine what your mother would have done if they'd caught you and put you on a bus to somewhere?"

She nearly dropped the glass, and held on tighter to the short stem. Her mother would have thrown a fit, but oddly, she found she wanted him to have saved her from being stolen because he hadn't wanted that to happen for himself, not her mother. "She would have had a heart attack," she said.

He held up his glass. "To us?"

"To us." She clinked the edge of her glass against his and took a sip. It was sweet, bubbly and smooth. She took another drink.

Carrying his glass in one hand, he took her elbow with the other and guided her back toward the sofa. Once they'd both sat, he said, "Your mother wasn't the only reason I didn't want you to be stolen."

"Oh?" She took another sip, acting as if another reason had never crossed her mind.

He nodded. "I wanted today to be everything you'd ever dreamed of your wedding day being, and highly doubted being stolen was part of that dream."

She couldn't remember a single time when she'd dreamed of her wedding. Marriage hadn't been something she'd spent a lot of time thinking about. Not until her mother had brought it up barely three weeks ago. That truly hadn't been enough time to get used to anything. Let alone dream about it.

"Did you want to be stolen?" he asked.

"No." She leaned back and looked at him. "I can't remember a time when I dreamed of what I wanted my wedding to be like."

"You can't?"

"No."

"My sisters did. That's all I heard about when they got married, that everything had to be just like they'd dreamed about when they were little."

She'd met his family, both sisters and his grandfather, a few times the past couple of weeks. They were nice and friendly, happy that he was getting married. She also knew that he'd paid for Willa's and Danielle's weddings, and that he continued to financially support their families. And now hers.

"Did your mother plan everything about today?" he asked.

"Yes. I told her whatever she suggested was fine with me." That wasn't completely true, she'd wanted it to be smaller, simpler. Shifting her thoughts to him, she said, "You said that was fine with you, too. Was it? Did you dream of something different?"

He laughed. "No, men, as far as I know, don't dream about weddings."

Truly curious, she asked, "What did you dream about when you were little?"

Without so much as a pause, he replied, "Being a pirate."

"A pirate?" His answer made her laugh, and question if he was teasing. "Really?"

"Yes." He flashed her another one of his signature grins. "But a good one. I didn't dream of stealing loot, only of finding all of the loot that the bad pirates had stolen."

She giggled. "An honorable pirate, that's a new one."

"Somewhat honorable. I was going to keep any loot that I found."

She laughed aloud, and realized that was something she'd done more since meeting him than she had the past few years. She'd forgotten how good it felt. After taking a sip of her champagne, she asked, "What were you going to do with all that loot?"

He winked at her. "I don't know, I only ever dreamed of finding it."

A new train of thought formed. "And now you're dreaming of acquiring Dad's airplane company."

"I can't say I'm dreaming about that, but I'm definitely working on it."

"What if he decides not to sell it?"

"He'll sell it." Randal stood, collected the bottle of champagne from the table and carried it back to the sofa.

"How can you be so sure?" she asked as he refilled her glass.

"Because in this world, everything is for sale. Carl's a businessman, he'll recognize a good offer when it comes from the right man." He filled his glass and set the bottle on the table next to the sofa before sitting next to her again.

"A married man," she said.

"Having second thoughts?"

It was too late for that. "No, I just wish I knew what Dad expected."

"What do you mean?"

She shrugged. "He believes a man needs a woman behind him, but what does he expect that woman to do?"

Randal refused to respond to the shiver that tickled his spine. Did Carl expect something specific? That wasn't what he'd assumed. "I think his belief is based more on the man. Marrying shows an ability to commit."

She frowned, but then nodded. "Perhaps."

He'd embarked upon this union with the best of intentions, and would remain true to that, despite the desire to kiss her that was still living large inside him. The one at the altar had been a sampling of something sweet and delectable, making him want more. But he wouldn't act upon that desire, not unless she demonstrated she wanted him to act upon it. "No matter what Carl may expect, you'll never be expected to do anything that will go against your will."

She nodded, but the light that had been in her dark brown eyes earlier was now completely gone. He didn't like that. Over the past two weeks, he'd come to see how heavily her family relied on her, on this plan. He'd also seen how controlling her mother was over everything, and that made him understand why Jolie would want to know what was expected of her. He believed that she'd had to walk a delicate line her entire life, one that hadn't left her a lot of freedom.

He took ahold of her hand. "I think it's time you start dreaming about being a pirate."

An enchanting smile slowly grew on her face. "A pirate?"

"Yes, a pirate."

"Why?"

Just looking at her made his lungs lock up. He had looked forward to seeing her, to spending time with her, the past couple of weeks, and hadn't been able to get her out of his mind when they weren't together. In fact, he'd looked forward to today, and wanted this marriage to benefit her as much as it would benefit him. "So you can figure out the treasure you want to find, and then start working on finding it."

Her smile remained as she nodded. "Is that all it will take?"

Attempting to sound like a pirate, he said, "Aye, mate."

She laughed aloud. "Did you dream of talking like a pirate, too?"

"Maybe."

"As long as you don't make me walk the plank."

Clinking his glass against hers, he said, "I have to get a ship first."

He loved the sound of her laugh, the gleam it put in her eyes and the shine it put on her cheeks. If he had searched for months, years, he wouldn't have found a more beautiful bride. Right up until the moment he'd seen her walking up the aisle toward him, he'd wondered if she might change her mind.

Relieved that hadn't happened, he relaxed deeper into the sofa and rested an ankle on his opposite knee.

"I don't understand why your mother was so set against you sewing your dress. It's beautiful. You're beautiful."

She bowed her head somewhat bashfully. "Thank you." With a shrug, she added, "Mother was afraid of what people might think."

"Think? That you're gorgeous? What's wrong with that?"

She took another sip off her glass. "Homemade isn't fashionable, isn't in style."

He didn't know a lot about women's fashion, but knew a beautiful gown and woman when he saw one. Something else clicked in his mind, too. All of her dresses were fitted, as if tailored just for her. "Do you sew all your clothes?"

"No. My mother would never allow that, but the past few years, she hasn't complained much about me re-making my old clothes to be more in style with what's being sold at the stores."

He was about to tell her how talented she was when the phone rang. He sighed. "I think people are wondering where we are."

She nodded as it rang again. "It's probably my mother."

"Do you want to answer it?"

She shook her head.

He reached over to pick up the receiver, but she grasped his other arm. "Don't answer it."

Dropping his hand away from the phone, he asked, "Do you want to skip the entire reception?" He wouldn't object.

"Yes." She emptied her glass and then stood. "But we can't."

He stood and took her glass. "You're right." Lifting a brow, he asked, "How is your ankle?"

"It's fine."

"You're sure?"

She made a point of testing it so he could see. "Yes. It doesn't hurt at all."

"That's too bad."

She laughed. "It might start hurting later."

He set both of their glasses on the table, and took ahold of her elbow to escort her to the door. "Just tell me when, cutting out early sounds good to me."

She eyed him somewhat critically, then nodded. "I like the way you think."

"I think we are more alike than we'd imagined." He paused before opening the door. "I envision you and I will make a good team."

"We have to, there's no other choice."

He heard her words, but it was the unfaltering smile on her face that made his heart thud a bit faster. Opening the door, he gave her a slight bow, "After you, Mrs. Osterlund."

She lifted her chin in a haughty, yet saucy way. "Why, thank you, Mr. Osterlund."

They took the main elevator this time, which was more opulent than the service one. The attendant greeted them by congratulating them on their marriage and swiftly delivered them to the main floor.

The lobby was full of people, of which many clapped and shouted with glee as the caged door of the elevator slid open. He draped an arm around her shoulders, to protect her as he had when they'd left the church.

A man carrying a camera hurried forward, meeting them as they stepped out of the elevator. "You left the church so quickly I didn't get any still shots. Can we do them now?"

Jolie looked up at him hesitantly. "He's the photographer Mother hired."

Randal nodded, already having figured that out at the church when the flashbulbs had gone off nonstop.

"Right over here will work," the man said. "Near this wall."

They moved to the spot the man directed, and posed for several pictures before the man asked, "Where's your veil? We should have you wearing it in some of the pictures."

"We don't need the veil," Jolie said. "And I think that's enough pictures."

"Your mother—"

"Is not the bride," Randal said, cutting the man off. "My wife is, and she said that's enough pictures." As far as he was concerned, Jolie being controlled by others was over as of today.

The somewhat surprised, yet happy, expression on her face was all the encouragement he needed. "Shall we, Mrs. Osterlund?"

Laughing, she nodded. "Yes, Mr. Osterlund."

They had barely made it ten feet down the hallway when her mother entered the hall from the ballroom.

"Jolie!" Eyes glaring, her mother stomped toward them. "Where have you been? I had the desk call your room! What were you thinking? Leaving the church like that!"

If necessary, he'd apologize tomorrow, because he didn't want to disrespect his mother-in-law, especially this early on, or cause undue issues, but Jolie had already had enough chastising over the wedding. "We were having fun," he said while steering Jolie around Amelia and toward the ballroom. "And will continue to."

"Well!" Amelia huffed. "Her veil is—"

Randal saw the veil as soon as they arrived at the entrance of the ballroom, hanging from one of the chandeliers. "We see it," he said over his shoulder to Amelia. Whispering to Jolie, he asked, "Should I tell her to be glad it's only your veil?"

"Dear heavens, no," Jolie whispered.

"I'll find someone to get it down," he offered.

"No. Leave it," she answered. "Your friends must be proud that they managed to steal something."

He appreciated her sense of humor about his friends and their shenanigans. It could have been far worse. Leading her toward their table, he said, "I'm sure they are."

"I'm happy it was only my veil."

"Me, too," he replied, glancing at where a number of his friends were gathered, laughing. Perhaps, within time, he'd miss being a part of the rowdier, single crowd. Only time would tell.

Chapter Six

The moment Jolie realized which table was theirs amongst the dozens upon dozens of tables draped with white tablecloths and hosting bouquets of flowers, she questioned twisting her ankle on purpose so she and Randal could leave. Both of their families, including Dad, were sitting with them, and she worried Dad would bring up her visit.

It had been an innocent meeting, but still filled her with guilt that she hadn't yet told Randal about it. She could tell him—put it in proper context he'd surely understand—but she didn't want him to know that she'd been wondering about love. Love had nothing to do with their marriage. Neither of them wanted that. It was about dreams and making them come true. But she didn't want to talk about that, either. Her dream had been squashed too many times in the past. If it got squashed again, if she'd have to give it up, she wouldn't have anything.

"Do you want to use the powder room before sitting down?" Randal asked. "I should have asked while we were upstairs, but didn't think of it."

"Yes," she said almost before he'd finished asking. Any excuse for a bit more time was welcomed. Even more welcome was Chloe walking toward them, carrying Jolie's purse. "I'll be back in a moment."

Jolie hurried forward, took the purse her sister held out. "I'm going to powder my nose."

"I'll join you," Chloe said. "Mother's been in a snit since the church."

"I saw her in the hallway," Jolie replied as they crossed the room toward another open door.

"You did? You looked really happy when you and Randal walked into the ballroom."

She couldn't stop a smile from forming. "We were laughing about my veil."

"You should have seen Mother's face when she saw that!"

"I'm glad I didn't."

"She was about as mad as she'd been at the church when you left. That had to have been the most exciting wedding chase ever! Tires squealing, horns honking. Did they chase you all the way to the hotel?"

"Yes. It was crazy, and exciting, and fun. Very fun."

"How did your veil end up hanging from the chandelier?"

They'd reached the doorway and Jolie glanced over her shoulder. Randal was near their table, but surrounded by his friends, and laughing. "Randal's friends. My veil got caught in the door of our hotel room when he carried me in and they wouldn't stop pounding on the door until he opened it and threw the veil in the hallway as a consolation prize."

"He carried you over the threshold?" Chloe asked gleefully. "Just like a fairy tale."

As the fairy-tale image of Randal slipping her shoe back on her foot formed, Jolie pressed a hand against her breast and the skipping of her heart.

"You're blushing," Chloe said.

"Because I was embarrassed. Randal had to carry me down the hallway and into our room because I'd lost my shoe when it got caught in the elevator track. We were racing his friends to get to our room so they couldn't steal me."

"That all sounds like so much fun."

It had been fun, and so had talking with him in the room. Jolie pulled her gaze off Randal and stepped into the hallway. "It was. Thank you for remembering my purse."

"You're welcome." Chloe slipped an arm around Jolie's elbow. "I'm sure you need to touch up your lipstick after all your kissing."

Jolie's cheeks warmed all over again at the thought of the entire church watching them kiss.

"You're blushing again." Chloe was still giggling as they entered the ladies' room.

Rooms actually. The first one was the waiting area, with flocked blue-and-cream floral wallpaper and a fainting couch covered in dark blue velvet, along with a floral-printed divider screen that gave privacy for those needing to reapply makeup or check their appearance in the mirror behind the screen. The door that led into the facilities room was beside the divider.

Finding her lipstick in her purse, Jolie stepped closer to the mirror as the door to the hallway opened.

"I'm telling you, it's homemade," a woman's voice said. "Katherine DeWitt sold Jolie the material just two weeks ago."

"Her new husband must not be as wealthy as he portrays," another woman said. "Or as wealthy as Amelia is claiming."

Jolie's hand trembled as her heart sank deep into her stomach.

"The whole wedding seemed fishy to me. So quick. And now a homemade wedding gown," the first one said. "Disgraceful. That's what it is."

"Deceiving, that's what it is. But I expected no less. We all know Amelia's been putting on airs for years, pretending as if her husband left them well off when he clearly hadn't. This just proves it," the other said.

"Yes, it does. And her veil hanging from a chandelier? I've never seen anything so distasteful. It's probably homemade, too."

The door to the toilet area opened and Jolie spun around. Chloe's lips were pursed and anger shone in her eyes. Catching her sister's attention, Jolie shook her head, knowing Chloe had heard everything and was about to respond—Chloe style. Her sister often spoke without thinking.

Hoping for the impossible, Jolie pressed a finger to her lips, but Chloe's eyes had already narrowed. A sure sign she wouldn't stay quiet.

Jolie's stomach sank deeper. Her dress certainly hadn't received the attention she'd hoped for, and her sister was about to make things worse.

"Well, if it isn't Mrs. Emmerson," Chloe said, with a tone Jolie knew well. "And Mrs. Goode. Clucking as usual."

Needing to act fast, Jolie shot out from behind the screen and grabbed her sister's arm. "Shush."

The eyes of both of the matronly women were wide and their jaws were dropped, leaving their mouths open.

"My sister—" Chloe started.

"Has her groom waiting," Jolie said, tugging Chloe forward, past the women.

"Sewed her dress because she wanted to, and Randal is far wealthier than either of you!" Chloe managed to get out before Jolie pulled her out of the door and into the hallway.

Jolie closed the door firmly behind them.

"You aren't going to let them—"

"Stop, Chloe. Don't say anything. Not to anyone." She pulled her sister down the hallway toward the ballroom.

"But, Jolie—"

"Please." Jolie's stomach was curdling. Her mother had been right. She should have bought a dress.

"Those old biddies don't know a beautiful dress when they see one. Did you see what they were wearing? Their dresses had to have been hanging in their closets since before I was born."

"Talking about others doesn't hurt them, it only makes you look bad," Jolie reminded, trying to get her own anger under control. She'd never imagined that sewing her dress would have made people question Randal's worth.

"They started it, and what they said did hurt you. I could see that on your face."

"No, it didn't hurt me," Jolie lied. "So don't worry about it." They turned to step into the ballroom, and as if she didn't already feel rotten enough, her stomach hit the floor. Randal was sitting at their table, talking with Dad. "Oh, no. No," she muttered.

"What?" Chloe asked.

Searching for an excuse, Jolie nodded at a nearby waiter. "The meal is about to be served."

"This wedding sure is a wingding," Chloe said. "Everything Mother wanted."

"Yes, everything Mother wanted," Jolie replied, huffing out yet another breath and wishing it was all over.

Randal stood as she arrived at the table and held her chair as she sat between him and Dad.

She pulled up a smile as a thank-you, but noted the way his brows were knit together.

"Is your ankle hurting?" he asked next to her ear as he took his seat again.

She shook her head.

"Then what does?" he whispered. "You're as white as your dress."

As if Chloe had heard him, she asked, "Randal, don't you think Jolie did an amazing job sewing her dress?"

Jolie shot a glare at her sister.

His arm was across the back of her chair and he cupped her shoulder, rubbed it as he looked at her. "Yes, I do," he answered. "Her dress is beautiful. *She* is beautiful."

The soft glimmer in his eyes made her cheeks grow warm.

"I think so, too," Chloe said. "Others—"

Jolie flinched, and twisted to respond to her sister, but her mother was quicker.

"Chloe," her mother interrupted with warning. With a smile that looked painted on—because it was, with bright red lipstick—her mother turned her attention on her. "Everyone agrees that Jolie's dress is pretty. Some of us were just concerned that she already had enough to do planning the wedding in such a short time, but as you all see, it turned out lovely, so we aren't going to worry about it."

"I wasn't worried, Mother," Chloe said. "Just like I'm not worried about her veil hanging from a chandelier."

Jolie balled her hand in a fist to keep from pressing it to her forehead, where a headache was starting to form.

Randal leaned next to her ear. "Who—?"

She stopped him by shaking her head.

"I think that the bride is exceptionally beautiful," Dad said. "And I like where the veil is hanging." Chuckling, he added, "That was quite the chase. I'm glad they didn't catch you."

"So am I," Jolie responded. "Thank you, Dad, thank you for everything." Remembering what Randal had said earlier, she continued, "I couldn't have dreamed of a more perfect wedding."

"It was an honor, Joey-girl." He leaned over and kissed her cheek. "I wish you all the happiness in the world."

Randal watched Jolie closely throughout the meal, noting how her smile never reached her eyes. He'd always been protective of his sisters as they'd grown up, and felt the need to protect Jolie ten times over. He wanted to put himself between her and everyone else at the table. He also wanted to know who had said something about her dress. That really got his ire up.

It seemed like hours before he and Jolie were able to make their way through the ballroom, taking the time to thank people while heading toward the exit into the hallway. Color had returned to her face, and if he didn't know better, he'd believe the happiness she portrayed was real. His, too. They were both happy to be leaving the room.

This entire plan, of marrying to advance his financial goals, had made sense when he'd created it, but now he was questioning the consequences. Somehow, he'd expected his life to go on as usual, but that wasn't about to happen. Not with the way his mind was full of her.

The day had a lot to do with that. Perhaps once it was all in the past, things would return to normal.

A new normal. One that included her.

Laughter pulled his thoughts back to the present, and his heart skipped a beat as Jolie pressed a hand against his chest, right over his heart. Her eyes were gleaming as she laughed, looking up at him.

Leslie Graham was laughing, too. Randal figured his friend had said something, a good-humored joke, that he was the brunt of, no doubt. Although he had no idea what had been said, he laughed and steered Jolie around the table that Leslie was seated at along with several other friends.

"You've been subjected enough to these geniuses," he told her.

The table erupted with more laughter at his teasing insult. Face aglow, she asked, "How long have you been friends with them?"

A part of him wished he'd heard what Leslie had said, only because of how happy she looked at this moment. "Too long." He'd been friends with some of them since grammar school, and right now, wanted to leave them in the dust as much as he had during the car chase. There were about half a dozen tables between them and the door. "How fast do you think we can make it to the door?"

Her forehead creased slightly, but she was still smiling. "I don't know, how fast can you run?"

Without a word, he grasped her hand and took off. He didn't run, but they both jogged at a good pace, side-stepping around chairs in their pathway and waving at the table occupants that they sped past.

The entire room started clapping and cheering, and once they reached the door, he paused and pulled her close with the intention of turning around to give a final wave. That changed the moment he looked down at her. The jubilance on her face struck him, and whether it was because people might have expected it, or because he thought it might be his last chance to do so, he cupped her face and kissed her.

Increased cheering from the crowd gave him a reason to continue the kiss. Or perhaps that came from within, too, because of her response. Her hands were on his chest, her fingers curled into the lapels of his suit jacket, and she was on her tiptoes, stretching upward as if she too wanted to prolong the kiss.

Few things in life had been difficult for him, and stopping the kiss was definitely one of them. Pulling his lips off hers was like losing a treasure, one he'd never expected to find, but he stopped the kiss, and winked at her before turning to wave at the crowd.

Jubilance followed in their wake, spilling into the hallway as they hurried to the elevator, past more people clapping and shouting congratulations.

Once in the elevator, their eyes met, and he joined her in a laugh that echoed in the shaft as the attendant closed the door and pulled the cord to take them upward.

Moments later, with the weight of the day behind him, Randal twisted his shoulders as he and Jolie entered their room. His back had been itching for hours, but with everything else on his mind, he'd ignored it. That was no longer possible, and as soon as the door was closed, he leaned against the corner of the doorjamb to scratch his back.

"What's wrong?"

"It must be the starch in my shirt. My back has been itching for hours."

"Take off your jacket and I'll scratch it for you."

Grateful for the assistance, he stepped away from the wall and shrugged out of his tux jacket.

"And your vest," she said.

He removed the vest, tossed it on the chair along with his tailed coat. The touch of her nails against the burning itch was like heaven, making him involuntarily arch into her scratching.

"I think I see the problem," she said.

Her hand was rubbing up and down his back, which felt nearly as wonderful as her scratching. Twisting his neck to look at her, he frowned. "Problem?"

Leaning around his shoulder, she nodded. "Yes. Problem. You have rice stuck between your dress shirt and undershirt."

He let out a growl and started unbuttoning his shirt.

"Careful." She grasped both of his shoulders. "Don't just pull it off, we'll have rice flying everywhere."

"What do you suggest I do?"

"Undo your cuff links and slowly remove your shirt. I'll try to keep as much as I can from falling on the floor."

Removing his cuff links, he asked, "There's that much?"

She rubbed his back again. "From what I can feel, there's enough to make rice pudding."

He could feel the grains of rice sliding down his back as her touch loosened it. "No wonder I've been itching for hours."

Grasping his shirt by the shoulders, she slowly lifted the material and pulled it back so he could slide his arms out. The action sent grains of rice into the waistband of his pants.

"Now it's running down my legs, into my shoes."

She giggled. "I'm trying to catch as much as I can in your shirt."

He pulled the tail of his shirt out of his waistband. "It sounds like you're enjoying this."

Her short silence as she completely removed his shirt was followed by soft laughter. "I can't believe you spent the entire evening with this much rice in your shirt."

He turned, stared at the amount of rice she held cupped inside his shirt. "I can't believe I didn't feel all that."

She set the shirt on the table. "Turn around, let me see if we got it all."

The touch of her hand on his back ignited the itching of his skin. Somehow sensing that, she gave his back a good overall scratching. "Thanks, that feels so much better."

Giving his back a final pat, she peeked around his shoulder. "I'm glad I could help."

"How about you? Do you have rice stuck inside your dress?"

"No. Between you and my veil, I barely got hit with any." Grinning, she walked farther into the room. "Thank you for that."

"You're very welcome." He crossed the room and sat

down on the sofa, kicked off his shoes and put his feet up on the coffee table.

She sat in the adjacent chair and did the same.

Grinning at her actions, he asked, "Tired?"

"More like worn out." She sighed. "It's been a crazy couple of weeks."

"It has." He couldn't take his eyes off her, and knew why. The kiss they'd shared at the altar was still alive and well inside him, and repeating it in the ballroom doorway a few moments ago had only reinforced how perfectly her lips fit against his. He had to be careful of his thoughts, and actions. Although he was comfortable around her, things were delicate between them. They barely knew each other.

Her hands were clasped together across her stomach, and her thumbs were slowly circling each other. Nerves? Probably.

He threaded his fingers and put them behind his head, leaning deeper into the sofa. "I think we should take it slow from here. Just let things play out as they may."

"What things?"

"Our marriage." Her frown had him explaining further. "As in us truly becoming man and wife."

Her gaze went past him, to the door that led to the bedroom. "So we won't…"

"Not tonight. That will happen when we are both ready." He could be ready in less than a heartbeat, but had come into this with his eyes open. However, the way the brows above her eyes knit together, he wondered if he'd spoken too soon. If he should have let the marriage become real tonight.

She glanced around the room, twiddled her thumbs

some more. "Your friend, Jerry, the one you said his wife was put on the bus?"

He nodded.

"Couldn't his wife attend the wedding?"

"They're divorced." He could elaborate, tell her how Jerry's wife found another man within months of their marriage, but he held his tongue.

"Oh. That's too bad."

He held his opinion. Jerry was doing better now, but would never be the same man. Learning his wife had been unfaithful and was carrying another man's child had devastated his friend. Randal had never seen a good man go bad so fast. All because of love.

"So what do we do now?" she asked. "It's too early to go to sleep."

He left the couch, walked to his suit coat and dug in the pocket. Holding up a deck of cards, he asked, "Cards?"

Her frown increased. "Do you always carry a deck of cards in your pocket?"

"No. Leslie gave them to me earlier today." His body jolted slightly, one specific part at the reason his buddy had given him the cards. The gift had been a joke, that all of his friends had laughed about, but it was early, and they did need some way to pass the time.

"Why?"

"To play poker."

"Poker?"

Strip poker had been the reason Leslie had given him the deck. "Do you know how to play poker?"

"Yes, my father taught me, but I don't have any cash."

He had a few bills in his billfold, but not enough different denominations to make the game worth playing.

Glancing at his shirt, he scooped out a handful of rice and walked back to the sofa. "We'll play for rice."

"Rice?"

Slowly releasing his pinky finger, he let a pile of rice funnel onto the table in front of her, and then a second pile on his side of the table. "Yes. We might as well put it to good use."

Eyes sparkling, she scooted off her chair and sat down on the floor near the table. Rubbing her palms together, she said, "All right. We'll split for the first deal."

Chapter Seven

Jolie picked the small, tightly corked bottle off the corner of the desk. The contents made her grin. No one would ever believe that she'd spent her wedding night playing poker, with grains of rice, and had won. Won Randal's entire pile. They'd played until late into the night, and the following morning, she'd collected her winnings in a handkerchief, telling him that had been the most she'd ever won in a game of poker.

Randal had found her the bottle that evening after they'd arrived home and every day since, the sight of it made her smile.

She stood and, holding the small bottle, wandered around the large room that she shared with Randal. The area with the large four-poster bed and matching dressers comprised of the size of her old bedroom, and that was a mere corner of this room. There was a large sitting area, complete with two armchairs and a long sofa, upholstered in a rich brown brocade that matched the draperies hanging on the long windows, and the bed covering. The walls were painted a pale green, except for the one that housed a large bookcase that went from floor to ceiling.

In another corner was the desk she'd been using all week, writing out thank-you cards for the many wedding gifts they'd received. Near it sat her sewing machine, having been delivered from her mother's house. She hadn't lifted the top, opened the machine, since it had arrived. There was no reason. Even the newspaper had specifically pointed out that *"the bride hand made her dress"* in their wedding announcement on the social page.

Hand made.

Not designed.

Not created.

Hand made.

That must be the polite way to say homemade. When would people understand that every woman's body was different? For a dress to fit properly, it had to suit a woman's unique figure. So did the undergarments. For some dresses, the undergarments were even more important.

She pushed the air out of her lungs and leaned against the back of the sofa. No one, it appeared, understood that.

At home there had always been something to do. A floor that had needed to be scrubbed, clothes to wash, meals to cook, but here, at Randal's house, the cook, maid and butler took care of everything. She did clean this room, because she was perfectly capable, but also because she didn't want anyone to discover that Randal slept on the sofa every night.

It was his house, his bed. If anyone should be sleeping on the sofa, it should be her. He wouldn't hear of that, though, even though she suggested it each night.

As she glanced down at the bottle in her hand, her

heart thudded. She knew why, and it wasn't only because of the poker game. The grains of rice reminded her of the two times Randal had kissed her.

With little else to do, she'd thought about those kisses a lot the past few days. People don't have to love each other to kiss. She'd kissed boys before, and certainly hadn't loved them.

People don't need to love each other to sleep in the same bed, either. She'd never done that, but knew it happened all the time.

She liked Randal, and wouldn't mind kissing him again. What she would never do was like him so much that she fell in love with him, or become jealous of everyone he spoke to, or live her life for him alone.

She'd spoken to Chloe and Silas, and her mother, and so far, they were doing fine without her.

She was the one not doing so fine.

Her plan to become a clothing designer had failed. With that, and with no one needing her, she had no idea what she would do now that she'd finished the last of the thank-you notes. All that was left was to carry the stack downstairs. The butler, Peter, would see that they were mailed.

Huffing out a breath, she pushed off the sofa to cross the room back to the desk. She shouldn't be so despondent. Her family's bills had all been paid, there were groceries in the cupboards, fuel in the car and money to buy more.

She'd just sat down at the desk when the bedroom door opened.

"Are you still writing thank-you notes?"

She stood, surprised to see Randal. "What are you doing home? It's not even noon yet." There were times, like right now, when her fingers would tingle, remembering the feel of his back. The hard muscles. The ripples of his rib cage. The firmness of his waist.

He entered the room and closed the door. "I took the rest of the day off."

"Why? Is something wrong?"

"No. I thought I'd take you out for lunch, and then we'd go for a drive or something." Stopping next to her, he continued, "Unless you are too busy with the thank-you notes."

"No. I finished the last few. They just need to be mailed."

His hand touched her elbow, then ran down her arm until his fingers wrapped around hers. The action stole her ability to breathe for a moment, and when her lungs did release the air locked inside them, a long sigh escaped.

He reached around her and picked up the stack of envelopes with his free hand. "We'll mail them on our way to the restaurant."

She gave her head a clearing shake because it was thinking about kissing him. "I need to get my purse."

His thumb ran over the inside of her wrist. "You won't need it for anything."

"How do you know that?"

He lifted an eyebrow. "Because you'll have me."

She bit back a smile. "And that's all I'll need?"

"Yes."

He could make her smile with nothing more than a look. "And if I need a comb or lipstick?"

"Your hair looks perfect." His gaze slowly moved from her hair to her mouth. "So do your lips."

Dear Lord, but the desire that struck right then weakened her knees. Why was she wishing that he would kiss her? Randal had married her in order to buy Dad's company, and she'd married him in order to have her family's bills paid.

"What are you thinking so hard about?" he asked.

She forced her thinking to clear. "Nothing. Just wondering if I'll need my purse or not."

"Not." He tugged her toward the door.

By the time they walked out the front of the house, his excitement had become so evident, it was seeping into her. "Where are we going?"

"I told you, out to lunch and then for a drive."

"I know what you told me, but something tells me you have more in mind."

He opened her car door and, once she was sitting on the seat, handed her the envelopes. "We'll mail these first."

He jogged around the front of the car, climbed in, and they were off, driving toward downtown. They made a quick stop at the post office, and then he parked near a cute little café where they sat outside, in the shade of an awning over the tables lining the sidewalk. She wondered if this had been his secret, because she sensed he had one.

"This is lovely," she said, after they'd placed their lunch order, referring to the flower boxes on the widows of the café as well as the vases of flowers on the table.

"I thought you might enjoy getting out," he said.

"I do, thank you." She hadn't been out of the house since their wedding. The next day, the house had been full for the gift-opening party and starting Monday morning, he'd left for work early each morning. Upon returning home, they'd spent the evenings downstairs, with his grandfather listening to radio programs or hearing Ness share many of his stories of years gone by. It was enjoyable learning more about Randal's family.

"I couldn't get away for a honeymoon, still can't, not until I know when Carl will put his company up for sale."

"I never expected a honeymoon."

"I know you didn't." He put his elbows on the table and leaned toward her. "You've been very unselfish about our arrangement from the beginning. The only thing you asked for was to sew your dress."

The newspaper announcement flashed across her mind and she had to look away. "I shouldn't have done that. I'm sorry."

"Sorry? Your dress was lovely and admired by many."

That article had been festering inside her since she'd read it, and the frustration of that was screaming to get out. "No, it wasn't admired. It was labeled homemade, and that made people question..." She swallowed the lump in her throat.

"Question what?"

Maybe that's what this was all about, her dream and how it had not only crumbled, it had affected him. "Your wealth," she admitted. "I never thought of the consequences of that."

"The consequences of my wealth?"

The weariness inside her grew. "Not necessarily the consequences of your wealth, but the consequences of them not believing you *are* wealthy."

"Them?" He shook his head and leaned back. "Did I miss a portion of our conversation? Because I don't understand how your dress could make people question my wealth."

She folded her arms across her midsection and leaned closer to make sure no one walking past or sitting near could hear their conversation. "The nation is in the middle of a depression, and anything homemade suggests that the depression is affecting your family, too."

"The depression is affecting every family in one way or another."

"Yes, but by sewing my dress, I gave people cause to believe that you may not be as wealthy as they'd once thought."

His frown increased, but he didn't comment as the waitress brought them the food they'd ordered and set it on the table. After the waitress had walked away, Randal said, "Did you enjoy sewing your dress?"

She unfolded her napkin and laid it on her lap. "Yes. I've always enjoyed designing clothes."

He lifted his knife and fork. "Good. Then that's all I care about."

"You have to care what people are thinking. It was printed in the newspaper."

His fork paused near his mouth. "What was printed in the newspaper?"

"That my dress was homemade."

He chewed and swallowed before gesturing at her plate with his fork. "Aren't you going to at least taste your food?"

She scooted a green bean around on her plate with her fork. "You don't seem to understand the implications—"

"Yes, I am understanding," he interrupted. "And I'm annoyed at what the newspaper printed, because I can see that it upset you. I also understand that we haven't had the chance to learn that much about each other, so

I should let you know that I'm rarely interested in what the newspaper says, or what other people think. Other than those I care about."

Although she attempted not to, Jolie looked up from her plate.

He'd set his fork down and was looking directly at her. "I care about what you think, and I hope you're interested in what I think."

She nodded.

"Good, because I think you shouldn't put much stock into what the newspaper or anyone else has to say. If you want to sew, to design clothes, then that is what you should do. Just like you did with your wedding dress. Your mother wasn't pleased about that, but you didn't let that stop you."

She shook her head. "It's not that easy."

"Why isn't it?"

Flustered that he truly wasn't understanding, she said, "Because what I do affects you, now that we are married."

"I'm aware of that." He reached across the table and ran a finger over the back of her hand. "And as your husband, I will support you in whatever you want to do." He grinned. "As long as it's legal."

He was still rubbing the back of her hand with the tip of one finger and the warmth spreading up her arm was affecting her ability to think. "Legal?"

A smile spread across his face as he removed his hand and picked up his silverware again. "Yes. I'm assuming there is nothing illegal about creating clothing."

"Well, no."

"Then I encourage you to continue doing so." He

lifted his fork to his mouth. "And I encourage you to eat your lunch, so we can go on our drive."

"You really don't care what other people think?"

"No."

"Yet, that is why you married me, because Dad thinks whoever buys his company needs a wife."

Once again, he waved his fork. "That is different. I'm simply abiding by his rules."

She considered that, but for only a moment because it didn't make sense. "I think you are talking out of both sides of your mouth."

"Perhaps, or maybe in this instance, I found a degree of agreement with his logic."

He sounded serious, but his eyes held too much of a twinkle to make her believe he truly was serious. "Logic?"

"Yes, logic."

That merely led her to have more questions, but his plate was almost empty, so she spent the next few minutes eating. During that time, her questions compounded, and she concluded that she didn't know much about the man she'd married at all. She also concluded that she liked him. Appreciated his honesty, even if she didn't understand his logic.

Upon leaving the café, he drove north out of downtown and then westward. Her mind was still in a quandary. She wasn't upset that she'd married him, wasn't even all that upset over the newspaper article or what others believed. Nor was she sure what any of that meant. Was there still a chance her dream could come true? She wasn't sure of that, either, but knew if there was a chance, she had to take it, but only if it wouldn't cause trouble for him. He might not put much stock into what the newspapers or others say, but that wouldn't stop others from putting stock in it.

When he pulled off the highway, onto a gravel road, she said, "This is the road to the airport."

"It is. I thought we'd drive out here, take a look at a few planes as one day, hopefully soon, we might own an airplane company."

He was driving with one hand. The elbow of his other arm was resting on the base of the rolled-down window and his fingers were curled around the top of the car. "We?" she asked, trying to decipher if she'd heard correctly.

"Yes, we. We're in this together. It'll be your company as much as mine."

She let that sink in for a moment. "If—if I wanted to be involved in the business, you wouldn't mind?"

"Why would I mind?"

"Some people don't think women should work, shouldn't have an interest outside of the house, their family."

"I'm not saying you have to."

"And I'm not saying that I want to, or don't want to," she said, confusing herself, but not wanting him to think she might not be interested.

"There's plenty of time for you to decide. Carl hasn't put it up for sale yet."

"But you're sure he will."

"Yes."

She already knew that. He wouldn't have married her if he wasn't sure. Drawing in a deep breath, she turned and looked out the window. There was truly something wrong with her. Nothing was making sense. She wanted to sew, and couldn't decipher why she also had a desire to help him with his airplane business. She couldn't do both...could she?

Randal saw the way she stared out the passenger window out of the corner of his eye and wondered what about her had gotten under his skin. And not in a way he was used to. He couldn't seem to get her out of his mind.

He wasn't impressed with the newspaper calling her dress homemade, that was for damn sure, and now he knew why she'd seemed so solemn all week.

Though she'd greeted him each evening with a smile, and had been content to sit downstairs, listening to a radio show or Grandpa telling one of his stories that everyone, less Jolie, had heard a million times over, when they'd go upstairs afterward she turned somber, quiet.

That's why he'd set this up today. Hoping if she saw the airplanes, rode in one, that she might understand why he was so interested in Carl's company. He'd known airplanes would be the wave of the future the first time he'd flown in one several years ago, and had started to invest in them. Now he was ready to have a company that others could invest in, and hoped that she'd see it that way, too, because it was a sure bet to be successful.

He pulled the car up near the hangar. A small silver plane with a red tail and wings was parked outside the big doors.

"Is that one of the planes that Dad's business builds?"

"No, though it is similar in size. Carl's business builds mail-carrying planes, but when we buy it, I plan on expanding beyond that, focus on passenger planes.

Right now, there are planes that carry up to twenty people. Someday, they'll carry a hundred."

"One hundred?" she asked, yet was smiling. "That would have to be as large as a bus."

"An airbus. I like the sound of that." He opened his door. "Ready to take a closer look at it?"

"I knew you had more in mind than just a drive," she said as he took her hand to help her out of the car.

"How did you know that?"

"The sparkle in your eyes."

His gaze lingered on her, because he couldn't look away. Nor did he want to. Her dark brown eyes were mesmerizing. They were twinkling like stars in the dark of night. Sharing a room with her each night had become an agony he hadn't expected. He had to keep reminding himself that they were taking it slow, getting to know each other, but he was ready for more. A man has needs and he'd planned on their marriage providing that. Love wasn't needed for that to happen. Love wasn't needed for anything other than heartache and misery. He wouldn't open himself to that.

"Randal!" Roger Wayne shouted from near the hangar. "I have her gassed up and ready to fly!"

"Are we going to watch it fly?" Jolie asked.

Randal took ahold of her hand and led her toward the plane. "No, we aren't going to watch, we are going for a ride."

She stopped walking and grasped his arm with her free hand. "In the airplane?"

"Yes, in the airplane."

Chapter Eight

Half an hour later, they were soaring over the countryside, but Randal was hardly aware of specific sights Roger and his co-pilot, Allen, pointed out to Jolie. He and she sat in the two back seats, and though their chairs weren't touching, she hadn't released his hand. Not because she was scared, but because she was excited, squeezing his hand every time there was something she wanted him to see out one of the windows.

The plane was noisy, stuffy, and smelled of hot oil, fuel and metal, but none of that deterred her enjoyment. He'd never have believed she could look more beautiful, but happiness did that to her. The way she went from looking out her window, to leaning across him to look out his, and peering between the front seats to look out the windshield, was captivating.

Roger had warned her about turbulence and airsickness, but she didn't appear to be bothered by either. Shortly after takeoff, she'd squealed softly at some of the rougher jolts the plane had made, but quickly had laughed at herself and assured him she was fine, and now acted as if she was a seasoned flyer.

It was hard to hear, so they had to yell almost directly into each other's ears, which didn't seem to faze her, either. All in all, the want to kiss her again was back with a vengeance. He'd dated, kissed women often, but had never once wanted to kiss anyone the way he did her. He was trying hard to not put much significance on it, but that didn't lessen the want.

She was far more attractive than any woman he'd known. He'd realized that from the start. She also fit into his plan better than anyone else ever would have. Neither of those facts should instill the kinds of desire that smoldered and leaped to flames out of the blue at numerous times. Such as now, and in the mornings when he'd catch her walking out of the bathroom, all fresh and clean and wearing one of her fitted dresses. And at night, when he'd see her climb into bed, wearing a modest, loose-fitting nightgown that somehow, on her, looked completely tantalizing.

He had read the article about their wedding in the society page of the newspaper, but hadn't picked up on the line that stated her dress had been homemade. The fact that she had, and had been disturbed over it, bothered him. Her dress had been beautiful, and she was talented. Anyone who noticed the way her clothes fit would have to admit that, if they were being honest. But some people were never honest. They'd rather be snobbish and rude, putting the blame on social standards or some other excuse, because they were jealous.

Her handmade dress showed talent, not poverty. If she wanted to design and sew her own clothes, then that is what she should do. He'd see to it.

In fact, her reaction to that newspaper article wasn't all that different to what he'd been dealing with his entire life.

The mention of her dress being homemade had instilled doubt in her. Something his family had done to him since day one. Both his father and his grandfather had created a competition within their family that had pitted them against each other, and him against both of them. The wealth his grandfather had amassed had become something that his father had been expected to double, and then it was down to him to double what his father had amassed.

That competition had been instilled in other things, too. If another boy had mowed one yard, he'd been expected to mow two. If they'd split one cord of wood, he'd had to split two, and so on and so forth. He'd worked hard to meet every expectation put upon him and had learned early on that there were no excuses. Rain shouldn't stop him from mowing lawns and blizzards shouldn't stop him from splitting wood.

There had never been encouragement that he could do whatever the challenge had been. Only doubt, because in the end, there was no way he could be better than his father, than his grandfather.

The stock market crash hadn't changed the expectations on him. Hadn't wiped out the tally sheet that had been held over his head for years.

Jolie squeezed his hand, and understanding the signal, he leaned closer so she could shout in his ear. "Look, there's another airplane!"

He leaned across her to look out the window beside her. "It's a passenger plane!"

"Look at how big it is! It looks too big to fly!"

He tried to focus on the plane, but he could feel her breath on his cheek as she spoke into his ear. Unable not to, he turned, faced her and placed a soft, quick kiss on the tip of her nose. "I'm glad you are enjoying this!"

"I didn't know what to expect in the beginning, but this is amazing! So amazing!" She looked at him for a long moment, smiling, eyes sparkling, and then leaned forward and kissed his cheek. "Thank you."

Holding back his desire to kiss her lips, deeply kiss her, nearly killed him. "You're welcome."

Her gaze went back to the window, and he leaned back into his seat, knowing what he was watching— her excitement—was more amazing, more captivating, than what she was seeing out the window.

The flight lasted for over an hour, and she was still excited, still enchanting, when the plane touched down and rolled to a stop. Upon climbing out the door, Randal turned around and grasped her waist. She laid her hands on his shoulders for him to lift her down. He lifted her out of the plane, but didn't set her down until he'd carried her out from beneath the long wing of the aircraft.

There he lowered her, and to his surprise, as her toes touched the ground, she didn't release him, but slid her arms around his neck and pressed herself against him in a tight hug. "That was wonderful. So wonderful!"

He folded his arms around her, keeping her against him. He'd felt a unique bond with her from the beginning, but at this moment it was so strong, so real, he felt it deeper, as if his soul felt it, needed it.

That was impossible and he released his hold.

She lifted her head, but rather than release him, she kissed him.

Soft and warm, her lips met his, tentatively at first. The idea of not returning her kiss crossed his mind, but only for a second. She knew where things stood between them, and wasn't expecting love any more than he was willing to give it.

Within a flash, her lips became as demanding as his, unabashed and holding nothing back. He didn't, either, thrilled to know he had chosen the ideal wife.

Jolie's heart was still pounding when they drove away from the airport. The airplane ride had been beyond exciting, beyond anything she'd ever imagined, but her heart was pounding because of what she'd done. She'd kissed him. The impulse had struck so fast and hard she hadn't been able to stop it. The moment their lips had touched, she had realized what she'd been doing, but then he'd responded and that had ignited some kind of flame inside her that just sort of took over.

There had to be a reason for that. Perhaps because inside, a part of her realized that she was no longer alone.

It could also have been because they were here, at the airport, a place her father had brought her to not long before he'd died.

He had been the backbone of their family, and that role had fallen to her upon his death. A role she hadn't wanted and one that had left her feeling completely alone in so many ways. While in Randal's arms, she'd realized that was no longer true. She and Randal were in this together. Their wedding hadn't brought them together because of love, but they were married and she admired him, liked him, and that was enough. There were probably many marriages that had less than that.

If the last few years had taught her anything, it was to appreciate what you did have, every day.

She appreciated him, and had more to be thankful for than she'd had in a long time. He'd said she could work if she wanted to, and she did want that.

"Why didn't we see any larger, passenger airplanes at the airport?" she asked as he turned onto the highway.

"Because that was just a small privately owned airfield where Roger and Allen store their plane," he said.

Before they'd boarded the plane, he'd explained to her that Roger and Allen worked for the utility companies and used their plane to plot out new electrical and telephone line routes. At that point she hadn't known what to expect, but hadn't been afraid because he'd been beside her and had held her hand the entire time.

"The passenger planes fly out of the main airport," he said. "It's owned by David Albright and his brother. They also own the A and R Railroad, but David saw that airplanes were the wave of the future a few years ago."

"Like you," she said.

"Yes, I've been intrigued with planes for years, but after Lindbergh made his transatlantic flight, I knew they were going to be the next era of transportation. The airmail planes that Carl's company makes fly out of the main airport, too," he said.

"Where is that airport?"

"Southeast of downtown. Haven't you seen it?"

"No. I've seen the planes overhead, and knew about the small airport we were just at because my father used to drive out here for exhibition shows. I assumed it was the only airport around here."

"There are actually several small ones. Carl's company has an airstrip, but it's only for testing their planes," he replied. "You haven't seen the main one? Or Carl's company?"

"No, Dad bought it shortly before my father died." Guilt struck again, at still not telling him about her visit to Dad. She needed to, but still didn't want him to know what she and Dad had talked about. Love. She didn't want him to think that was what she expected from their marriage. "I've only seen Dad a couple of times since my father's funeral."

He took ahold of her hand, held it firmly. "Losing a parent is hard, painful. That pain never really goes away, but it does get easier to carry over time."

She knew he was talking from experience, and wanted to offer him some of the support he'd been showing her. She laid her hand over the top of his. "Yes, it does."

"Would you like to see the main airport and Carl's company?"

"Yes, if you don't mind, I would."

They discussed airplanes while driving. He told her that there were several books and magazines in the bookcase in the bedroom that she could read to learn more. Finding enough money to keep her mother's household going the past few years had been all she'd been able to focus on, and it felt good to know that she now had more time to read, to learn about other things.

The Albright airport had several large passenger planes, some solid gray with the numbers on their tails painted in black, and others brightly painted, including their aviation numbers. Randal explained how those numbers identified and also confirmed the registration of the airplanes like a car license plate. She liked how he would present things in a way that she could easily understand.

All the planes had long rows of windows for the passengers to look out once they'd boarded the planes via the tall ladder that was rolled up next to the door.

"Have you ridden in one of those?" she asked as they watched one of the planes take off.

"Yes." They were leaning against the front of his car, side by side, and he leaned over, bumped her shoulder with his. "We'll take a trip so you can fly in one of them."

"A trip to where?"

"Wherever you want."

His arms were folded across his chest as he stared ahead, at the airplane that was flying higher and higher. His profile made her smile. She could see how much the planes meant to him, feel how badly he dreamed of owning them. Folding her arms, she bumped him in the arm like he had her. "Where would you like to fly to?"

"South Dakota."

"Why?"

"To see the building of Mount Rushmore. They've been working on it for over five years, and although I've seen pictures, I'd like to see it in person."

She'd read about that, too, how the carving of George Washington was expected to be completed by next year. "That would be very interesting to see. I read recently that President Roosevelt had signed an executive order to place Mount Rushmore under the jurisdiction of the National Parks Service."

He glanced at her. "I read that, too, and that the pictures don't do it justice."

"They say it's truly massive. I'd like to see it, too."

"All right then, that's what we'll do. Fly to South Dakota and see Mount Rushmore."

The idea was exciting, but having been broke, searching for pennies to buy eggs and bread for so many years, she had to ask, "Is it expensive to fly?"

"Some think it is, but we can afford it."

"I wasn't implying that you couldn't, I just…" She let

her voice trail off, not sure how to explain the knot that formed in her stomach when she thought about money, about spending it.

He touched her shoulder. "Those worries are over for you."

Involuntarily, she leaned toward him, as if her body ached for a form of support because her mind knew it wasn't that easy. After not having money for so long, no longer worrying about it couldn't happen overnight. Even while writing out the thank-you cards, she had calculated the cost of each card, each stamp. Every time she sat down at the table to eat at his house, she couldn't stop from adding up how much had to have been spent on the food. That had all become a part of her, and she wasn't sure she wanted it to go away because it made a person think before they spent.

Randal's arm slid around her shoulders. "Shall we drive past Carl's company now?"

"Yes."

He kept his arm around her as they walked to the passenger door, and she missed the weight and the comfort when he removed it for her to climb in the car.

The airport was on the outskirts of town, and they headed farther into the countryside. As they drove, he told her more about Dad's business, how he made the mail-carrying planes because it was a government contract, and how that was enough to make the company fruitful, but how that was also holding him back from making it as successful as it could be because the contract kept them compliant, and not branching out into other models and ventures.

His motivation and determination had her commenting, "You must have been encouraged to never give up as a child."

"I can't say *encouraged* is the right word," he replied. His tone was light, but it was laced with something heavier. "Why?"

"I was told not to fail. I was given goals that I had to meet, then surpass, double, triple. There was no other option."

"What sort of goals?"

"I started mowing yards for the neighbors when I was seven. By the time I was ten, I was mowing ten yards a day, but that still wasn't enough. I was expected to find more customers. I started on the first yard at six in the morning and didn't get home until dark, but that was an excuse."

"An excuse? You were expected to mow yards in the dark?"

"That was one option, but I found another option."

"What?"

He stopped at a stop sign and waited for a car to pass before crossing the road. "Hire someone to help me."

She grinned because she would not have thought of that. "That certainly was another option."

"When I turned fifteen I sold my lawn mowing business to a competing company, and used a portion of the money to buy my first trades."

"And saved the rest?"

"No, I bought my first car. Brand-new."

"You had to have been proud of that. And your father had to have been proud, too."

"I was, but my father was furious."

The idea of anyone being upset at him after he'd worked so hard irritated her, and filled her with sympathy for him. Reaching over, she laid a hand on his arm. "Why?"

"Because I'd failed."

"Failed? How?"

"I hadn't diversified enough." He glanced at her. "I'd put my eggs in one basket, instead of five, or ten. It was a lesson learned, and one I've remembered."

"That's why the stock market crash didn't hurt you as badly as it did others, because you were more diversified in your investments?"

"Yes, it worked in my favor."

"Is that why you want to buy Dad's company? To be even more diverse?"

"Yes, and no. I'm willing to invest far more in buying the company than I have in any other investment. It's a chance I'm willing to take because I've researched it thoroughly. I know what I'm getting into. The past few months I've been working on balancing incoming funds with the outgoing funds so that we'll be fine until the investment starts to pay off."

She knew all about incoming and outgoing funds, and guilt struck hard. "I'm sorry. I know my family—"

"It's all part of the investment," he said. "And doesn't affect the bottom line any more than my family does."

She flinched slightly at being referred to as an investment. She also wondered about his family. Danielle and James lived in the same house as them. Willa and Don didn't, but visited regularly. Don worked at his father's drugstore as a pharmacist and James was a photographer. Did he consider them all investments?

"This is Carl's company," Randal said, gesturing toward an area that had several large buildings and a few airplanes in a field behind the buildings.

The yellow-and-red planes were much smaller than the passenger ones. "Those planes do look like the one we flew in."

"On the outside. Inside there's only room for one pilot, the rest is cargo space." He continued to explain more about the planes and the company as they drove around the buildings, past the planes, and then back out to the road.

She found it all interesting, but had so many other things on her mind, she was having to compartmentalize things: the number of people he was financially supporting, within her family and his, the airplanes and Dad's business, and how badly he wanted his dream to come true.

"I have one more place I'd like to stop," he said as they entered the city again. "If that's all right with you?"

"Of course."

The smile on his face was like earlier today, at the house. A secretive one. Like a pirate would have. She glanced out the side window and bit her lips as her smile formed.

"What are you smiling about?"

"You," she admitted, looking at him. "And your pirate smile."

"Pirate smile? What's a pirate smile?"

She twisted in her seat so her back was toward her door and it was easier to look at him. "The one on your face. It was there earlier, too, when we left the house."

He glanced her way. "Was it?"

She slapped his arm playfully. "Yes, and you know it. It's a smile that says you have a secret. So what is it this time?"

"You'll see."

Chapter Nine

It had been a long time since he'd enjoyed a day this much, and Randal wasn't ready for it to end. This had been the most significant amount of time they'd spent together since their wedding day, and it had given him a deeper understanding of Jolie. He sensed he'd barely scratched the surface, but liked what he had discovered and had no doubt the trend of that would continue.

"Here we are," he said pulling up next to the curb.

She glanced out the window, at the department store, and then back to him. "What do we need here?"

He flashed her a grin and pulled open his door.

A quizzical frown still tugged on her brows when he opened her door and took her hand to assist her out of the car and into the store.

He didn't know much about sewing, but had seen bolts of cloth and other sewing notions near the back of the store, and that's the direction they walked.

She quickly caught on, and as her steps slowed she shook her head. "Randal—"

He pressed a finger to her lips. "If my wife wants to design clothing, then that's what she's going to do."

"But—"

He pressed the finger more firmly against her lips. "I want you to pick out whatever you need. However much you need."

Shaking her head again, she closed her eyes.

Sliding both hands over her shoulders and down her arms, he wrapped his fingers around her wrists. "I like the clothes you design." He held her arms out at her sides. "I like how they fit you." She was wearing the same blue-and-white polka-dot dress as their first date. Then, he'd noticed the fitted waist, but now, like her wedding dress, it was the way it fit around her breasts that really caught his attention. It wasn't tight or revealing, just fit her in a way that emphasized the perfection of her figure.

He brought his eyes back up to her face, and the redness of her cheeks said she'd known exactly where his gaze had been moments ago.

"May I help you?"

Keeping his eyes on Jolie, he told the clerk, "Yes, my wife needs material for several new outfits. She designs and sews clothes, and I admire that very much."

Jolie shook her head again, but this time, she was biting back a smile.

He liked that, but liked how dark her eyes had grown even more. "It's just one of the many things I admire about her," he said.

The clerk made a mewing sound along with a long sigh.

Jolie's smile broke free as she whispered under her breath, "Stop it. You're going to make her swoon."

"I don't see why. Everything I've said is the truth." It was either kiss her, or release her, so he released one of her wrists and waved a hand at the bolts of cloth lining the wall. "I'll help you pick out some material."

"Do you know anything about material?" she asked.

"No, but I like how the blue of your dress makes your eyes that much darker."

The clerk, a short woman with curly blond hair and a double chin, met them at the fabric wall. "We have some lovely blue eyelet embroidered batiste that just arrived the other day."

He had no idea what eyelet embroidered batiste was, and looked at Jolie for help. She shook her head, but then shrugged and nodded.

"Let's take a look at that," he told the clerk.

"Randal," she whispered. "This isn't necessary."

"Yes, it is." He winked at her. "I want to witness the start-to-finish process."

Her cheeks pinkened again, and she rolled her eyes, but stepped forward to examine the bolt of material the clerk held.

It was pretty, and he encouraged Jolie to tell the woman how many yards she'd need, but other materials caught his attention, especially a deep blue silk. He laid the bolt on the counter for the clerk to cut next. From there, he pointed out others that caught his eye, and watching her expressions, knew when he'd found one that she too liked. Those all went on the counter with the others. Every so often, he'd purposefully picked out some he knew she wouldn't like, just to make her laugh.

She would pay him back by finding an equally ugly one and hold it up against his chest, threatening to make a shirt for him out of it.

When they'd reached the end of the bolts, he pointed out the lace and ribbon section. "You'll need some of this stuff, too, won't you?" A spool of thick braided cording caught his attention and he lifted it off the shelf. "Especially this."

She frowned. "What would I need that for?"

He unwound a large section off the spool. It was white, with specks of gold in it, and as soft as spun silk. Holding the spool in one hand and the loose end in his other hand, he looped it over her head and let it fall down her back. Once it landed near her waist, he wrapped the lose end around his palm, increasing the tension it to pull her close. "I can think of several things I'd use it for."

She planted her hands on his chest to keep from colliding against him. "I don't believe it's intended to be a lasso."

"It works as one."

Glancing over her shoulder, at the clerk who was indeed watching them, Jolie whispered, "Put that back."

"Why?" he asked innocently.

"Because you're causing a spectacle," she whispered.

"Am I?"

"You know you are."

He wound the rope tighter around his palm, bringing her even closer. "So you want me to let you go?"

"Yes."

She was looking up and he was looking down, making them almost nose to nose, but it was lips to lips that he wanted to be. "What will you give me?"

"Give you?"

"Yes." He lifted a brow. "To let you go?"

Her giggle was soft, almost silent. "Am I being held for ransom?" She lifted a brow. "By a pirate?"

"Aye, mate," he hoarsely whispered.

Laughing, she wiggled against his hold. "Will you stop? And let me go before you turn us into a real spectacle."

"Kiss me," he said. "That's your payment. One kiss."

Her lips parted as she gasped. "You can't be serious. We're in a store."

"I know where we are. What I don't know is how long you're willing to stand here, caught in my pirate rope." Shrugging, he added, "I could stand here all day."

She searched his face for a moment. "You're serious, aren't you?"

He nodded. "I'm not moving until you kiss me."

She glanced around, but he kept his eyes directly on her. He was indulging himself, fully aware that he hadn't had this much fun, felt this young and carefree in…well, forever. He'd dreamed about being a pirate while mowing lawns, wished he could just find a treasure chest of gold big enough to satisfy his father and grandfather so he could go have fun like the other kids he knew.

"Oh, good grief," she whispered, then stretched onto her toes.

Her plan was a quick peck, he knew that, but he had his own plan. As soon as her lips touched his, he parted his and caught her bottom lip between his, not letting her pull back. He felt the moment the tension left her body and she gave in to the kiss. He took full advantage of that and teased, tasted her lips with his for several sweet moments. The kissing didn't last nearly as long as he'd have liked, but he, too, was aware that they were being watched and didn't want to embarrass her.

When he finally released her lips, she was fully up

against him, with her finger curled within the lapels of his suit jacket.

"You're incorrigible," she whispered.

He understood she was trying to blame him for how much she'd enjoyed the kiss, and was more than willing to take the blame. "And you're beautiful." He kissed her forehead before unwinding the cording from his hand and lifting it back over her head.

Her breasts rose as she drew in a breath of air while stepping back. "Now put that away."

"This?" He held up the spool.

"Yes."

"No." He wound the cording back onto its spool. "I'm buying this. I've always wanted a pirate rope."

Jolie was so overwhelmed she could barely think. Not from all the material and sewing notions, but from kissing him in the middle of a department store, in full view of clerks and customers alike. She tried to calm herself by picking out thread, buttons, trimmings and such, but by the time they carried everything out to the car, she had no idea what all he'd purchased. Other than the entire spool of white cording with gold specks. And a couple yards of pearl-gray linen with enough tint of blue in it that it matched the color of Randal's eyes to perfection. The prospect of making him a shirt out of that material elated her. She couldn't wait to get home and open up her sewing machine.

He took the last package from her and set it in the trunk of the car. Now that they were outside, away from being overheard, she said, "Thank you, but this really wasn't necessary." He'd just spent an extravagant amount on sewing supplies.

"I felt it was." He closed the trunk and stepped in front of her, trapping her between the car and him. "I admire your clothes and look forward to seeing the new ones you create."

No one had ever supported her dream, and she appreciated that he did, but couldn't get over the fact that it would affect the way society looked at him.

He brushed her hair from one temple. "You worry too much."

There was no use pretending that she wasn't, he'd see through it. "I'm just afraid of what people might think."

"I don't care what people think, and I wish you didn't."

She shrugged. "It's embedded in me."

"It's funny how that happens, isn't it? How things end up living inside us, driving us, even though it's not how we really feel."

He was clearly referring to something embedded inside him, leaving her unsure how to respond. She wished that wasn't so, and wondered how she could help him. Lifting her chin, she smiled. "Maybe that's something we can work on together."

"I like that idea." He placed a tiny, soft kiss on her forehead and slid his arm around her shoulders to walk her to the passenger door.

She truly didn't know what to think about the way he made her feel. Every touch filled her with a warm excitement. Perhaps because she'd never had a boyfriend. She had dated a small amount while in school, but then the stock market crashed and her father died, and life had completely changed.

"You're worrying again." He pulled open the car

door. "I can tell because right here." He touched her forehead. "Between your brows, a little wrinkle forms."

No one had ever teased her the way he did. Like everything else when it came to him, it made her happy. "And you think that's funny."

"I didn't say that."

She pressed a finger into the tip of his chin. "You didn't need to. I can see it in your eyes. They're twinkling."

"Twinkling?"

"Yes." She stretched up on her toes and whispered next to his ear. "Just like a pirate."

He poked her in the ribs with one finger, the absolute most ticklish spot on her body. That was her downfall. The one thing she couldn't control at all. Being tickled.

The way his eyes sparked, she knew he knew, and jumped in the car before he could tickle her again.

He laughed, closed the door and was still laughing when he climbed in the driver's door.

She pinched her lips together and stared straight ahead.

"You're that ticklish?"

"I'm not ticklish."

"Yes, you are."

"No, I'm not."

"Yes, you are."

She huffed out a breath, fighting both laughter and looking at him. "Just drive." Was there no rhyme or reason to her? One second she was worried, the next second she was breathless from his simplest touch— or more specifically, kisses, which truly did more than take her breath away—and the next second, she was laughing, happy.

"Where else are you ticklish?" he asked.

Continuing to refuse to look at him, she replied, "No-where."

"Just the ribs, then."

"No. I'm not ticklish at all."

"Liar."

She saw his hand move from the steering wheel out of the corner of her eye and reacted swiftly, grabbing his wrist in hopes of stopping him from touching her in the ribs.

He laughed as his hand settled on the gear shifter and he shifted gears.

Not trusting that he'd only shifted to prove that he hadn't been going to touch her, she kept her hand wrapped around his wrist, and he kept his hand on the shifter.

Their hands remained like that until he pulled into the driveway at his house. Their house now, as it was where she lived, too. She'd accepted that readily enough, it was the obligations that went along with it that she was still uncomfortable about because she wasn't sure what those obligations included.

"Time to unload the trunk," he said.

Nodding, she released his hand. He turned off the engine and then wrapped his fingers around hers while opening his car door with his opposite hand. He tugged her to follow him. She scooted across the seat, passed the gear shifter and steering wheel to climb out his side of the car. Cautious, because her body was still sensitive at the idea of being tickled, she scanned his face as she swung her legs out of the door.

"I'm not going to tickle you," he said.

Not certain she could completely believe him, due to his broad smile, she asked, "Promise?"

He released her hand and stepped back, holding both hands up, palms out.

"That's not a promise," she said.

Laughing, he walked to the back of the car.

She climbed out, shut the door and kept her distance as he opened the trunk. It might be foolish. Many people found tickling funny. She didn't. She hated the way it left her with no control over her body.

"You're worrying again, Jolie."

Today had been fun. More fun than she'd had in a long time, and here she was, worrying about a silly thing like being tickled. She walked to the trunk to assist him in collecting packages.

With their arms full, they entered the house, through a door that the ever-somber-looking Peter held open.

"Would you like me to take those for you, ma'am?" he asked.

"No, thank you, I have it," she replied.

"We're good, Peter," Randal said. "Thanks. We just picked up a few things that my wife needed."

Peter closed the door and gave a genteel nod. "Very well, sir."

Jolie waited until they were out of earshot before she said, "I didn't need anything. This was all you."

"Yes, it was," he answered as they crossed the foyer.

"Then why did you say I needed a few things?"

"Peter would never believe that I needed yards of material."

She glanced at him as she started up the stairway to the second floor. "Or pirate rope?"

"He's probably never seen pirate rope. I hadn't until

today." He leaned closer. "Nor had I met someone so worried about being tickled."

A shiver rippled over her. "You promised."

He lifted a brow. "No, I don't think I did."

She shot up the steps so quickly a bag slipped from her hands. There wasn't time to stop and retrieve it. He was right behind her. Even though she didn't want to be tickled, she couldn't help but laugh at the excitement that raced through her as she ran up the stairs.

He landed at the top of the steps at the same time she did, and with a laughter-filled squeal, she ran down the hall toward the bedroom. His laughter echoed off the walls, and though she wondered what others in the house might think, she didn't let it slow her down.

At the bedroom door, she grasped the doorknob, twisted it and shot inside, but Randal was too close for her to get it shut in time to keep him out. She dropped the two bags she was still carrying and ran toward the bathroom door, seeking sanctuary there. Barely a step later, Randal caught her around the waist and lifted her feet off the floor.

"No! Please don't tickle me," she pleaded. "Please!"

He set her feet on the floor, pivoted her around to look at him. "Give me one good reason not to."

"Because I don't like it."

Excitement was racing through his veins. Not only had he not chased someone up a flight of stairs in years, he'd never enjoyed doing so more than today. He slipped his hands around her waist, to the small of her back, and pulled her closer. "Why don't you like it?"

She planted her hands on his biceps. "Because there's nothing I can do about it."

The way she was looking at him, full of sincerity and honesty that penetrated clear to his bones, he felt rotten about teasing her. She was so prim and proper, so sweet and innocent, he'd enjoyed seeing her blush, but he sincerely didn't want to hurt her. Not now or ever. He also knew how hopeless a person could feel.

"I won't tickle you. I promise." He touched his forehead to hers. "Cross my heart."

She sighed softly. "Thank you. I know it's silly, but—"

"It's not silly. We all have things we don't like."

"What is something you don't like?"

Failure, but he wanted to keep things light, so he said, "Beets."

She leaned back and looked up at him. "Beets?"

"Yes. I've never liked beets."

She smiled. "Well, if I have the opportunity, I'll make sure you don't have to eat any."

"Thank you. I appreciate that."

Halfway through her nod, she gasped. "Oh!"

He twisted, glanced over his shoulder to see what she saw. Bags and packages were spewed across the floor, as well as their contents.

"Look at the mess we made!"

"I'll help clean it up."

"Yes, you will," she said, laughing. "You helped make it."

Chapter Ten

Once everything was put away, to her specifications, which meant stacked neatly on the small table that was sitting near the desk, he crossed the room and removed his suit jacket, tossing it over the back of the sofa in the sitting area.

"As long as you are taking things off, remove your shirt, too, please."

He spun, stared at her. "Excuse me?"

Her back was to him as she dug in a basket. "Take off your shirt, please."

"Why?" he asked, as he began unbuttoning his shirt. A dozen things raced through his mind. She'd been open to kissing today, but he wasn't completely sure she was ready for things to advance that quickly.

Turning, she held a tailor's measuring tape in one hand and a pencil and paper in the other. "Because I need to take your measurements."

"What for?"

"The first thing I'm sewing out of the material you just purchased is a shirt for you," she said, crossing the room.

Removing his shirt, he tossed it on the sofa with his jacket. "I didn't buy material for me, I bought it for you."

She twirled a finger in the air, indicating he should turn around. "I know, but I picked out material so I could sew you a shirt." She set the pencil and paper on the table beside him. "Now turn around and hold still."

He spun about. She stretched the tape measure across his shoulders, and down his back, pausing to write numbers on her paper between each action. Then told him to hold his arms out at his sides.

Many tailors had measured him over the years, and she had the lightest touch he'd ever felt. The simple brush of her fingers made his breath stick in the back of his throat.

"Turn around," she said. "I need to get your chest and waist measurements."

Keeping his arms out at his sides, he shuffled in a half circle to face her. "Like this?"

"Yes." Her cheeks flushed as she used both arms to stretch the tape measure around his back and then pull it taut over his chest.

By the time she finally wrote a number on her piece of paper, Randal figured it would take a good ten minutes for his heart to slow down to a normal beat again. Then she wrapped the tape measure around him again, this time his waist. The back of her knuckles brushing over his lower stomach sent more than his heart throbbing. He tried to make light of that. "It's like my pirate rope."

She pinched her lips together. "No, it's not. It's a tape measure and I'm not holding you captive."

He trailed a finger along the side of her face. "You could."

"Both arms out and hold still."

"Why do I have to put both arms out?" He touched her earlobe.

She tried to brush his hand away with her shoulder. "So I can get an accurate measurement."

"My arms aren't attached to my waist."

"I know your arms aren't attached to your waist, but I need both arms held out at your sides."

He exaggerated a sigh, and held both arms straight out long enough for her to get a measurement, but before she could reach for the pencil, he caught hold of both of her elbows. "Aren't you going to ask for ransom before you let me go?"

"No."

"Why not?"

"I already said that I wasn't holding you captive."

"Why aren't you?"

"Arms out again. I need to measure the circumference of your upper arm."

He'd never been vain, but as he held his arms out again, he considered flexing his biceps, in hopes of impressing her. His entire body was reacting to her closeness, and the blush on her face said she wasn't unaffected, either.

She measured both arms, wrote them down and then looped the tape measure around his neck. "One last measurement."

"Then I have to kiss you?" he asked, hopeful.

"No."

Using a knuckle, he lifted her chin so she was looking at him instead of the tape measure at the base of his neck. "But I want to."

She nibbled on her bottom lip and glanced away. "I

thought we were taking it slow, getting to know each other."

He cupped the back of her neck. "We have been. We've been married a week."

"Tomorrow will be a week."

"I know."

When she looked at him, with her eyes sparkling, he could barely remember his name.

"Fine." She tilted her face, brought it closer to his.

Not dipping his head and capturing the lips she was freely offering was the hardest thing he'd ever done, but he wanted her to know she was in charge. It was her choice. The seconds that ticked by were some of the longest in his life.

And worth the wait. Her hands cupped his neck and pulled his head down to meet her lips.

It wasn't just one kiss, nor was it one-sided. As soon as their lips parted, they came back together in mutual agreement that more was needed.

When he'd come up with this plan, when she'd agreed, he'd known their lives would become entwined, and had expected they'd form a friendship, a mutual agreement of fulfilling obligations, and grow accustomed to each other, but he'd never expected the overwhelming desires that filled him.

At first, he thought the sound was merely his pulse, echoing in his ears, but when she broke the kiss and bowed her head, preventing him from capturing her lips again, he heard the knocking on the door.

Damping down his frustration, he responded to the knocking by saying, "Yes?"

"Forgive me for the intrusion, sir." Peter's voice came through the door. "You have a telephone call."

Peter had been with them for years, and wouldn't have disturbed him if the caller had been willing to leave a message. "I'll be right there." Regretting having to leave, he rubbed her shoulders. "I have to take the call."

"Of course." She stepped back and scooped the pencil and paper off the table.

He picked the tape measure off the floor and handed it to her. "I'll be right back."

Not bothering with his shirt, he crossed the room and pulled open the door. The bag Jolie had dropped during their run up the stairway was sitting on the floor. Smiling at the memory, he picked up the bag, set it inside the room and hurried down the hallway. He'd never spent enough time in his bedroom to merit having a telephone line extension installed in that room, but he would have Peter order one as soon as possible.

The caller surprised him. Carl Jansen, inviting him and Jolie to a dinner party the following night. Randal accepted the invitation and encountered his grandfather on his way back toward the staircase.

"I was wondering," Grandpa said, leaning on his gold-knobbed cane.

"About what?" Randal asked.

"This marriage of yours, to a girl you'd never mentioned until you announced your engagement."

He'd been expecting this conversation, had been surprised it hadn't happened before now, and at this moment, didn't want to take the time to have it. "You should be happy. You've been telling me to get married for years."

"You insisted you didn't want to get married," Grandpa pointed out.

"I didn't, until I met Jolie."

Grandpa grinned. "Then why have you been sitting down here every evening? Listening to the radio when you should have been up in your bedroom? The reason you needed to get married was to carry on the Oster-lund lineage. You're the last male."

That had been shoved down his throat for years. "Because we didn't want to be rude." He stepped around his grandfather. What was between him and Jolie was no one's business but theirs, yet he couldn't stop from saying, "It's good to know we no longer have to worry about that."

"Dinner will be served soon."

"Same time as always," he replied, already leaping up the stairway.

A unique sense of excitement was still singing through Jolie's body, so strongly it was hard to concentrate on the people or food. Randal was sitting at the head of the table, next to her, and all she could think about was kissing him. She tried hard to not think about it, but it was impossible. Nearly as impossible as remembering the sight of him without his shirt on.

Why did she find him so attractive? Would that make things more complicated? Or would it make things easier? It certainly made kissing him easy. Or was it because he'd bought enough material that she could sew to her heart's content?

Dear Lord, was she already turning into her mother? Rather than sitting home crocheting doilies, she'd sit home sewing clothes? Or was he trying to turn her into her mother? He'd said he didn't care what others thought, that she should sew if she wanted to, but he would when the gossip started, and spread, about them having *handmade* clothes. That couldn't happen. She wouldn't let it. She would show him how well she could sew. Men and women's clothing, and then show him how she would never depend on him for everything. That she could and would contribute to their partnership.

She was glad when the meal ended and when Randal explained she had some sewing she wanted to complete. Before dinner, she'd had time to create a pattern from tissue paper and had told him she wanted to get it cut out yet tonight.

She would do more than that.

Randal escorted her upstairs, and when he entered the room behind her, she said, "You can go listen to the radio show."

"No, I'll stay up here with you."

She glanced toward the table where she had the material laid out.

"I won't bother you." He walked to the sofa. "I'll just keep you company." Removing the suit coat he'd put on for dinner, he asked, "Or will that bother you?"

"It won't bother me." Chloe had often sat in her bedroom, talking while she'd sewed at home. She could have his shirt done in time for him to wear it to Dad's dinner party tomorrow night. The dinner party invitation made her nervous, but they had to go.

"I'll just sit over here, as quiet as a mouse, and read," he said. "Unless there's something I can do to help?"

"Actually, do you know if you have an ironing board and an iron?"

"Yes, I know we do. I'll go get them."

"Thank you, and a bowl that I can use for water?"

His frown had her quickly adding, "I need to sprinkle it on the seams when I press them open."

"Okay. I'll get a bowl, too."

She was in the midst of cutting out the pattern pieces when he returned, along with Peter. The two of them set up the ironing board near the sofa, where there was an electrical outlet handy, and she bit her lips together to keep from smiling at the size of the bowl he'd brought her. It had to be the biggest mixing bowl in the kitchen. One a tenth of that size would have been more than sufficient.

Assuring that all was exactly as she needed it, she thanked Peter and then sat down at her machine to stitch the first pieces together. Once done, she carried it to the ironing board. Randal had filled the bowl with water for her use and had set it on the table in front of the sofa, where he sat reading a magazine.

"I wasn't sure how much you needed," he said.

She grinned at how the bowl was filled to the rim. "This is perfect." Carefully, she dipped her fingers in the bowl and sprinkled the water over the seams.

"Why do you do that?"

"Pressing the seams open prevents any tiny puckers when I'm sewing on the adjoining piece, and the water creates steam, so they hold their shape and stay in place," she explained, while ironing. "What are you reading?"

"An airplane magazine."

"Tell me about the article." She collected the material and walked back to the sewing table to pin on the sleeves.

"It won't bother you?"

"Not at all."

* * *

The hours that passed were truly enjoyable, with her sewing and him reading the articles in the magazine aloud and then the two of them discussing what he'd read. It was about passenger planes and the airlines that owned them, how they'd hired young nurses to be stewardesses to take care of the passengers and their frequent airsickness. They had hired young men at first, but the article explained that nurses were better equipped to know how to care for the passengers who frequently threw up.

"When you buy Dad's company, who will you sell your planes to?" she asked, walking to the ironing board again. The shirt was complete, except for attaching the collar and cuffs, buttons and buttonholes.

"No one."

She sprinkled the pocket she'd just sewn on with water. "No one?"

"No, I not only plan on building planes, I plan on creating an airline." He set the magazine on the coffee table next to her bowl of water. "I figure it will take about five years before we see a return on our investment."

Setting aside the iron, she picked up the shirt. "Five years? It'll take that long to build the planes?"

"Not the first few, but it'll take at least that long to build up the company. Once the first plane is built, staff will need to be hired to fly and maintain it while more are being built. Within five years, I hope to have enough planes in the air, filled with enough passengers, to make back my investment as well as ongoing operating costs."

"That seems like a long time." And costly. Everything was costly, and she couldn't help but think about the money he'd spent on all the material today.

"Don't worry. I have plenty to get us through."

She couldn't help but worry, and waved a hand for him to stand up. "I need you to try this on so I know if I need to make any adjustments before putting on the collar and cuffs."

He stood and she told herself to look away as he un-buttoned his shirt, but for the life of her, she couldn't. In an attempt to not focus on his chest being revealed, she spun around and turned off the iron, then unplugged it from the outlet.

"You don't need to iron anymore?" he asked.

Still keeping her focus off him, she coiled the cord around the handle, being careful of the still-hot metal. "Not tonight. I'll mark any adjustments and finish it in the morning."

"Say, this fits really well."

She set the iron on the board before looking up. Not gasping was hard. The pearl blue-gray material did match his eyes perfectly.

"It's not tight across the shoulders at all," he said, testing the fit by pumping his arms in front of his chest. "And the length is perfect."

"Let me see." She twirled a finger for him to turn around so she could examine the back first. Pride filled her as she smoothed the shoulder yoke. The material tapered exactly as his body did, framing him perfectly. "Put your arms out," she said, watching as he lifted both arms to make sure the material didn't pucker or constrict movement.

"It feels good," he said.

"Turn around." Once again, she smoothed the material, this time along his arms, down his sides and across his chest. Then she held the two front sides together in the center, to check for fit once the buttons were attached. Once again, she was proud of how perfectly it fit.

"I like it," he said.

"So do I," she admitted. "There's still plenty of length on the sleeves to add the cuffs. Do you like one or two buttons on your cuffs?"

"One. I rarely use the second one."

"All right then. You can take it off. I'll finish it in the morning."

"I can't believe you sewed a shirt in one evening."

Even though she'd been examining the shirt, it had been the body underneath that she'd felt. The muscles that rippled his arms, chest and shoulders, and that had her hands trembling. Once again, she turned about in order to not stare as he removed the shirt. "It's not done, and it's after ten." Seeing the water bowl, she picked it up to carry it into the bathroom.

"Where should I put this?" he asked.

"You can just leave it..." Words escaped as she looked up, saw nothing but his bare chest, splattered with dark hair, and immediately her hands began to tremble again.

"I'll get a hanger so it doesn't wrinkle," he said.

She closed her eyes to block the view. "Okay." Drawing a deep breath to collect her bearings, she took a step. A very stupid thing to do with her eyes shut, and made worse because her knees were oddly weak, and didn't want to work. A yelp escaped her throat as the water sloshed and the bowl slipped from her fingers, landing upside down on the sofa. "Oh, no! I'm sorry! So sorry!"

* * *

An hour later, she was not only sorry, she was mortified. The water-soaked cushions meant that Randal was
in the bed beside her. Right beside her. She could hear
him breathing, feel the covers move up and down with
each breath. Feel the heat radiating off his body. Feel the
slope of the mattress because of his weight next to her.

The mortifying part was what all that did to her body.
Her heart was pounding, her palms sweating, and a tingling sensation zipped up and down every inch of her.

"What do you think of Air America?" A second later,
he said, "Sorry. Didn't mean to wake you."

"You didn't."

"Then I didn't mean to startle you. I felt you jolt."

She swallowed and licked her lips, knowing nothing would settle her heightened nerves. "What is Air
America? I've never heard of it."

"I'm thinking that's what we could call our airline."

"Oh." She silently repeated the name several times.
"That sounds like a good name."

"Our planes will fly to every airport in America," he
said. "Someday, every airport in the world."

"Will it really take five years to earn back your investment?"

The bed shifted as he rolled onto his side. Her eyes
had adjusted to the muted darkness some time ago, and
she could see him looking at her, with one elbow in
the pillow and his head propped on his hand. "If we're
lucky, it'll only be five years."

She rolled onto her side to face him and tucked both
hands beneath the pillow under her cheek. "Won't that
be a long time with no money coming in?" The past

few years had taught her that money going out and none coming in didn't make for an easy life.

"That's where other investments will come in. Keep us fluid."

So many people expected him to keep them fluid.

He touched the spot between her eyebrows. "There you go, worrying again."

"I can't help it."

"Just like you can't help caring what people think?"

"Yes, because I do care what others think, and you will, too, when they are gossiping about your wife and her homemade clothes. How you can't afford for her to buy new things."

"I can and will always be able to afford to buy you whatever you need, but you like designing clothes, and you're good at it. Your wedding dress, the shirt you made me, are amazing, and show how talented you are." He rubbed her upper arm. "Designing clothes makes you happy, so that's what you should do, despite what anyone says."

There was so much more to it. More than she could explain. "I don't want you to be embarrassed because you married me."

"Do I look embarrassed?"

Hardly. He looked wonderful. Even in the dark, she knew exactly what his bare chest looked like, how beautiful his eyes were, how his face was perfect in every way. And the rest of him. The parts she hadn't seen unclothed. Embarrassing herself with her own thoughts, she closed her eyes. "I don't mean right now. But it will happen."

He rolled onto his back and put both hands beneath

his head. "Why do you care so much about what others think?"

The memory that struck was painful, so dark and ugly, a tear slid out of her eye. She'd kept it hidden, refused to think about it for so long, that it gave her a chill. Grasping the blanket, she rolled over and pulled the blanket up over her shoulder, tucked it beneath her chin.

He laid a hand on her shoulder. "I'm sorry. I didn't mean to upset you."

"You didn't." She sucked in a breath. "I've never told anyone."

"Maybe it will help if you do." He tugged on her shoulder, until she rolled onto her back again. "I won't tell anyone."

His gaze was thoughtful, sincere. Uncurling her hand from the blanket, she drew in a deep breath. "When I was in grammar school, some kids held me down on the playground and tickled me until I wet my pants," she said quickly, before she lost her nerve. As soon as the words were out, she added, "I can't believe I just told you that. I've never told anyone. My mother doesn't even know about it."

"The school never told her?"

"No. Thank goodness. Mother would have been mortified that I'd done something like that. The nurse gave me dry panties and an ugly brown skirt, that she had to pin to make it small enough to fit around my waist. I had to wear that skirt all day, until I got home and threw it away." Even with the pin, she'd had to hold on to the waistband of the skirt to keep it from falling off, and everyone had noticed.

"Didn't the other kids get in trouble?"

"For what? Making someone laugh?"

His fingers wrapped around hers. "For holding you down."

"All the teacher saw was them tickling me, and didn't think there was anything wrong with that."

His other hand slid beneath her neck and pulled her up against him. "I was born peeing my pants. Did it for two, three years, straight."

Her mortification disappeared as she fought smiling. She snuggled her head deeper onto his shoulder. "That's not the same."

Randal tightened his hold around her and kissed the top of her head. He hadn't thought of Amy since his first date with Jolie, but was now, because a sixth sense told him Amy was one of the kids who had held Jolie down, tickling her until she wet herself. Amy was not only mean, she was sly, would have known they wouldn't get in trouble for tickling. That was part of the reason he'd dated her, because she wasn't likable, and therefore, no one, not even his grandfather, would have expected or encouraged him to marry her. That had kept him safe, because he would never enter something that was sure to fail. That was also why he chose to marry Jolie. Their marriage wouldn't fail, as long as they both got what they wanted out of it.

All thoughts shifted back to her. "I know it's not the same, I was just trying to make you feel better. Some memories stick with us. Affect us more than we realize."

"Your lawn mowing business?" Jolie asked quietly.

That was one that had stuck with him over the years. "Yes, I should have learned what was expected when I was told that one lawn should be two, two should be four, four should be eight, and so on."

"Learned what? You built a business that you sold when you were only fifteen."

He grinned at the mixture of pride and indignation in her voice. "I learned that failure's not an option."

"You didn't fail!"

He rubbed her arm, tightened his hold on her. In his father's eyes he had failed and had vowed it would never happen again. Not in any aspect of his life.

She snuggled closer to his side. "I'm proud of you for being so young and successful."

She'd would never know how much her words meant to him. "Thank you." He rested his chin on her head. Whoever those kids had been that held her down, he'd like to find each and every one of them. More than that, he wished he'd been there that day, to make them stop before they'd hurt her, embarrassed her. "Is that when you started sewing? Because of that ugly brown skirt?" He'd heard loathing in her voice when she'd mentioned it, more than when she'd mentioned the kids that had held her down.

She lifted her head, looked at him. "How did you guess that?"

He'd wanted her all day, and the way she was looking at him with those shimmering brown eyes, increased those desires. Pressing her head back onto his shoulder, he replied, "Because you always look perfect. Your hair, your clothes." Her body and face and everything else. "I can believe that wearing an ugly brown skirt, pinned to fit, would have been traumatic for you."

"It was. I ran all the way home and upstairs to my bedroom before anyone could see me, but it was actually Dad's wife, Anna, who introduced me into sewing a few weeks later. I'd gone over to their house with my father, which I did a lot, and she was sewing. She let me help, and when I went home that day, she put together a small sewing kit for me. Material, thread, straight pins, the measuring tape I used on you today, everything I needed. I sewed clothes for my dolls and my cat and—"

"Your cat?" He couldn't help but interrupt.

"Yes, Thomas, my cat."

He loved how happy she sounded. "Was he fond of that?"

Her soft laughter made her entire body jiggle against his. "Well, I still have a scar on my thigh from one particular dress that he really didn't like."

He wanted to see that scar. "Because he was a boy, wearing a dress?"

"No, he never minded that. It was the pin I'd accidentally left in the dress that poked him right under his little kitty arm."

"Ouch."

She giggled again. "You might want to remember that when you're trying on clothes for me."

"I will."

There was a short length of silence. A nice, comfortable silence.

"My father bought me my sewing machine for my birthday a couple of years before he died, and I sewed some clothes for myself, but Mother would never let me wear them in public."

"Because it wasn't fashionable?"

"Back then it could have been because they weren't very good. But she never knew about the dresses I fixed. Ones she bought me that didn't fit right. I'd put in darts or pleats to make them fit better. She never noticed. Not until after my father died, and to keep our wardrobes in style, I had to make things over. Or make two old dresses into one new one. I did that for all of us. Even my brother. I remade most of my father's clothes to fit him as he grew."

Another silence ensued, and he wasn't sure if he should break it.

"I did some sewing for neighbor ladies, but it wasn't until my wedding dress that I totally designed and sewed a dress completely from brand-new material."

At that moment he'd never been happier about a purchase than he was the material he'd bought today. "I would have never guessed that."

"Thank you for all the material you bought today."

"You are very, very welcome."

The silence that followed was so long, he wondered if she'd fallen asleep.

"Randal?" she asked, in barely a whisper.

"Yes?"

"I…I like you."

The warmth that rushed through his system was like nothing he'd ever known. He pressed his lips against the top of her hair and held them there for a long time. Feeling the warmth. Inhaling her sweet, flowery scent. "I like you, too." Very much, and that was something he could live with, because they would be living together for the rest of their lives.

Chapter Eleven

"My Anna never cared for cigar smoke," Carl said, lighting the end of a stogie. "I try to not expose other women to that, but I do enjoy one after a fine meal."

"The meal was delicious." Randal sat back in the solid leather chair in Carl's den. "Thank you for the invitation."

"I'm glad the two of you could make it." Carl took another puff off the cigar, blew out smoke. "I also wanted a moment of your time to mention something."

Randal gave him a nod.

"I have this little airplane business," Carl said, "that not a lot of people know about."

Randal picked his drink off the table, trying to hide the excitement that zipped through him.

"And I thought you should know," Carl continued. "That it's in my will to go to Jolie."

Randal's excitement froze. He lowered his glass, swallowed the bourbon in his mouth, let the burning sensation in the back of his throat, down into his chest, overtake his senses for a moment, giving him time to form a response.

When the burning eased, he asked, "Is Jolie aware of that?"

"No." Carl tapped the ashes off the cigar in an ashtray on the table between their chairs. "We didn't discuss that when she came to see me about marrying you."

For the second time in a matter of minutes, Randal was taken aback. He'd assumed Jolie's mother had contacted Carl about paying for the wedding. Not Jolie. She'd never mentioned talking to Carl about their marriage. "I was more than willing to pay for the wedding," Randal said.

"I'm sure you were," Carl said. "That's not why she came to see me. She needed some fatherly advice on love."

Love? Randal's insides churned.

"I was happy that she'd sought me out, and offered—actually, insisted—that she let me pay for everything." Carl drew on his cigar again as he glanced at an oil painting hanging over the fireplace. "Anna and I never had a daughter. Just our two sons, they were our blessings and I'm proud of them. But Joey-girl, she stole our hearts. I'm her godfather, you know."

"She mentioned that," Randal answered. Jolie had mentioned that, but hadn't mentioned that she'd gone to see Carl for fatherly advice about love. What kind of trick was she trying to play?

His stomach somersaulted. Had she known about Carl's will, but figured he wouldn't give her the company if she wasn't married? And needed to know if love had to be a part of that marriage?

He didn't want to believe there was a conniving bone in her body, but there certainly was in her mother's, and the apple doesn't fall far from the tree. His jaw tightened.

It would be a major failure for a man to make a fortune on a company that had been given to his wife. Doubly so for him. That certainly wasn't the Osterlund way of doing things. His father would roll over in his grave and his grandfather would probably fall right into his if the family fortune was expanded that way.

"Her father, Joseph, and I were best friends," Carl said. "Had been for years, long before he married Amelia. She never liked me, Amelia that is. Anna used to say that Amelia was a young bride and jealous of the time Joseph spent with me because that meant he wasn't with her. We did a lot of business together, Joseph and I. I tried to get him to invest in things outside of the market, but that's where he was making the bulk of his money and he just wasn't willing to take the risk. I didn't blame him for that, nor did I blame Amelia. No one should come between a husband and wife, and I tried hard to make sure that I never did that."

Randal nodded, but was only half listening. His mind was still reeling that Carl was willing to give away the very company he wanted to buy to increase his fortune, his status in the business world. If he did that with a company given to his wife, people would think that was the only reason he'd married her—for her money.

"Because we made money together," Carl continued, "Amelia never stopped Joseph from coming over, and she never stopped him from bringing Joey-girl with him. Anna and I treasured those visits." He stubbed his cigar out in the ashtray. "Joseph is the one who came to me with the idea of the airplane business. He was intrigued with them. Went out to watch exhibitions at the airfield west of town regularly. If the stock market hadn't crashed, we would have been partners in the company. I went ahead and bought it and I told Joseph the company was half his. He wouldn't hear of it, and…"

Carl shook his head, sighed heavily. "A month later, he was dead. The day of his funeral, I changed my will. Told my boys that the airplane company goes to Jolie when I die."

That explained why Carl had refused offers to sell the company. Randal had known about offers, and had been using those numbers as a base for the one he'd been preparing. "How did your sons respond to that?"

"They have other businesses, other interests, and are fine with my decision, because it was my decision to make. They are quite a bit older than Jolie, but knew how much Anna and I loved her. She's called me Dad from the time she could talk, because that's what Anna called me and Jolie just assumed that was my name, or maybe she just assumed all men were called Dad. I loved having her call me that, and still do."

Randal was having a hard time swallowing all this. On one hand he was happy for Jolie, that she'd had Carl and his wife's devotion for so many years, but on the other hand, his dream had just been destroyed. He'd have to find another business to buy. Which wouldn't be easy.

Worse yet, this would mean his marriage was a failure, too. Jolie wouldn't need him, or his money, once she inherited the company.

His guts knotted together. "When do you plan on telling Jolie all this?"

"Well, that's why I'm mentioning it to you first. She's a good girl. Good woman. Strong, dedicated and stubborn. I wish she would have come to me when they were in need, but that would have been going against her mother, and she wouldn't do that." He shrugged. "I considered contacting her, giving her the company more than once over the past few years, but I was afraid of what might happen. Of men coming out of the wood-work to marry her, just for the company. Unsavory men. Jolie deserves to be loved. Deeply and wholly. If she hadn't come here, needing advice, I may have questioned if she was marrying you just to save her family. I know you paid the taxes on their home."

"I did," Randal replied, but withheld the fact that he and Jolie didn't love each other. Never would. They'd agreed to that.

Carl winked at him. "And let me say, I agree with you giving Amelia a monthly allotment. She was another reason I couldn't give the company to Jolie earlier. Amelia has never been good with money. What little Joseph left them only lasted as long as it did because of Jolie."

Randal nodded, having already figured out all of that, and asked again, "When do you plan on telling Jolie of what she will inherit?"

"That depends on you," Carl answered. "I want you to have time to get all your affairs in line."

"My affairs?"

"It's my understanding that you are quite diversified in your investments, and that you were able to manage losses due to the market crash far better than most. That takes considerable time and effort. I have an excellent manager at the company. Duane Mills. He's trustwor-thy and handles the day-to-day affairs with no issues, but there is room for growth within the company. I'm too old to put in that time and effort. You aren't. Jolie may not want anything to do with the company but it will be hers, so she can sell it, keep it as is, or look to expand. Personally, I hope she keeps it, and that as her husband, you will dedicate your time and expertise in helping her succeed."

"I don't mean to sound..." Randal searched for the right word. "Indelicate, but it's difficult to plan when someone might inherit something."

Carl laughed. "I did forget that piece, didn't I? I'm not waiting until I die to give it to her. I want to do it soon, within the next few months. Can you arrange things so you'll have the time to assist her by then?"

His affairs were already completely in order to dedicate all of his attention to the airplane company, but he'd need more than months to find another company to buy and put another plan in place. Even longer to make it be worth more than the company Carl was giving his wife.

He didn't like the idea that Jolie was not the woman he should have married, but it sure appeared that way.

"You can review the time you'll need, and we'll talk again in a few weeks." Carl stood. "Right now, we better get back to the rest of the guests. I invited David Albright and his wife tonight because I'd like you two to get to know them. David owns the main airport in town and will be a real asset when you and Jolie take over the company."

Randal knew what an asset David Albright would be, and he hated the conflict battling inside him right now. Sleeping with Jolie in his arms last night had been heaven on earth, and now he felt like he'd been plunged into hell. A man who became rich off his wife was no real man. He didn't want a failed marriage, either. Right now, it was one or the other.

"Oh, and one final thing," Carl said. "Let's keep this between the two of us. I want it to be a surprise to Jolie when I give her the company."

Jolie had been making small talk for what felt like hours, with people she barely knew, and some she'd only met tonight. Dad, wanting to enjoy one of his cigars without exposing anyone else to the smoke, had asked Randal to join him in his den some time ago, and they still hadn't returned to the room.

"Sit here. There's plenty of room."

The invitation, including the patting of the cushion beside her, had come from Jane Albright, a beautiful blonde woman, who was very pregnant. They had been introduced earlier this evening, before the meal had been served.

"My feet couldn't take standing any longer and I'd love to have someone to talk to," Jane said.

"Thank you." Jolie sat, glad that the doorway was within eyesight. Her nerves were a jumbled mess, wondering if Dad had told Randal about her coming to see him for fatherly advice. Waking up snuggled up against him this morning had been the most wonderful thing. She'd never felt so safe, so content. She should have told him about visiting Dad last night, while they'd been lying in bed talking. But she hadn't.

"I heard about your wedding dress," Jane said quietly. "I wish I could have seen it."

Jolie's spine stiffened. Jane Albright had seemed so nice and kind earlier.

"Oh, horse feathers!" Jane said. "I should have said that I heard your gown was absolutely stunning. That's what I meant. Forgive me, please? I'm usually not such a simpleton. I swear this baby just steals my mind at times." She rubbed her stomach. "Which is fine, but I truly didn't mean to insult you. I used to sew all my clothes. When I lived in California. My sisters did, too. But from the sounds of it, we never created anything as lovely as your gown. And don't worry about what the newspaper printed. They wrote unflattering things about me when I first arrived in town, and my family in California even heard about it." She laid her hand on Jolie's arm. "And now I'm rambling. Just tell me to shut up. I won't mind. Just, please forgive me, and my baby."

Jolie grinned at the woman's honesty. "There's nothing to forgive. Is this your first baby?"

Jane's face glowed as she laid both hands on her stomach. "Yes. If it's a boy, his name will be Gus. Augustus David Albright. Named after the two most wonderful men on earth. Gus is David's grandfather and he's absolutely delightful."

Jolie heart skipped a beat, wondering if she'd ever know the happiness that exuded off Jane. "And if it's a girl?" she asked.

"Mary Jane. Mary after David's grandmother—Gus's wife—and Jane because David insists." She sighed. "He's so wonderful, but so is your husband. I've never met him before, but I've sent him a thank-you note every month for years."

"You have?"

"Yes, from the soup kitchen. I chair the fundraising committee. Randal is one of the few that when the need increased and donations decreased, he doubled his contribution, and has continued to be one of our largest donors every month. Many people have benefited from his generosity."

Jolie didn't know what to say. "Randal is a generous man."

"Yes, more than many others." Jane let out a huff. "I was so glad when his past affiliation ended. The only person Mr. Casswell has donated to is his daughter, making her an even bigger spoiled brat." Jane slapped a hand over her mouth. "I'm sorry. I did it again, and believe me, I know that no wife wants to talk about her husband's former girlfriends."

Jolie was liking Jane more and more. "That's all right. Amy is a spoiled brat."

"Such a brat her father had to send her overseas to find a husband." Jane twisted her shoulders and leaned back against the sofa, as if trying to get comfortable. "Just blame it on the boobs."

"Excuse me?" Jolie asked.

Jane laughed. "See, there went the brain again. I was talking about mine, not Amy's." Leaning closer, she whispered, "They've gotten so big and uncomfortable. I swear, half the weight I've gained has gone straight to my boobs. David says they're beautiful, but he doesn't have to carry them around. And they don't fit into any bra."

Glancing around to make sure no one was within listening distance, Jolie wasn't sure if she should laugh or be embarrassed over talking about such personal topics.

"If I find one big enough for my boobs to fit in, I have to tie knots in the straps to keep them from falling off my shoulders, and then it doesn't fit around the middle so it's always riding up. Like right now." Jane fidgeted with the sides of her dress. "But the alternate, one with straps that don't fall down, is worse. So tight

I can't even breathe once I manage to get it on. And the way they squash my boobs is painful."

Jolie could relate to that. She'd had issues with bras since she'd started wearing them. Not because her *boobs* were overly large. At any size it was difficult to find a fit that was comfortable because women were all made differently. "I could help you with that," she whispered.

"Pulling it down?" Jane asked, still tugging at her sides, although discreetly.

Jolie giggled. "Well, if you need, I could do that, too, but I've sewn my own bras for years and they are much more comfortable than anything you can buy. I sew them for my sister, too, and for a couple of elderly women that used to be my neighbors."

"Sew them? I never thought of that." Jane slapped the cushion between them. "If you could sew me one that's comfortable, I'd empty my husband's bank account to pay you." Jane's expression was serious. "And he wouldn't mind because ever since I became pregnant, I've been complaining about my boobs."

With another glance to make sure they were still not being overheard, Jolie said, "I would have to measure you, or tell you how to measure yourself." Lowering her voice even more, she added, "With no clothes on. I need exact measurements to get the exact fit."

"I have two sisters," Jane said. "We measured each other all the time, you just tell me when and where. I'd do it right now if we had a tape measure."

"Well," Jolie said, glancing around, not sure if she should take advantage of what she knew.

"Well, what?" Jane asked excitedly. "Do you have a tape measure?"

"No, but Dad's—Carl's—wife, Anna, her sewing

room is just down the hall. I knew her very well, and
her sewing items might still be there."

"Seriously? Can we go check?" Jane shook her head.
"Please don't think badly of me. I love being pregnant,
knowing David and I created a life, and that it's inside
me, safe and warm, and growing until it's ready to come
out, but I'm so frustrated by being so uncomfortable."

"I don't think badly of you," Jolie assured. "Let's go
see if Anna's supplies are still there."

Hurrying beside her across the room, Jane whispered, "Thank you! I've even tried going without, but
that wasn't any better."

"I'm positive I can make one that will work for you."
Jolie led the way down the hall, past the closed door
of Dad's den and into Anna's sewing room. Memories
flooded, making her eyes sting as she noticed everything was in the exact same place as when she'd been
here years ago.

"Oh," Jane said softly. "You must have really loved
Carl's wife."

"I did. She was like a grandma to me. She gave me
my first sewing kit." Jolie shook her head in order to
focus on the task at hand. Opening a drawer of the cabi-
net that held Anna's sewing machine, she took out the
tape measure. She also retrieved a pencil and paper.

Jane was already removing the stylish, short black
jacket that was over her cream-colored dress. "I'll have
to ask you to unbutton the back of my dress."

"Of course." Jolie stepped around and quickly unbuttoned the dress.

"You'll see where I tried to take in the sides, but it
didn't help."

Jolie did see the stitches on the sides of the bra, and

how the bunched-up material was leaving red marks on Jane's skin. "Your bra is made of tightly woven cotton and that doesn't give, nor does it move with the body. Also, the elastic is stitched on, which makes it lose its ability to stretch." Anna had been the only person she'd been able to talk to about sewing, and being in her sewing room, Jolie just couldn't seem to stop. "And the whole seamless bra that they are touting is ridiculous. Without seams, it won't fit any woman's body, furthermore, if your underclothes don't fit your shape, your outer clothes won't, either. I use darts, four of them, so the material conforms, but I also use two layers of material, back-to-back, so there are no seams to irritate the skin or distort the outer clothing."

"Do you have one on right now?" Jane asked as she stepped out of her dress. "Could I see it? I know that sounds crazy, but I'm usually not a complainer and I really want to be comfortable and enjoy every part of my pregnancy. I'm so excited that you could make that happen."

"Sure," Jolie agreed. Randal was wearing the new shirt that she'd completed this morning, but she was wearing a red-and-white dress that she'd remade before their wedding, which buttoned down the front. She unbuttoned it and let it fall off her shoulder.

"Oh, my goodness! That is so pretty! Is it silk?" Jane asked.

"Yes, but cut on the bias so there is some elasticity to it, and the elastic is inserted through a hemmed fold, so it doesn't bind."

Jane laughed. "I never thought I could be this excited over a bra, but I am!"

"Me, either," Jolie admitted. "I'm excited, because I know I can help you."

The two of them laughed and talked and laughed some more. Once Jolie had all the measurements she needed, and they were both fully dressed again, they left the room. The door to Dad's den was open and the room empty, causing Jolie's heart to skip a beat. It skipped another one as soon as she entered the front room and saw Randal. His smile filled her with a delightful warmth as their gazes met.

"Oh, good, our guys are together," Jane said, her arm looped through Jolie's. "Let's go tell them that you and Randal are coming to dinner on Monday night." Giggling, she added, "I'm so excited, I'm giddy."

Jolie had promised to have a bra for Jane by Monday at the latest. It wouldn't take her long to make one—after her shopping trip with Randal, she had all the materials needed—but she didn't feel comfortable saying she'd sew it tomorrow. A bra was not something she'd want Randal to see her sewing. It seemed too personal.

"Hey, there, big guy," Jane said to her husband as she slid her arm around his back. "Did you miss me?"

"You know I did, doll face." David wrapped his arm around her shoulders and kissed his wife's upturned face, before he said, "We were wondering where you two were off to."

Randal rested a hand on her lower back and Jolie, longing for what she saw between Jane and David, had to stop herself from snuggling up to his side. She and Randal didn't love each other the way Jane and David did. Nor would they. Ever. She didn't want that and neither did he. She was just caught up in the excitement of helping Jane.

"Someone said the two of you disappeared together," Randal said to her.

She would have replied, but the smile he'd flashed moments ago was gone and the dullness in his eyes stole any reply that might have formed.

"Outfit mishap," Jane said. "And Jolie was kind enough to help me. The two of you are also invited to our house for dinner on Monday night."

"Splendid idea," David said. "Randal and I have a lot to discuss."

Randal nodded, but his stiffness, his aloofness, made Jolie's stomach sink.

"Seven o'clock?" David asked.

"That sounds fine," Randal replied.

"Oh, good! I can't wait!" Jane wrapped her other arm around her husband's waist.

David pulled Jane even closer as he laughed, and Jolie felt a longing that she couldn't describe. And regretted.

They visited for a few more minutes, before the couple took their leave, and a short time later, she and Randal thanked Dad and bade him good-night.

"Come see me again, soon," Dad said as he kissed her cheek.

"I will." Her emotions were all mixed up because she knew Dad had to have mentioned her visit to Randal.

Shortly after he'd driven out of Dad's driveway, Jolie squared her shoulders, knowing she had to get it over with. "Dad told you I'd come to see him before our engagement, didn't he?"

He never took his eyes off the road. "Yes, he mentioned that."

"I was going to mention it to you."

All he did was nod. It was dark outside, and in the car, but she saw his head move, slightly, and she waited for him to say something. But he didn't.

"I didn't mention it," she said, "because I didn't want you to think I was attempting to undermine your chances of buying his business."

"Why would you think that I would think that?"

She'd never heard him sound so distant. Berating herself for not telling him, she looked out the side window. "I don't know. I didn't know you at the time, so I didn't know what you would think."

"Did you talk about his airplane company?"

"No. It never came up. I went to see him because I wanted to know what he expected. What would be expected of me if I did marry you. You'd said that he'd only sell to a married man, and I wanted to know why. What a wife had to do with a business deal."

"What did he say?"

"He didn't. He assumed I was there for a different reason."

"Assumed?"

"Yes."

"What did he assume?"

She huffed out a breath. "That I didn't know what love was."

"And that's what you expected?"

"No." She bit down hard on her bottom lip, forcing her emotions to not get involved. There was no reason to be upset about any of this. "That's what Dad expected, and I couldn't tell him otherwise, or he would have..."

He waited for a long time before asking, "Have what?"

"I don't know, maybe tried to stop me, or maybe

figured out that you only wanted to marry me so you could buy his business." That was the only reason he'd married her, and she knew it, so why did it bother her now? "I acted like he was right, and agreed when he set the date."

"Carl set the date? Not you? Not your mother?"

"Yes, he set the date. He said true love shouldn't have to wait."

Chapter Twelve

Randal stayed downstairs after they'd returned home, nursing a drink and staring at a newspaper that he had no intention of reading, sitting in the room that had been his father's office, waiting until he was certain that Jolie would be in bed, and hopefully asleep.

As if it wasn't bad enough that he'd never be able to buy the company he'd set his goals on owning, he'd seen something in Jolie's face tonight that made him feel like a total heel. That's what he was, as much of a blackguard as any pirate ever had been. It was disgusting. He'd pulled her into this because he'd wanted to outdo all of his past accomplishments. Turn a company from earning hundreds to making millions. Like his grandfather had. Like his father had. Like what was expected of him.

He'd put everything in place, so nothing could fail.

But it was. His perfect plan was quickly becoming a plan of shambles.

Not just because of Carl giving the company to Jolie, but because of him.

When he'd seen Jolie walk into the room while he'd

been talking to David Albright, his body had reacted. Had remembered waking up next to her, with her head on his shoulder, the sweet scent of her filling the air. For a brief moment, all Carl had said, hadn't mattered. What his grandfather expected hadn't mattered. What anyone else might think or expect hadn't mattered. In that brief moment, when he'd seen her, he'd remembered how she'd said that she liked him last night, and how he'd admitted he liked her.

He'd thought that was fine, for them to like each other, but now...

He took a sip off his drink.

Now, he knew that Jolie wanted more.

Anyone around Jane and David Albright saw the love between the two of them. Jolie had seen it, and she wanted it. He'd seen the longing in her face as she'd looked at Jane and David.

Carl was right. She deserved to be loved.

Randal squeezed the glass in his hand harder. He couldn't give it to her.

This very house had once been filled with love, but he'd seen his father brought to his knees when his mother had died. It had changed his father into someone who'd hated everything and everyone around him. Love had done that.

Randal shook his head. There was no way he'd ever give a woman that kind of power over him. Cause him to fail.

Not even Jolie.

Another thought washed over him.

Carl would give her the airplane company before long and Jolie wouldn't need him for money when that happened. That had been all he'd had to offer her, and she would no longer need it.

Randal's throat burned at the reality of that.

He stood, crossed the room and stared out the window into the dark night. He had a choice to make. Continue being a heel, a blackguard by forcing her to stay married to him, or call the entire sham off, have their marriage annulled so she could someday find the love that she wanted.

There truly was no reason to continue it. His dream of buying Carl's business no longer existed, and he could never give Jolie what she wanted.

He'd had every intention of sharing the company with her if he bought it, but having it given to her, he couldn't claim it as his. Couldn't take advantage of something that belonged to her to further himself and the Osterlund name. It wouldn't be right.

No man could be proud of that.

He hated the idea of failure, but there was nothing he could do.

"What are you still doing up?"

He turned, saw his sister Danielle in the doorway. "Just thinking."

"About what?"

"Nothing in particular," he lied. "What are you still doing up?"

"Hoping to talk to you." She walked into the room. "James is going to talk to you tomorrow, but I saw the light on and saw you, and…" She closed the door. "Oh, Randal, I hope you will understand."

"Understand what?"

She sat down on a chair, looked up at him with a frown. "When I got married, I said that I'd stay here and run the house as long as you needed me to, and I'm—we—are hoping that now that you're married, I can turn those duties over to Jolie."

He leaned against the windowsill and crossed his legs at the ankles. "I would need to speak to Jolie about that." Requiring anything from Jolie was not something he was open to committing.

"She already knows everything I do. We've talked about it."

"About her taking over your duties?"

"No, not taking over, just what I do. You know, approve the menus and shopping lists, check that everything was cleaned to Grandpa's standards." She sighed and threw her arms out at her sides. "Make sure the help doesn't steal the silver."

Caught off guard by that, he stared at her.

"Of course, no one is going to steal the silver. It's just a saying, I was joking. Criminy, Peter's been here longer than I've been alive. Mrs. Hoover almost as long, and I've never made a change to her menus, and as for Darla, she needs this cleaning job to feed her children. She wouldn't chance losing it for anything."

"Darla?"

"She cleans, three times a week, you've never met her, but Jolie has, and all of the staff like Jolie, everyone is glad that you married her. Even Grandpa. Haven't you noticed that he's not as grumpy these days? He was worried that you might marry Amy. We all were."

Randal was not willing to comment on any of that.

His silence gave Danielle the opening to continue. "Grandpa really likes Jolie. He likes how she listens to his stories. Did you know that after you leave for work in the morning, she stays at the breakfast table, talking to him? She does the same at lunch. Tonight, at dinner, he asked me why you are making her sew in your bedroom, when the bedroom next to yours is empty. She could turn the entire room into one just for sewing. He's going to tell you that tomorrow."

"Why do you need to give up your duties?" he asked, needing for his own sanity to change the subject.

"Please don't tell James that I told you."

He was growing tired of secrets. Very tired. "You haven't told me anything."

"Like I said, James is planning on talking to you tomorrow morning, to tell you, that…well, he and I would like to move out."

"Move to where?" Without waiting for her to answer, he continued, "I said I'd buy you a house—"

"We don't want you to buy us a house."

He wouldn't insult her or James, but without his help, they couldn't afford to buy a house.

"We want to rent an apartment."

"Why?"

Her face lit up like it used to when she was little and he'd come home from school. "James and I are going to have a baby."

That didn't surprise him, he'd expected it sooner than later. "Wouldn't you want to stay here, so you have family to help?"

She stood up and walked to the desk, ran her hand over the top of it. "You're my big brother, Randal, and were more of a father to me than our father ever was. Even though you worked as long, as hard, as much as he did, you still had time for tea parties, bedtime stories and to teach me how to ride a bike, amongst many other things. I've always appreciated all that you've done for me. I love you, will always love you, and I know that no matter what, or where, or when, that if I need something, I can come to you. But James is my husband. I love him and he loves me. He and I are a family now, and he wants to take care of his family. Provide for his family. I want that, too. We, James and I, want to build something, just like Grandpa did when he came to America."

Love. His jaw grew tight. It's not the wonderful thing people think it is, but Danielle didn't want to hear that. She thought it was, and she thought she knew what she wanted.

"James has his pride, Randal, and so do I, please understand that."

He did understand that, and he also knew Danielle wouldn't listen to reason. He'd tried that when she'd announced that she and James were in love and getting married.

Jolie couldn't lie in bed any longer. If she'd been going to fall asleep, that would already have happened. She climbed out of bed, picked up the robe she'd left lying across the foot of the bed, and shrugged it on while crossing the room to turn on the light.

Randal must still be downstairs, where he'd stayed upon their arrival home. Should she go make sure he was all right? Or just leave him be? She hadn't expected him to be this upset over her meeting with Dad that he... She shook her head, stopping the thought because it would only make her eyes sting all over again.

She reached the light switch and clicked it on, just as the door opened.

Silent, she and Randal stood still, staring at each

other for a long moment. She was relieved to see him, but he didn't look relieved.

Breaking eye contact, he walked into the room and closed the door. "I thought you would be asleep."

She considered not responding, but only for the briefest of moments. "I said I was sorry."

He loosened his tie, pulled it off and tossed it on the back of the sofa, all the while toeing off his shoes. "No, I don't believe you did."

Unable to recall their conversation word for word, she accepted that he might be right. "Well, I am. I'm sorry that I didn't tell you about meeting with Dad."

His suit coat landed on the back of the sofa, atop his tie.

"What more do you want me to say?" She should have told him, wished that she had, but there wasn't anything she could do about that now. Other than feel bad, which she did. She felt awful.

"Nothing. You met with Carl because you wanted fatherly advice. End of story."

"If it's the end of the story, why are you still mad at me?"

The shirt she'd made for him landed on his coat. "I didn't say I was mad at you."

Flustered, she crossed the room, collected the shirt, coat and tie, and carried them to the closet. "You don't have to say it. Your face shows it."

"Whatever my face is showing isn't anger at you. I'm not mad at you."

She took down a hanger and hooked the coat over it. "Then who are you mad at?"

"Myself."

Hanging up the coat, she took down another hanger

for the shirt. "Why?" She couldn't fathom a reason for him to be mad at himself.

"For believing in a plan that will never work."

A shiver rippled her spine as she hung up the shirt and hooked the tie over a hanger holding several others. "Yes, it will." It had to work. There was no other option.

He opened the wicker trunk beside the sofa, took out the pillow and blanket.

A lump formed in her throat, reading what that meant. "Why do you think it won't?"

Tossing the pillow and blanket onto the sofa, he walked back to the door.

"Where are you going?"

"To shut off the light. Do you want to climb into bed before I do?"

"No. I want to know what's happened. Why are you mad? Why are you saying this won't work?"

He pivoted, looked at her. "Why do you think it will?"

"Because you are good at what you do. You'll be able to create an airline from Dad's business, just like you planned."

"So, I'm good at making money?"

"Yes. And providing for your family. And..." The things coming to her were all personal. Too personal to say out loud. Like how he made her feel happy, safe, secure, and how she wanted to help him make their agreement work.

He turned, walked toward the door. "You're right. That's what I'm good at. Making money." He clicked off the light. "Go to bed, Jolie."

"If you tell me what happened—"

"The only thing that happened was that I started something I shouldn't have." He reached the sofa, sat down.

She could see the outline of his body, how he had his head bowed. "Something must have happened."

"When we discussed this plan, I told you I wasn't looking for love."

Another shiver zipped up her spine. "I know." She had to swallow before continuing, "And I agreed. I was—I'm not looking for love, either."

"I don't believe you fully understand the consequences of what that means."

"Yes, I do." She knew the consequences better than most, and would not turn into her mother. Loving a man to the point that nothing else in life mattered. Not even her own children.

"Do you really want to live the rest of your life with a man who doesn't love you?"

It felt as if a knife had struck her right in the heart, which made no sense, because she hadn't changed her mind. "Yes. That's what we agreed to." She kept her chin up, even as it began to shake. "We like each other, Randal." At least they had… Right now, she wasn't so sure. "I'm sure some marriages don't even have that." She didn't want love, so there was no reason for his statement to hurt her, yet it had. Walking to the bed, she said, "Good night."

Randal squeezed his temples with one hand, wanting to inflict pain on himself. He'd just gone from a heel to a complete bastard. He had to give her the option to get out of their agreement, but he didn't have to hurt her, be a complete ass in the process. He didn't want to fail, especially not at this magnitude, but he couldn't hold her to something that should never have happened in the first place.

He left the couch, crossed the room and sat down on the bed. "I'm sorry. I shouldn't have taken my frustration out on you."

She rolled onto her back, looked at him. "Why are you so frustrated?"

Her voice sounded shaky, sad. The strong, deep ache inside him kept growing. He couldn't tell her why he was frustrated. Not tonight. Tomorrow, he'd call Carl and tell him that this was a secret he couldn't keep. Jolie needed to know, now, so she could decide what she wanted. He would abide by whatever she chose. Couldn't hold her in a marriage that she no longer needed. "Nothing you need to worry about."

"I can't help it. Just…just because we don't love each other doesn't mean we can't care about each other, and I care that you are frustrated."

This was a mistake. He should have stayed on the couch, let the guilt eat him alive. He put a hand on the bed to push off.

She grasped his wrist. "I won't stop caring just because you're on the sofa."

He wanted this day to end, but why? All of his issues would still be there in the morning. Not only with her, but with Danielle. Maybe that is something she could help him with. Talk some sense into his sister.

Sinking back down into the mattress, he said, "Danielle asked to speak to me downstairs."

Releasing his wrist, she sat up, pulled the blanket up and tucked it under her arms. "Why? Is something wrong?"

"She and James want to move out. Into an apartment."

"You don't want them to?"

"No."

"Why?"

"There's no need. There's plenty of room for them to live here."

"And?"

Of course she wouldn't simply agree with him. "They can't afford it," he said. "James is a good photographer, excellent at it, but he doesn't make much money. It will be years before he can afford to take care of his family. I should have seen this coming. Right from the start he wouldn't take any financial backing from me. That's why they've lived here, so he could invest profits back into his company, build it up, and why they need to continue to live here. Baby or no baby."

"Baby? Danielle is pregnant?"

"Yes, she just told me that downstairs."

"They are starting their own family, Randal, and want to do it on their own."

"That's what Danielle said, but she's my responsibility, has been since she was born."

"You were only seven when she was born."

"Old enough to know she needed to be taken care of. She was only a few months old when our mother died from pneumonia, and our father was so mad. Mad at Mother for dying." He clenched his back teeth at the memory of how he'd been mad, too. Because that's what had been expected. "We went through a slew of nannies. Grandpa has mellowed over the years, but back then, he and my father were tyrants, and nannies didn't last long. Some no more than a day. It was up to Willa, who was only five, and me, to take care of Danielle." She'd been so afraid of their father, of his shouting, anger at everything. Randal closed his eyes at remembering how he'd tried to shield both of his sisters from that, and how he'd worried about Danielle while he'd been at school or mowing lawns.

"Did Willa live here after she got married?"

"No. Don's family owns a drugstore and have other investments that have done well for them. James doesn't have any of that. His father died when he was little and his mother was one of our nannies. He and Danielle have known each other since grammar school. He and his mother had moved out of town for several years, and when he returned, he and Danielle dated, and then got married."

"Can I ask you a question?"

"Yes."

"Would you want to live with my family? In their house, have them provide everything we needed?"

"It's a man's duty to provide for his family."

"James is a man."

That's why she'd asked. It was a trick question. "Danielle is my sister. My family. My responsibility. I can't fail her now."

"You aren't failing her. James is her husband, and they love each other."

There it was again. Love. Nothing but trouble is what it should be called.

"They are going to have a baby together," she continued. "And James wants to be the one to provide for both his wife and child. He wants the privilege of providing for his family. Can't you give him that?" She touched his hand. "Very few people want to be dependent upon someone else, because there's no pride in that, but there is pride in taking care of your family. And there are many ways to do that. Can't you let them try? You can always help if they need it."

Randal wasn't sure if it was her well-meaning pleading, or the warmth of her hand, that was softening everything inside him. Or the fact that she was right on a few points.

There was a gentle, serene smile on her face as she scooted back down, beneath the covers. "It's late. We should get some sleep."

After last night, he didn't want to sleep on the sofa and wondered what she would do if he lay down beside her. He huffed out a breath. The sofa was lumpy and short, but it was where he should sleep.

"Lie down and go to sleep, Randal."

Chapter Thirteen

Rolling over and finding the space next to her empty, didn't stop a smile from forming on Jolie's face. Randal had slept there. She'd lain awake until she'd been sure he'd fallen asleep.

Love had not been a part of the deal, and still wasn't. But she'd been honest when she'd said she cared about him, and right now, was worried. She knew the pressure of taking care of siblings, and could relate to his concern about not failing Danielle.

She sat up and scanned the sofa. The back of it was all she could see, but when Randal slept on it, his feet always stuck over one arm. There were no feet there, and the bathroom door was open, the room empty.

After climbing out of bed, she made it, then collected a dress from the closet and entered the bathroom. Before going to Dad's dinner party last night, she'd bathed and her hair had still been damp when she'd pinned it into stylish rolls on both sides. A quick brushing left it hanging in waves around her face.

On her way to the door, she noticed the pillow and blanket were still on the sofa, in the same places they'd landed when Randal had tossed them there. She smiled the entire time she returned them to the wicker chest. He had already provided her and her family with so much. Knowing she'd helped him with his troubles last night made her feel as if she'd given him a little bit in return, even if it was just understanding.

Danielle and Grandpa, which is what he insisted she called him, were sitting at the table when she walked into the dining room. "I'm sorry, I hope you didn't wait on me this morning."

"We just sat down," Danielle said, while pouring coffee for the three of them. "James and Randal ate before they left."

Jolie nodded as if she knew that as she took her regular chair.

"Randal told Peter to get that other room set up for you today. 'Bout time if you ask me," Grandpa said.

Jolie's fingers shook so hard her cup clattered against its saucer. She placed her hands in her lap without picking up the cup.

"Grandpa." Danielle shook her head and handed him the bowl of scrambled eggs. "I think Randal wanted that to be a surprise."

"Well, she'll see Peter carrying everything out of the bedroom," Grandpa replied.

Jolie's heart was sinking deeper and deeper. Was he still intent upon things not working between them?

Danielle rolled her eyes. "Randal is having Peter create a sewing room for you in the room next to yours, the room that had been Willa's. She took all of her furniture when she moved out, and it's never been replaced, but there are a few things in the attic that will work for a sewing room, including a big table and a chest of drawers for all your material."

Squeezing her hands together to ease their trembles as relief flooded her, Jolie nodded. "Oh, that sounds wonderful."

"It's no sense using up all the space in your bedroom when there are other rooms just sitting empty." Grandpa passed her the platter of bacon that he'd nearly emptied onto his plate. "My wife, Virginia, used to sew. She made me a smoking jacket. A green velvet one. I loved that jacket. Wonder whatever happened to it." He was looking at Danielle.

"I don't know, Grandpa, I've never seen it," she answered.

"Would you be interested in having me sew one for you?" Jolie asked.

Grandpa took a bite of bacon. "I think I would."

"I don't have any green velvet, but I do have some blue," she told him. Randal had picked out a dark, royal blue velvet from the store the other day.

"I look good in blue," Grandpa said.

She also had several yards of blue silk that she could use for lining for the jacket. Jolie gave him a nod. "Then I will make you a blue one."

"I used to wear that jacket when Randal was little," Grandpa said. "I remember bouncing him on my knee while wearing it." He continued, carrying his memories into a long story that lasted until they'd eaten and the table had been cleared.

"I'll show you the room and the items in the attic," Danielle offered during a brief moment when Grandpa had paused to remember what he'd been talking about.

"Yes, do that," Grandpa said. "And tell Peter to scrounge up anything else she needs."

"I'm sorry he ruined Randal's surprise for you," Danielle said as they walked side by side out of the dining room.

"It's fine," Jolie said. "I hear congratulations are in order."

"Yes! We are so excited." Danielle pressed a hand to her throat. "I just hope Randal gives us his blessing to move into our own place. Between you and me, we are going to do it either way, but I don't want to upset Randal. He's... I know he's my brother, but he's more to me than that. He raised me. I know he's worried about us financially, but James wants the chance to prove he can provide for us. It's very important to him."

"I'm sure it is, and he deserves the opportunity. You both do."

"I don't think Randal thinks that."

"Maybe you just need to give him a little time to get used to it," Jolie said. She wasn't sure that would happen, but wanted to provide Danielle with hope.

"Did he discuss it with you?"

"We talked about it last night."

"I'm sorry I kept him down here so late."

"It was fine," Jolie replied. The conversation changed to her new sewing room as they continued along the upstairs hallway, to the stairs that led to the attic, where Jolie felt as if she'd just entered a treasure vault. There was a large, framed, freestanding mirror, stools, a dressmaker's mannequin and so many other things, she was speechless at times.

"I don't remember ever seeing any of this," Danielle said as she uncovered another treasure, a trunk full of material, lace, ribbon and a large roll of tissue paper. "It must have belonged to my grandmother."

"Do you think Grandpa will mind if I use it?"

"Of course not. He said to scrounge up whatever else you needed." Danielle stepped over a crate of books to gain access to another trunk. "And we're scrounging."

"Yes, we are," Jolie agreed, lifting a chair off an old dresser to see behind it. She then pushed aside a wardrobe screen. "Danielle, there's a baby cradle back here."

Climbing over more crates, Danielle made her way over to take a look. "Really? I have to see."

"There's also a crib and high chair," Jolie pointed out.

Danielle pulled open a dresser drawer and used it as a step to reach over the dresser and push the screen completely away. "And the table and chair set I had in my bedroom when I was little." She leaned over the top of the dresser and giggled. "Randal used to have tea parties with me at that table."

"He did?"

"Yes, he did." Danielle let out a long sigh. "Oh, I hope everything is going good between Randal and James."

Jolie rested her elbows on top of the dresser and stared at the baby furniture. "I'm sure it's going fine." She had far more thoughts about Randal than just his talk with James. Plenty of her thoughts included her. Although she tried not to judge people, she did consider herself a decent judge of character. Randal was a man of excellent character. She wholly believed that. She also believed that Danielle and James were not the only things that had been bothering him last night. She couldn't help but wonder if he'd been thinking about children, after seeing Jane so pregnant. Did he want that? Was that why he'd brought up living with a man who didn't love her?

"This means so much to me and James." Danielle turned around. "It's not that we aren't grateful, but no one wants their brother to pay for everything, forever. We know the depression has hit everyone hard and that photography isn't something that everyone needs or can afford, but James is very good at it."

"I'm sorry that we didn't hire him for our wedding," Jolie said. That hadn't been something she thought of before. She hadn't questioned anything her mother had suggested, other than her dress. Perhaps she should have.

"The apartment that is for rent is only a block away from James's photo shop. I could help him every day, wait on customers while he's developing photos or out taking photos. I know our leaving means work for you, and I'm sorry about that, but..."

Jolie frowned, not sure what Danielle meant, but remained silent.

"You already know what I do running the household," Danielle continued. "It's not hard. Peter takes care of most of Grandpa's needs and I could come back and help you whenever you need."

"I would prefer that you simply come back to visit, regularly," Jolie said. Contributing was something she wanted to do, too, and running the household would be a good place to start. It wasn't as if her few sewing projects would keep her busy. They'd be completed in no time. However, she had to wonder if Randal would object to her taking over for Danielle. Yesterday morning, she would have thought not. So much had changed in a very few hours.

"Oh, I will, I promise." Danielle stepped out of the dresser drawer. "Let's get this stuff hauled down to your new sewing room."

Between the two of them, they carried a large portion of the items they'd found to the empty bedroom, only needing Peter's help for the larger and heavier items, including a long table perfect for cutting out material.

An organizing of the room came next, along with a detailed cleaning of the items. She and Danielle were putting the dressmaker's form back together when Jolie spotted someone in the doorway. For a moment, she was annoyed at herself for being disappointed that it was James. Only James. Randal was nowhere in sight.

"And?" Danielle asked James.

Tall and slender, with short, wavy blond hair, James nodded and his face lit up as he said, "Yes. He agreed."

Danielle squealed and ran into her husband's open arms.

Jolie attempted to focus on the mannequin, giving the couple privacy, but she was smiling, very happy for Danielle and James. At the same time, she couldn't help but sympathize for Randal at how difficult that decision had been for him. There was also a part of her that wondered if rather than trying to put things in perspective last night, she should have agreed with him. She, of all people, knew what it was like to live with next to nothing, and it wasn't easy. It had been a considerable strain on her entire family.

"Thank you, Jolie," Danielle said. "Thank you."

"I didn't do anything," Jolie insisted.

"Yes, you did. If you hadn't married Randal, we wouldn't have this opportunity." Danielle then asked James, "Where is Randal?"

"He had someone he had to go see," James said. "He asked me to let you know he'll be back later, Jolie."

She smiled her thanks, damping down more disappointment. "Well, you two must have some planning to do."

"I thought we'd go see when we could move into the apartment," James said to Danielle.

"Oh, yes, but just let me finish helping Jolie—"

"Nonsense," Jolie interrupted. "I have this all under control." She waved her hands in a shooing motion. "You two go on, go see your apartment."

Danielle clasped her hands together. "I'll help you as soon as we get back."

Jolie appreciated the offer, but more than that, she loved the happiness shining on both James's and Danielle's faces. "Go. Now."

Laughter of happiness echoed in the hallway, and Jolie stood there for a moment, wondering if things were starting to make sense, or if she was just looking at them differently.

Randal shoved his hands in his pockets and rocked back on his heels in order to hide the frustration that was reaching a whole new breaking point. "Do you know when he will return?" he asked the butler who had answered Carl Jansen's door.

"Approximately two weeks, closer to three," the man responded.

"Weeks?" Randal took a moment to grasp his options. Waiting weeks was not one. He needed resolution now. "Is there a telephone number where I could contact him? I'd really like to speak with him."

"I'm sorry, Mr. Osterlund, there is not. Mr. Jansen and his sons are taking their annual fishing trip at their cabin near Springfield. He left for the airport a short time ago, and I don't expect to see or hear from him until he returns." The butler appeared concerned. "Is Miss—forgive me, Mrs. Osterlund all right?"

"Yes, yes, she's fine." More than fine. She's beautiful, kind, caring. He hadn't been able to leave her bed until the sun was coming up because lying next to her had been amazing, and had made him think about certain things differently than he'd ever have expected.

"If I do hear from him, sir, I will forward the message you wish to speak to him."

"Thank you." Randal held in a pent-up sigh. "Thank you, very much. Good day."

The butler stepped back to close the door. "Good day to you, sir."

The air seeped out of his lungs as Randal walked toward his car. The last thing he wanted was for Jolie to believe she'd been made a fool. That she'd married him when she truly hadn't needed to. At the same time, he couldn't defy Carl's request to not tell Jolie about her upcoming inheritance. There had to be a way he could talk to Carl now. Get it out in the open, let her choose if she wanted their marriage to continue, or to end.

That was a conflict inside him. He knew what he wanted, and what he should want. They weren't the same thing.

Maybe Carl's flight hadn't left yet. There was a chance of that.

He jogged the last few yards to his car and drove

straight to the airport. A large plane was coming in for a landing as he arrived in the parking lot; it was an amazing sight to see, and thrilling. The entire industry was thrilling, especially the potential that was there for the right investor. He'd dreamed of being that investor and had been so close, but Jolie had upheld her end of their bargain without a single complaint. Before he could decide what his next step should be, Jolie needed to know Carl's plan.

He left the car and entered the small building where passengers purchased their tickets.

The young woman behind the counter told him the plane for Springfield had left a short time ago, but that there would be another flight to Springfield in three days.

Randal thanked her, said he didn't need a ticket to Springfield and stepped away from the counter. Three weeks of holding a secret of this magnitude, of this importance, was not going to work. Maybe he should buy a ticket to Springfield. It couldn't be that hard to find Carl's fishing cabin. He could buy two tickets. Jolie wanted to fly in a passenger plane, after all.

The shine in her eyes, the glow of her face, when they'd talked about seeing Mount Rushmore flashed in his memory, and like some kind of magician's trick, made his heart tick faster. There were times when she looked at him that he became incapable of doing anything except staring back. In those moments, he couldn't even remember his own name—however, when she kissed him, when she was in his arms, he knew who he was and that he didn't want their marriage to fail.

"Randal? How did you know I was flying home today?"

His spine stiffened as he turned. Passengers from the plane that had landed were entering the building, and near the door, blocking the way so others had to skirt around her, stood Amy.

Her short, black hair was covered with a white pill hat and her lips were coated with bright red lipstick, and he wondered how he had ever been remotely attracted to her. Right now, he couldn't fathom it because there was nothing friendly, kind or even pretty about her. "I didn't know you were coming home." Nor did he care.

Her smile was much more of a sneer. "Then why are you here?"

"To buy tickets." He pivoted to approach the counter again.

The hand she laid on his arm made his skin crawl. A flash of anger filled him at the idea of her holding Jolie down, of humiliating a little girl who would never have hurt anyone.

He pulled his arm away and walked to the counter. The next flight to South Dakota was over four weeks away, but he still bought two tickets.

Amy stood in his pathway to the door, held out a hand. "Here are the tickets for my luggage. You can give me a ride home so I don't have to wait for a taxi. I have been traveling for well over a week and the flight out of New York was at a god-awful hour this morning."

Ignoring the ticket stubs in her hands, he stepped around her. "No, I won't give you a ride."

"Randal!"

He kept walking, wondering all over again why he'd aligned himself with her for so long. However, he wouldn't be in the situation he was now if...

His stomach fell. Amy obviously hadn't heard he'd

married Jolie, and was not going to respond well to the news. He wasn't going to respond well to her reaction, either, because he wouldn't tolerate a single moment of her hatred projected toward Jolie.

He wouldn't accept anything hurting Jolie, not from anyone. She was his wife, and that meant she had his full protection.

It wasn't love, but it was something he could give her. He contemplated that on the drive home.

Lunch was being served when he walked into the house, and the laughter coming from the dining room made him pause near the doorway. Jolie's laugh was a form of music all on its own. Light and lyrical, it had the ability to not only instill happiness, but evoke it.

"Are you just going to stand there, or are you going to join us?" Grandpa asked.

Randal stepped around the corner. "I was waiting to hear what you two found so funny."

Grandpa laughed harder. "You."

Randal lifted a brow at Jolie's blush. "Really?"

Covering her mouth with one hand, she nodded.

No one had ever made him desire something so badly, and he highly doubted anyone ever would. She was unique. Special. In so many ways.

"I was telling her about when you were little, not in school yet, and your mother told you to hurry and put on a pair of shoes if you wanted to go to the store with her."

"Ah, yes." He knew the story well and sat down next to Jolie. "Mother had told me to put on shoes. She hadn't specified that they had to be my shoes."

"So you put on your father's shoes and wore them

to the store?" Jolie's eyes were still shimmering, her cheeks still flushed.

"Yes. Peter had just polished Father's shoes, so they were in the kitchen. Mine were upstairs in my room, and she'd said to hurry."

"How could you even walk in them?" she asked.

"I don't remember, but I'm sure it wasn't easy." What he did remember was his mother laughing about it while telling his father, and how she'd looked almost as pretty as Jolie was right now. That was rare. Him remembering things about his mother. Specific things, but right now, he could almost hear her laugh. His father's, too. That was a rare memory. After his mother died, he never heard his father laugh.

"Jolie is sewing me a smoking jacket," Grandpa said. "A blue one. She got that sewing room of hers all ready to go and measured me so it'll fit just right."

Pausing as he spooned food onto his plate, Randal looked at Jolie.

She poured coffee into his cup. "Grandpa said he looks good in blue."

"Did he?"

"Yes, I did," Grandpa said. "I do look good in blue. So do you."

"So does Jolie." Randal hadn't seen her not look good. She was wearing a simple white blouse today, along with a black skirt, and looked as lovely as she had on their wedding day. As enticing as she had last night when he'd opened the bedroom door and saw her standing there, with her robe open, exposing a nearly translucent nightgown. It had nearly gutted him, to think of giving her up, and still did.

"She'll show you the room after lunch," Grandpa

said. "She found all sorts of things up in the attic. It's good to know they'll be used rather than sitting up there gathering dust."

"Yes, it is," Randal agreed.

Half an hour later, he was impressed by the transformation that had taken place in the once empty room, and was instantly drawn to the table, where dark blue material was laid out with tissue paper in odd shapes pinned to it. "Is this the smoking jacket?"

"Yes." She pointed to more material draped over the back of a chair. "I'll line it with this."

Twisting, leaning a hip against the table, he couldn't stop from voicing his disappointment. "I thought you'd make a dress for yourself from this material."

"I will. There's more than enough for both."

"When?" Regret rose up in him at the way she glanced down at her attire. "You look beautiful in everything you wear. I just thought that's what you wanted to do, sew clothes for yourself."

"I enjoy designing things for others, too." She walked around the other end of the table, touching the material. "Things that they want. Like a smoking jacket."

He believed that. She liked helping others. "All right then. Anything I can do to help?" He walked over to a shelf where material was stacked along with some notepads. "Need a bowl of water?"

Her laugh was soft as she picked up a pair of scissors. "No, but thank you."

He lifted a notepad off the shelf and flipped through the pages of drawings. Dresses and blouses, shirts and pants. All drawn in pencil. A page caused him to stop flipping. They were drawings of underclothes. Specifically, women's underclothes. With his blood flowing a bit faster, and hotter, he glanced across the room. She was bent over the table, cutting the material along the edges of the tissue paper pinned to it. He wished her blouse was transparent because he wanted to know if she was wearing a brassiere like the one in the drawing.

Really, most definitely, wanted to know.

Chapter Fourteen

"Oh, my word, Jolie! It's not only comfortable, it's so pretty! I can't wait for David to see it. He's going to love it!" Jane Albright twisted, looking at her image in the mirror; one of several mirrors in the very large dressing room that held four mirrors, two freestanding closets, racks of shoes and a lovely dressing table amongst other things. Jolie had barely walked into the house on Randal's arm when Jane had asked for the men to excuse them and brought her up here, where Jolie had taken the bra, wrapped in tissue paper, out of her purse. She'd sewn it this morning, and had worried all day if it would fit or not.

"I bet Randal can't wait to watch you undress every night," Jane said.

Jolie's face burned and she had to turn away. Randal had never watched her undress, but the idea of him doing so certainly made her body react. Holding her breath at the rapid increase of her heart, she counted to ten, then breathed. It didn't help much, the idea was still there, but she turned about. "I'm glad it fits and I hope you find it more comfortable than your others."

"It already is more comfortable. I love it." Jane stuck her arm in a sleeve of the sleek, gold silk dress she'd unbuttoned to her waist to put on her new bra. "I'm burning those other ones. They are torture traps compared to this."

"Here, let me help you." Jolie held up the back of the dress for Jane to slip in her other arm.

Once the dress was buttoned again, Jane twisted, glancing at her image in the mirror. "Look at that. It makes my dress fit better. Look better. How can that be?"

"It's the way I sew the cups together in the front," Jolie explained. "I sew material between them to separate your boobs instead of bunching them together."

Jane examined her reflection again. "That's exactly what it does. And being so silky smooth, the material of my dress doesn't catch on anything." Wiggling and lifting her arms, she added, "No matter how I move." She then spun around and planted her hands on her hips. "You are a genius."

"Not hardly." Bras had been the one thing she had been able to design and sew that her mother never complained about. Mainly because she never knew about them.

"I think you are." Jane hooked their arms together. "And I think we better get back downstairs before the men come looking for us."

The men were in the living room, along with David's brother, sister-in-law and grandfather, Gus, who was as charming as Jane had insisted. He kept them laughing throughout dinner. Afterward, she and Randal and Jane and David retired into a game room where they played several games of whist, during which the conversation included airplanes. Randal's knowledge not only filled her with pride, it held her captive. He didn't just know about airplanes—he was passionate about them. She could see it on his face, hear it in his voice and feel it.

That's why he'd married her, and she knew another why. This, the airplane business, was the pirate's treasure he'd been seeking for his entire life.

She sincerely wanted him to find that treasure. He'd told her in the beginning that he wasn't looking for love, and she certainly hadn't married him for love. But she was going to help him do whatever she could to make this dream of his come true. She liked that idea, and how it made sense. Life wasn't always about your own dreams. It was also about helping others find theirs.

"What are you thinking so hard about?" he asked later, as they drove home.

"Nothing." She couldn't tell him that she was considering talking to Dad, simply asking if and when he might put his airplane business on the market.

"Didn't you enjoy the evening?"

"Yes, very much. Jane is a delightful person, and it was interesting listening to you and David talk about airplanes."

He had to stop and wait for a car to turn before driving forward again. "Would you like to invite them to our house for dinner one evening?"

"Yes, I would." That could give her a reason to call Dad, and casually bring up the topic of selling his company. "Perhaps a few others as well."

"Sure, whoever you want."

"I was thinking Dad."

His silence gave the air an odd tenseness. Then he let out a sigh. "He's out of town for a few weeks."

"Oh? I didn't hear him mention that."

"He's gone on an annual fishing trip with his sons."

"At their fishing cabin? My father went there with him all the time." Fun, warm memories filled her and she leaned back against the seat. "Our entire family went once, but Mother didn't like it, she said it was like living in the dark ages."

"I can see your mother not appreciating that. What did you think about it?"

"I loved it. We'd swim all day, cook fish over the fire outside and chase lightning bugs until we were so tired, we fell asleep as soon as we laid down. Mother only went that once, but Silas and I went almost every year. So did Chloe when she got older and Mother was certain we wouldn't let her drown. Anna was there most of the time, too, and the way she cooked that fish, oh, I can almost taste how good it was." How had she forgotten how much fun that had been? "Have you ever gone on a trip like that?"

"No. My father was always too busy working for anything like that."

That was sad and she made an instant decision. "Then we'll go someday." The prospect excited her. "I know Dad will let us use the cabin."

"Do you know where it's located?"

"On a lake with a sandy bottom and surrounded by big climbing trees." She laughed. "Dad will give us directions, tell us how to get there." More memories were filling her mind. "My father and Dad were always betting on who would catch the first fish, and the biggest fish, and the most fish. I won all three one day and was dubbed the Fishing Queen."

"That's a royal title if I've ever heard one."

His teasing said his mood had lightened. "Thank you very much, you may call me Your Majesty whenever you're inclined."

"Should I bow at your feet, or kiss your hand?"

She hadn't realized they'd arrived home until he took ahold of her hand and kissed the back of it.

The heat of his lips raced all the way up her arm. She'd missed their kisses the past couple of days. Missed the way they made her feel. "Either, or."

His smile reflected in his eyes as he opened his door. "Allow me, Your Majesty." He slid out the door, still holding her hand.

She scooted across the seat and stepped out of the car, laughing again as he gave her a deep bow.

Her laughter lodged in the back of her throat as he stood so close that if she took a step, their bodies would touch. A tingling sensation took over her entire body, especially her breasts, making her wonder if he would like to see the bras she sewed. Specifically the one she was wearing right now.

The need, the want for him to pull her close, kiss her was so great, she couldn't move. Couldn't breathe. That grew harder as he stood still, staring at her. She sucked in a deep breath while asking, "Is something wrong?"

"No. No, nothing's wrong."

"Then why are you staring at me?" That wasn't what she'd wanted to ask. It was more centered on why he wasn't kissing her, but she couldn't quite make those words form.

* * *

"I'm merely admiring the Queen." Randal forced out a laugh to go along with his answer. In truth, he'd been convincing himself not to kiss her by coming up with every excuse under the sun. Or moon. For that's what was shining down upon her. A soft, muted silver ray that highlighted her amongst the shadows surrounding them.

She was so beautiful, so…perfect in every way. The desires inside him were so strong they were painful. He couldn't pretend that she didn't mean anything to him. She did. More than anyone had in a long time. He didn't want her to get hurt in all of this, which was tearing him up inside. The two forces inside him couldn't find common ground. She hadn't wanted to marry him, she'd been forced to for money, and the idea of ending it wasn't sitting well inside him. Not just because it would be a failure.

"There's not that much to admire," she said.

"I think there is." More than he could ever have imagined, and for the first time in his life, he wished he was someone other than Randal Osterlund.

He stepped aside so she could move away from the car. Closing the door, he tightened his hold on her hand to escort her into the house.

Grandpa was sitting in the living room and waved them into the room. "How was your dinner party?" he asked.

"Fine," Randal answered. "What are you still doing up?" Grandpa was usually tucked in bed long before ten.

"Enjoying my new smoking jacket." Grandpa's gaze was on Jolie, along with a smile. "What's the use of having such a fine jacket if you don't enjoy it?"

"It certainly looks good on you." Jolie walked to Grandpa's chair and kissed his cheek. "I'm glad you like it."

"It's the finest jacket I've ever had." Grandpa rubbed one of his sleeves. "I may never take it off."

"It will need to be laundered from time to time," Randal warned as he crossed the room and sat down on the sofa.

Grandpa lifted a brow in challenge. "I see you're wearing the shirt Jolie sewed for you."

"Yes, I am. It's become my favorite shirt." Randal didn't mind admitting that. It not only was more comfortable than any other he owned, he liked knowing she'd made it for him.

Shaking her head at both of them, Jolie sat down on the sofa next to him. "You two are two peas in a pod."

"I've been called worse," Grandpa said.

Randal laid his hand over the top of hers. "Me, too." He was still waiting for the desires inside him to subside, but had to be honest enough to admit that wasn't going to happen anytime soon.

"Was Gus at the dinner party?" Grandpa asked. "I haven't seen him in some time."

That led into a conversation that lasted for almost an hour, mainly due to Jolie sharing that they would be hosting a dinner party of their own soon, and that Gus would be included on the guest list. That had lit up Grandpa's eyes and soon he'd been rattling off a list of others he'd like to invite.

By the time Randal escorted Jolie up the stairs to their room, guilt was rolling around in his stomach. "I'm sorry Grandpa got so carried away."

"I'm not." She stepped out of her shoes and carried them to the closet. "It will be good for him to see all of his old friends."

He loosened his tie while crossing the room. "It will be a lot of work for you."

"I'm not afraid of work, it'll be fun." She removed her earrings and placed them in a glass container on the dressing table. "Besides, that's part of being your wife."

His throat tightened.

"Our agreement included me performing social duties." She turned, looked at him directly, chin up as if bracing herself. "Unless you've changed your mind about that."

He pulled off his tie and unbuttoned the top button of his shirt, needing air. Her dress was white and pale green, with a large bow tied above her breasts, and all night he'd been wondering about the drawing he'd seen of a brassiere, curious if she was wearing one like that.

"Have you?" she asked.

"No." He took off his suit jacket. "I haven't changed my mind."

"Then what have you changed your mind about?"

"Nothing."

She shook her head and looked away. "I'm sorry I voiced my opinion about Danielle and James moving out. You were frustrated and I just wanted to help. I didn't mean to interfere."

Regret at how he'd acted that night struck again. He stepped in front of her. "You weren't interfering. I appreciate what you said, how you made me look at things. You were right to do so. Danielle and James are adults and they deserve the opportunity to make it on their own. Even after they got married, I still thought of them as two kids and they aren't."

Looking down, she played with the bow of her dress.

"Have I done something else that upset you? That wasn't right?"

"No. Not at all."

"So this is just…" She closed her eyes.

"Just what?"

"Part of taking it slow. Getting to know each other."

He wanted to kiss her so badly his entire body was throbbing.

"Yes."

She nodded and turned around.

He balled his hands into fists to keep from grasping her shoulders, spinning her back around to face him and kissing her.

"Oh, good grief!" Her soft exclamation included a frustrated huff.

"What's wrong?"

"Nothing." She leaned closer toward the mirror attached to the dressing table. "I just pulled the wrong tie on my bow and now have a knot."

Her reflection showed how she was attempting to see the knot in the mirror. He laid his hands on her shoulders. "Turn around. Let me see if I can help."

"I'll get it."

He could see in the mirror that her fidgeting was tightening the knot. "You're making it worse because you can't see what you're doing." He forced her to turn around and pushed aside her hands. "Lift your chin up so I can see what I'm doing."

She tilted her head back and stared up at the ceiling.

Biting back a grin, he loosened the knot almost immediately, but kept pretending that he was working on it. Even though he knew he was playing with fire, he liked it.

"Can't you get it?" she asked.

"Yes, I can get it." He loosened the knot more, letting the silky material fall through the loop.

She bent her head down. "The material didn't snag, did it?"

He undid the second loop. "I don't think so, but your face is in the way, I can't see."

She lifted her face and stuck her tongue out him.

His reaction was to laugh, at the same time his hands slid up and grasped the sides of her face. Then, he bent down and covered her mouth with his. He also took advantage of her parted lips, slipping his tongue between them. A thrill rippled over him at the warmth, the sweet taste of her, and he delved deeper, entangling his tongue with hers.

Her arms slid around his sides as she melted against him and returned the kiss, tongue twist for tongue twist.

Having her close at hand, next to him, had become natural, but holding her, kissing her, was beyond that. It felt right. So right. The thought that struck next wasn't as welcomed as others would have been, because he wondered if it felt right to her. But it couldn't. He'd told her he could never love her, and she wanted that. She may think liking each other is enough, but there will come a day when it won't be. Tonight had confirmed it. He'd seen how she'd looked at Jane and David again.

He pulled out of the kiss, and unable to meet her eyes, pulled her into a hug, kissing the top of her hair. Then he released her and walked into the bathroom, needing time to cool the raging inferno inside him.

Chapter Fifteen

Jolie was overjoyed when Peter informed her that Chloe and Silas were there to see her. She had missed them both dearly, had thought about them each and every day since moving out of her mother's house. Not worrying about them wasn't an option. That had been her role for too long, and it kicked in high gear as soon as she walked into the living room where they were both seated, waiting for her.

She forced a smile to remain on her face until after giving and receiving hugs, and they'd all settled in chairs. Letting her seriousness show, she looked at each of them. "Spill."

The look Silas and Chloe shared made her stomach sink. "What's happened?" she asked.

Slender, with curly dark hair, Silas resembled their father. Always had. Right now, she saw even more of that. It was the set of his mouth, as if he didn't want to admit to anything.

That made her turn to Chloe.

Her sister let out a long sigh. "We never realized how much you protected us from Mother."

"Not necessarily protected us," Silas interjected, always the peacekeeper. "Shielded is a better way to describe it."

Jolie clenched her teeth together. "One of you tell me what she's done."

Chloe threw her hands in the air. "She's finding people for us to marry."

"What? No. That's—" Jolie stopped before saying that's why she'd married Randal. It had been, and was working out, but she didn't want her siblings subjected to the same thing. "Not possible. It can't be true."

"It is." In his slow, calm way, Silas shrugged. "It appears that she believes it worked so well with you and Randal, that she's convinced she can get three times the amount of money Randal has promised to provide her monthly, by doing the same with Chloe and I."

Why hadn't she seen this coming? Enough had never been enough for Mother, so it wouldn't be now, either.

"I have decided to quit school and obtain employment. I'm hoping that will placate her until—"

"No!" Jolie stood and paced the floor, needing to release some of the anger building inside. "You will not quit school." She turned to Chloe. "And you will not run away. I will figure this out."

"It's no longer your problem, Jolie. You've already sacrificed yourself for us. For our family." Silas shook his head. "I shouldn't have let you do that."

"Sacrificed myself? Do I look like I've sacrificed anything?" Jolie didn't wait for either of them to answer. "No, I don't, because I haven't. Randal is truly wonderful, and I assure you, I have gained everything and lost nothing." Anger reached a new level inside her. The truth of the matter was that he'd lost, financially, by marrying her. Breathing deep to calm herself, she continued, "The only things that I miss are the two of you." And it appears, the ability to protect them from their mother.

"We miss you, too, Jolie. But if I don't act, don't obtain employment, I fear Mother will request more funds from Randal. She has already spent her monthly allotment."

Never riled, Silas always maintained his composure and spoke eloquently. Someday, he would make a fabulous teacher. Jolie had to make sure that happened. "I will fix this," she said. "I just need some time to think about it."

Holding both hands up, so they would remain silent, she sat down on the sofa. Her mother would not extort more money out of Randal. Would not. There was no way on earth that she would let that happen. She pinched her lips together, thinking of the kiss they'd shared last night when he'd untied the knot on her bow. Randal had slept on the sofa last night, but that kiss had meant something to him. She could tell by the way he looked at her. It had meant something to her, too. She wanted other things, too. In fact, she'd spent a portion of the morning wondering how she could accidentally spill water on the sofa in their room again.

Chloe jumped to her feet, took her turn at pacing, and that forced Jolie's mind back to the business at hand. If only she had a way to make money, to placate her mother until her siblings were grown and on their own.

"We've both been looking for jobs," Chloe said, "but so is half of Chicago, and the only jobs we've found expect their employees to work all day, every day. The only way we can do that is to quit school."

"You aren't quitting school. You haven't even graduated high school." Jolie looked at Silas.

"We can't let you do this on your own, Jolie," he said. "You've done enough. If we have jobs, Mother can't blame us for not contributing to the family income."

That is exactly how their mother would play on their senses. She should have known once Mother got a taste of having money again, it would only increase. "I need some time, need to discuss this with Randal."

"No, Jolie, we don't want you to ask him for more—"

"I'm not going to ask him for more money," she said, cutting off Silas. Randal would give her mother more money, and that couldn't happen. He might need it before his airline business became profitable. "This is not his problem and I won't let it become his problem. But he might know of someone who is hiring. Someone who wouldn't mind employees who must work around their school schedules."

"Do you think that is possible?"

She hoped it was a possibility. "I won't know until I ask him." She would also be talking to her mother. "Does Mother know you came to visit me?"

"No." Chloe plopped down in the chair again. "She's having lunch with Mrs. Turner at a café downtown."

Louise Turner put on airs as strongly as their mother. Jolie stood. "Well, then, the two of you will have lunch with Grandpa and I, he'll enjoy that, and when you get home, you can let Mother know that I'd invited you to lunch and that I'll be over to see her later this week. By then, we'll have a plan in place." She wasn't convinced that she'd have a plan by then, but wouldn't let them know that. She waved a hand for both of them to stand. "Come, let me introduce you to Grandpa. You met him at the wedding and will enjoy getting to know him better."

Grandpa was in his study, wearing his smoking jacket and was delighted to have company. Jolie left her siblings with him while she went to inform Mrs. Hoover that there would be two more for lunch. She knew the additions wouldn't be an issue as Danielle and James would not be home for lunch because they'd received the key for their new apartment.

Danielle and James were so excited, and Jolie sincerely hoped all went well for them. Not only for their sakes, but for Randal's. He'd done so much for so many, including her family. If only Dad was in town. She could ask him about jobs for Silas and Chloe, and ask about his business. He would be home in three weeks, but that might be too late. It had only taken her mother days to marry her off to Randal.

Ironically, that had proven to be the best thing her mother had ever done.

For her.

But it hadn't been for him.

Randal rarely came home for lunch, but the kiss he'd shared with Jolie last night still had his heart pounding, not to mention other parts. He should stay away from her. That would be the smart thing to do. Yet, here he was, driving home on the pretense of needing lunch. His office was surrounded by places to eat. Restaurants he frequented so often they knew his likes and dislikes.

He just couldn't get Jolie off his mind today. She'd tossed and turned all night. He'd heard her. It hadn't kept him awake. He'd been unable to fall to sleep knowing she was only feet away, in a bed large enough for two, while he'd been on a sofa, not large enough for one.

He'd never gone back on his word, but keeping Carl's secret was killing him. Three weeks was too long to wait. If Jolie decided she wanted out of their agreement, it should happen sooner than later, before any more damage was done.

Pulling in the driveway, he didn't recognize the old Cadillac, but heard his grandfather's laughter as soon as he entered the house. Curious as to who the visitors were, he walked down the hall to the study. As he rounded the corner of the doorway, it was Jolie he saw first, and how her face lit up.

"Randal."

His heart pounded even harder as she hurried across the room to meet him. It took a moment for him to make his voice work. "I thought I'd come home for lunch today."

"That's wonderful." She stretched on her toes and brushed her lips over his as if it was the most normal thing in the world.

He was sure it was a manufactured welcome for the others in the room, but it flooded his system with something he couldn't explain. It went beyond enjoyment, beyond joy.

"Silas and Chloe stopped by and I asked them to stay for lunch." Jolie wrapped her hands around his arm. "Your timing is perfect. We were just on our way to the dining room."

He heard her, but in his mind, was wishing that her simple kiss had meant as much to her as it had to him, even though he knew he shouldn't wish that. There was still no place for love in his life, but there was room for like, and he liked her. He was still searching for another business to purchase, while also considering ways he might be able to help her with Carl's company. For multiple reasons, he didn't want their marriage to fail, but ultimately, he didn't want anyone to think badly of her. She'd been right about that. He did care what others thought, especially when it came to her.

He greeted her siblings, and escorted her into the dining room.

If he'd expected lunch to be an awkward affair, he couldn't have been more wrong. That also had him wondering about her greeting upon his arrival. Her siblings knew about their arrangement, so there had been no need for her to kiss him.

He'd met her siblings several times, but had barely heard either of them speak. Today, there was no lull in the conversation as they ate, especially when Jolie told her siblings that Carl was at his fishing cabin. All three of them were then full of stories, reminiscing about their trips to the cabin in the past.

Grandpa joined in by sharing his own fish tales, ending one particular story with a long sigh. "I used to go fishing a lot in the old country, with my grandfather." Grandpa looked at him. "It's too bad you and I never went fishing, Randal."

"It's not too late," Jolie said. "You still can. Randal and I are going to go. I'm going to ask Dad if we can use his cabin. You can come with us."

Grandpa shook his head. "You young ones wouldn't want me tagging along."

"We would love to have you join us," Jolie insisted. "The more the merrier."

"There is plenty of room," her sister said. "There are

two bedrooms and an overhead loft, which my mother forbade me from sleeping in because she thought I'd fall off, but since she wasn't there, my father let me sleep up there. One end had a huge window and I swear, the stars felt close enough to almost touch."

"Do you remember the year you won the fishing contest?" her brother asked Jolie.

Randal grinned at how Jolie laughed as she reached over and touched his shoulder.

"I told Randal about that last night," she said.

The warmth of her hand on his shoulder spread into his chest. "Her Majesty did tell me that last night," he replied, bringing a round of laugher to the table.

She let a soft sigh as she patted his shoulder and then removed her hand. "It was my favorite place to go as a child."

At that moment, Randal wanted to put her in the car and drive to the cabin, wherever it was.

"Well, then, when are we going?" Grandpa asked.

"I'll call Dad as soon as he returns to town," Jolie said.

Though he kept it hidden, Randal's heart sank, knowing Carl's return could very well change her mind.

As soon as lunch ended, her siblings took their leave, and while Jolie was seeing them out, Grandpa planted both elbows on the table. "You've done well for yourself, Randal. I'm proud of you."

Those were words he'd never heard. He'd wanted to hear them, especially when he'd been young and striving to prove himself. A shiver tickled his spine when he noticed his grandfather's gaze was on the door that Jolie had exited moments ago.

"A man can be proud of all of his achievements," Grandpa said. "But the greatest is his family."

Those were words Randal had heard before, many times. The importance of providing for his family had been drummed into his head at an early age, and repeated over and over again.

"I remember the first time I met your grandmother. She was washing milk bottles. I'd only been in America a few months and didn't have a pot to piss in, but I told her if she married me, I'd see to it that she never had to wash milk bottles again in her life." Grandpa laughed. "That meant I had to wash them. It took more than a year before that first well hit oil."

That, too, was something Randal had never heard. His grandmother had died when he was an infant, and like his mother, no one spoke of her very often.

"There's nothing like the love of a woman to put the drive inside a man to become more than he'd ever have become on his own. Your grandmother did that to me, and your mother did that to your father. Now, it's your turn."

Randal was aware that he was expected to make more money, build the Osterlund wealth beyond what the previous generations had acquired, but had never heard it put that way. That his grandmother and mother had been behind both Grandpa and his father. He wasn't sure what to think about that.

"Well, I guess I better return to work." Randal stood. "I'll see you tonight."

"I'll be here," Grandpa said. "The one wearing the spiffy smoking jacket."

Jolie had already made a large impact on his entire family. He hadn't expected that.

Outside, he stood beside Jolie as her siblings drove away. Her smile as she glanced up at him appeared strained and, knowing it would be natural for her to miss her siblings, he put an arm around her. One more thing that their agreement had done, taken her away from her family. "There's a car in the garage you can use to go see them whenever you want."

She leaned against him. "Thank you. I may do that later on this week."

He rested his head against hers, relishing in the connection. She'd changed something inside him. Opened a part of him he hadn't realized had been closed off. That made him wary. He'd never needed anyone, especially a woman, and didn't want to consider what that meant.

This couldn't go any further. He had to tell her about Carl.

And would have, right then, if not for the two-seated roadster that pulled in the driveway.

"It's Jane," Jolie said.

He'd already recognized the blonde woman. "I see that." He wasn't nearly as excited as Jolie sounded, only because the disruption meant they couldn't talk right now. Other than that, Jane was good people and he was very glad Jolie and Jane had become friends so quickly.

"Hello!" Jane climbed out of the car. "I hope I'm not intruding."

"Not at all." He leaned down and brushed a kiss over Jolie's lips. Not for show. It was because he wanted to kiss her. "I'll see you tonight."

"All right." She tugged at his tie, straightening it. "Have a good afternoon."

He winked at her. "You, too." With a nod at Jane, he walked toward his car.

"Don't you just love when they come home for lunch?"

He heard Jane's question, and held his breath as he walked, listening for Jolie's reply.

"Yes," Jolie replied. "It's wonderful."

He couldn't have stopped the smile that tugged at his lips if he'd have wanted to.

Chapter Sixteen

"Two dollars?" Jolie pressed a hand against the way her heart fluttered. "I couldn't possibly sell them for two dollars. Bras are only forty-nine cents in the department stores."

Jane held her arms out at her sides. "Forty-nine cents for torture devices."

No one in their right mind would pay two dollars for a bra, but to say that aloud would be saying Jane was crazy. She wasn't. She was just excited. Had been since they'd walked into the house.

"I'm telling you, Jolie. Women will pay two dollars without blinking an eye." She waved a hand toward the coffee table, where forty dollars lay. "In advance. I was going to call you yesterday, but told myself to wear the bra all day first, just to be sure, and am I sure! And David is thrilled. Not only because I'm comfortable. It's so pretty. Did I tell you that he thought I'd changed my outfit on Monday night? He said he knew right away that something was different, but was sure that I was wearing the same dress."

"Yes, you told me," Jolie replied with a laugh. It was

obvious that Jane liked her new bra, but that didn't mean others would.

Jane slapped her hands against her legs. "I can't stop telling people about it. My sisters, my mother, my sister-in-law, four very good friends, they all want bras now." She brushed her long blond hair off her shoulders. "My only request is that you make me one more first. At least one." Giggling, she added, "David told me to buy a dozen. And I will, but I'll let a few other people have one first."

Jolie rubbed her hands over her thighs, calculating how much money she'd need to buy the supplies. "I'll gladly make more, for you and the others, but I won't charge two dollars apiece for them. Fifty cents will be more than enough to buy all the material I need."

"I'm sure it will, but they are worth so much more. That's what you need to realize. Look at it this way. Besides the material, you need to be paid for your time, and more importantly, your design. It's perfect. And it's needed. Women need comfort as much as they need style. Your bras are both. Everyone who wears one is going to want more, and they are going to tell more people about them." Jane picked up the money. "This is proof."

"Two dollars seems so expensive."

"So is flying, but that doesn't stop people from buying tickets."

Jolie shook her head.

Jane nodded hers.

Attempting to compromise, Jolie asked, "How about one dollar?"

"No. I'm paying you two dollars for the one I'm wearing, and for each of the others I want you to sew for me, and that's the price I told everyone else, and they are more than happy to pay it." Jane fluttered the bills in the air. "I have my car. We can go shopping for supplies right now. I'll even come back and help you. I have everyone's measurements, told them to measure themselves just like you'd measured me."

Jolie scratched her head.

"I know you're busy, being just married and everything, but I will help," Jane offered.

"It's not that. I have plenty of time," Jolie insisted.

"Then what is it?"

Jolie huffed out a breath. "I'm not a designer, I'm not—"

"Yes, you are." Jane threw her arms in the air. "You are the designer of Jolie's dream bras. That's what I've been calling them."

"Jolie's dream bras?"

"Yes." Jane leaped to her feet. "Now, let's go shopping. I will help as much as I can between now and four. I have to be at the airport by then. I promised David."

By four o'clock, all of the patterns had been created, the material cut and several bras completed, besides the one Jane had taken when she'd left. Not only that, Jolie was very optimistic that both Silas and Chloe could soon have jobs that would work with their school schedules. Jane had to be at the airport in order to sell tickets and assist passengers when a plane landed. She'd explained that planes didn't fly in and out enough times a day to have a full-time employee manning the counter all day, but when they did land, at least two people were needed. Although many people were looking for jobs, few only wanted to work three to four hours each afternoon during the week. More planes flew in and out during the weekends, so those shifts were longer, but David was having a hard time finding people to fill those shifts, too.

Trusting her new friend, Jolie had explained that her siblings wanted to work, but were still in school. Jane had thought Silas and Chloe would be perfect for the positions, and promised to talk to David about it as soon as she arrived at the airport.

Jolie was very grateful for Jane's assistance, and was relieved that she wouldn't have to ask Randal to help her family even more than he already had. She was also grateful for the money from the sales of the bras she was making. What was left over after buying material would be enough to keep Mother placated for a couple of weeks.

Two dollars apiece seemed like an extravagant price, but again, because of Jane, and in a way, Randal, she'd accepted that price because she'd insisted that a percentage of every bra sold would go to the soup kitchen. Jane had agreed and Jolie sincerely hoped the other women loved the bras as much as Jane, because she liked the idea of how her bras were not only helping women, but those in need of food as well. Having been in that situation, though her mother would never have allowed them to visit the soup kitchen, she knew how it felt to have empty cupboards.

That led her to wonder if other married women's husbands would like the bras as much as Jane said David did, mainly because she wondered if Randal would like them.

If he ever saw one.

It was crazy, but when she thought of him seeing her

wearing one, warmth spiraled inside her body, leaving her tingling all over.

That warmth was there at other times, too, and it was a feeling that she liked. Just feeling it made her think of Randal.

A knock sounded and the door opened before Jolie had time to stand up from her sewing stool.

"I'm sorry for disturbing you, but I have to tell you about the apartment!" Danielle hurried into the room and closed the door. "I scrubbed all the floors and windows today."

Spinning her stool around to face Danielle, Jolie waved a hand toward a chair. "Sit and tell me all about it. I want to hear everything."

"There are two bedrooms, a living room, bathroom and kitchen with black-and-white linoleum. It's so cute. It's on the third floor and the kitchen window overlooks the street, the ones in the bedrooms overlook the alley." Danielle's smile never faltered as she plopped down in the chair. "It's small compared to all this, but I know we'll be happy there, even if the money is tight for a while." Sighing, she added, "I truly wish there was a way for me to help James get more customers."

Jolie wanted James to get more customers, too. Wanted this to work for him and Danielle. For them and for Randal, so he wouldn't have to worry so much about taking care of everyone. She'd been thinking about it a lot lately, including while her siblings had been here earlier. She'd told them about flying in the plane with Randal, and that had made other thoughts form. "I had a thought earlier today," she said cautiously.

"Oh? About what?"

"More customers for James."

"You did?"

Jolie nodded. "Two thoughts actually." The other idea had come about when Chloe asked if she'd hem her dress soon, so she could wear it when school started up for the class picture.

"What are they?" Danielle asked.

"The first one is about the schools, how he takes group pictures of each classroom. Perhaps he could take pictures of each child individually. The younger ones. Right now, it's just the high school students, those graduating who get individual pictures. The parents might really like that, and buy extra copies to share with family."

"Oh, my goodness, that is a wonderful idea! James knows all of the school principals, and, oh, that's just an amazing idea. I'm sure parents would like it." Danielle clapped her hands together excitedly. "What's your other idea?"

"It's very different, and has to do with Randal's friend Roger. Do you know him?"

"Roger Wayne? Yes. He and Randal have been friends for years. He uses his plane to scout new routes for the electrical and telephone companies."

"Exactly." Jolie wasn't sure about this idea, but offered it anyway. "My thoughts were about those companies. Perhaps they'd like pictures of the routes Roger finds, taken from the airplane."

Danielle's mouth fell open. "Wow. That's a very good idea. Roger says that sketching the routes, making the maps, is the hardest part. Pictures would help him immensely." She leaped to her feet. "Why didn't I think of that? Or of the schools!" She crossed the room, arms open for a hug. "You are the best, just the best."

Jolie returned her hug. "I hope one or the other of my ideas is helpful."

"I think they'll both work." Danielle hugged her again. "I can't wait to tell James about them." Stepping out of the hug, Danielle continued to stare at the sewing machine behind Jolie. "Are you sewing bras?"

Jolie spun her stool around. "Yes, I am."

Danielle picked up one of the finished bras. "It's so pretty, and soft and silky." She glanced at the table of cut material pieces. "How many are you making?"

"A few. I'll make you one, if you'd like."

"I'd like that, but how many bras do you need?"

Jolie laughed. "They aren't all for me. They are for... friends. I'll need your measurements to make yours fit properly."

By the following afternoon, Jolie had all the bras sewn, including a couple for each of Danielle and Willa. She then cut out a dress from dark blue sateen to wear to the dinner party they were hosting next weekend.

She and Randal spent Saturday helping Danielle and James move into their apartment, and on Sunday, they took Grandpa to Willa's for lunch and then to see James and Danielle's new apartment.

Randal appeared happy, but something troubled him. She could see it in his face, especially his eyes when she'd catch him looking at her for no reason. It would quickly disappear and he'd smile, even kiss her at times. Soft, sweet kisses. She liked those kisses. More than that, she liked being comfortable with him. More than comfortable. She liked the way he laid his hand on her back to escort her through a door, and held her hand to assist her out of the car, and draped an arm around her shoulders and rubbed her upper arms. Soft, gentle caresses that sent those spirals of heat throughout her body and made her wish that she'd come up with a way to spill water on the sofa again. She hadn't. He was still sleeping there every night.

She also wished she knew how long this getting to know each other time would last. They were married, there was no reason for them not to sleep in the same bed.

Not only did Jane insist that David liked her new bras, so did Danielle and Willa. Jolie wanted Randal to see her wearing one, wanted to know if he would like how it looked on her and if it would lead to what the others said it led to.

She wasn't exactly sure when she'd concluded that. Sometime over the weekend, while the orders for more bras had been coming in. Everyone who wore one wanted more, and told others, who also wanted one or two.

On Monday morning, she'd called the department store and asked them to deliver the material she needed so she could continue to sew until it was time for Randal to return home from work. She'd made sure to still spend time with Grandpa after breakfast and lunch, and to assist Mrs. Hoover and Darla with preparations for the dinner party they would be hosting on Saturday evening.

The rest of the week followed suit, with her sewing from the time Randal left in the morning, until he returned in the evening. He still slept on the sofa each night, but there was a closeness growing between them that filled her with a soft sense of contentment.

She still wanted more, but felt she understood why

Randal was continuing to take it slow. Grandpa had told her about Randal's mother's death, that his father had been angry afterward and how that had affected everyone. How Randal, especially, had never let himself get close to anyone ever since. Until her.

She'd let Grandpa believe she had cracked Randal's shell, as he'd put it, even though she knew she hadn't. She hoped time would do that, and she would give Randal all the time he needed.

He was on her mind every hour, as she continued to take more orders for bras. Jane stopped over almost daily, to pick up bras, drop off more measurements and money, and would often stay, insisting upon helping by cutting out pattern pieces while Jolie sewed.

They talked about a large variety of things, including about how David had hired both Chloe and Silas—which Jolie already knew because her siblings had called her, very excited about the jobs. Her mother had called, too, disgusted that Jolie had helped her siblings find work. To placate her mother, Jolie had driven over, visited and had given her the money. That had truly delighted her mother, as Jolie had known it would.

She and Jane also discussed the guests of the upcoming dinner party to the point that Jolie felt as if she already knew everyone who would be in attendance.

By the time Friday afternoon arrived, Jolie figured she could sew a bra in her sleep. Having made so many the past two weeks, she had it down to a very efficient system that allowed her to sew one in less than an hour. There were stacks of tissue-wrapped bras, with women's names on the little tags, ready to be distributed by Jane, Danielle and Willa, who would all be at the dinner party tomorrow night. She had just pulled the door closed on her sewing room when she heard Peter greet Randal at the front door.

Her heart raced at the sound of his voice, and she hurried down the hallway to greet him. They met on the stairway, with him going up and her going down.

He caught her by the waist with both hands. "Where are you going in such a hurry?"

Because she was still one step up from him, they were eye to eye and her entire body warmed at the way his silver-blue eyes glowed. She laid her hands on his shoulders. "To say hello to you."

"Aw, well, in that case, go ahead."

Giddy, she said, "Hello."

He lifted a brow. "Is that it?"

She wanted to kiss him, and knew that was what he was expecting, yet teasing him by not doing so was almost as delightful. "How was your day?"

He shook his head.

Acting as if she didn't know that he wasn't referring to his day, she patted his shoulder and offered her best frown. "Oh, I'm sorry that you had a bad day." Her lips tingled at the way he kept looking at them. "Is there anything I can do to make it better?"

"A kiss might help."

Not ready for the game to end, she leaned forward and kissed his cheek. "Is that better?"

"No."

She kissed his other cheek. "How about now?"

"No."

Rubbing his shoulders, she leaned close again. "It must have been a very bad day."

He pulled her hips closer, until she could feel the heat of his body. "Actually, it was a good day. A very good day." Their mouths were so close, his breath mingled with hers. "Because I came home to you."

Her heart nearly melted, as did her bones, the moment his lips met hers. It was a long, sensual kiss that left her dizzy, clinging to him and biting her lips together to keep from begging him to sleep in the bed tonight.

Chapter Seventeen

Standing there, holding her and trying to catch his breath, Randal knew he couldn't take any more. He'd tried to keep his promise to Carl, but he couldn't keep going on like this. The desire to carry her up to their bedroom and consummate their marriage was so great, not doing so might be the death of him.

Yet, he couldn't do that, not without her knowing the truth. Ultimately, making their marriage real had to be her choice. "How about we go out to dinner tonight?"

She lifted her head off his shoulder and nodded.

It might all be him, but he could have sworn he saw disappointment flash across her face. "You can wear one of the new dresses you've been sewing."

"I'm saving it for tomorrow night."

He eased his hold of her enough for them to climb the steps side by side. "I'm looking forward to seeing it. You've been sewing all day, every day, this week."

"Yes, well, the dress is done. You'll see it tomorrow."

The dinner party tomorrow night almost made him change his mind, but this living in limbo had gone on long enough. Having her so close yet so far away. Once she knew the truth, and decided what she wanted to do, he'd be able to plan his next steps. Never before had his decisions, his actions, depended so deeply on someone else. Not even his father or grandfather. Their never-ending prodding hadn't affected him the way Jolie did. His life had changed the moment she'd entered it. He didn't regret that, but was struggling with a way to make it work.

The drive inside him to succeed was still there, it was just different. He was no longer thinking of the bottom line, the money he could make. He was thinking about the people. How it would affect them.

Them.

His focus was on only two people.

Her and him.

He hoped he wouldn't regret his decision to tell her the truth.

They went to the hotel restaurant. It held good memories. She was wearing the white-and-green dress, with the bow that he'd untied. The idea of doing so again heightened his senses as they discussed the menu for the dinner party and how she'd helped Darla polish the silver, along with other preparations. He was interested, and the excitement on her face about hosting the party pleased him, and all the while he wondered about bringing up the subject of Carl's company.

He had to bring it up. Had to know if she would choose him, or the business. He was willing to help her with Carl's company, but would she want that? After they'd eaten and were sipping on cups of coffee, he did the inevitable. "I have something I need to tell you."

She set her cup down. "What is it?"

He spun his cup in a circle on its saucer. "Carl isn't interested in selling his airplane company."

Her face fell and she reached across the table, laid her hand atop his. "Oh, no." She shook her head. "I could talk to him. Find out why, or if he might reconsider."

"I know why, and he won't reconsider."

"I'm so sorry." She folded her fingers around his. "Why won't he sell?"

"Because he's already put it in his will."

Nodding, she sighed. "For his sons."

"No." He had to quit beating around the bush. "For you."

She pulled her hand off his and sat back in her chair, wringing her hands together. "Me?"

"Yes, you."

"No." She shook her head. "Whoever told you that—"

"Carl told me. The night of his dinner party. The company has been in his will, to go to you, since your father died. Per Carl, the two of them were going to be partners in the company, but then the stock market crashed. Carl bought the company, wanted your father to still be a partner, but your father died and—"

"Stop." She pressed two fingers against her temple. "I don't want to inherit it. I don't want to inherit anything."

His idea of telling her at the restaurant was failing. They should be at home, where he could hold her. "I'm sorry, Jolie."

"It's not your fault." Sadness filled her face, dulled her eyes. "I don't want to be in Dad's will."

"Well, you won't be. He plans on giving you the airplane company when he returns next week. He asked me to keep it a secret, but I—you needed to know. That's all there is to it."

Frowning, she leaned forward. "If he gives it to me—"

"It will be yours, Jolie."

"Ours, Randal."

He held back the need to take her hand. "Yours, Jolie. Carl considered giving it to you before, but was afraid that your mother might mismanage things."

"She would have."

"There was that chance," he admitted. "But the bottom line is that if he had given it to you, you wouldn't have had to marry me."

She leaned back, stared at him.

"You don't need to stay married to me, either. The agreement we had…" He shrugged, not wanting to continue. Not knowing what to say.

"Don't need to—"

"No."

Pressing a hand to her stomach, she closed her eyes, then pushed away from the table with her other hand. "Excuse me."

He stood, reached for her. "Jolie—"

"I need to go to the powder room."

Watching her hurry away, he knew he'd screwed this up tighter than a corkscrew. Why hadn't he asked if she wanted to stay married to him? Ask her opinion rather than just laying out the facts. Because he was an idiot, that's why. He was responding to this like a business deal, had been since the beginning. That's all he'd ever known. Business deals.

But this wasn't a business deal.

Not at all.

* * *

Jolie held her breath all the way to the powder room, fearing as soon as she breathed, she'd cry. She wasn't going to do that. Not here. She was responding to the idea of not being married to Randal, knowing deep down, that was the one thing she didn't want. But he didn't want to be married to her.

Thankfully the powder room was empty. She walked to the sink, leaned heavily against it, gulping for air as one thing played over and over in her mind. The same thing that had echoed in her head at the table. Dad had told Randal about the company the night of his dinner party. The exact same night that Randal had asked her if she wanted to live the rest of her life with a man who didn't love her.

She'd been so foolish.

This whole time he didn't want to be married to her. Her hands began to shake.

The door opened and she quickly turned on the water, pretending that she'd just arrived at the sink, and stuck her hands beneath the running water.

"Well, if it isn't Miss Perfect."

Jolie's spine quivered at the same time her stomach turned. Why would *she* be here? Now?

"Aren't you even going to say hello?"

Jolie turned off the water and lifted the towel off the rack. "Hello, Amy."

"You don't appear happy to see me."

Jolie lifted her chin and did her best to not feel anything. Amy's black hair was cut short and styled perfectly, her makeup impeccable. So was her burnt orange two-piece dress. As usual. Everything about her was always impeccable.

Amy stepped around her and leaned toward the mirror to reapply her dark red lipstick. "Randal certainly was happy to see me." She smacked her lips together to set the lipstick in place. "When he met me at the airport." She dropped her lipstick into her purse. "Sunday before last. It was so sweet of him to welcome me back." Smiling at herself in the mirror, she added, "He always bent over backward for me."

Jolie's entire being was trembling and things were echoing inside her head again. Sunday before last. That's where Randal had gone after his meeting with James. To the airport. To meet Amy.

"You didn't think that would change just because I was gone for a few months, did you?" Amy made a show of slapping her own cheek. "Oh, my, are you really foolish enough to think that Randal would choose you over me? Fall in love with someone like you?" Laughing, she added, "Oh, poor little Jolie. Tricked again." Amy wiped the smile off her face. "There's only one reason Randal married you, and everyone will soon know the truth."

It took all the control Jolie had to replace the towel on its rack and leave the room without saying a word or breaking out in tears. At the table, she retrieved the purse she'd left on the floor near her chair.

Randal had stood as she'd approached the table. "I've already paid the bill."

She picked up her purse, and started for the door.

He touched her elbow.

She pulled it away and walked faster, through the room. She couldn't help but search the tables on her way to the door, looking for Amy, but she wasn't anywhere to be seen. If not for the pungent scent of Amy's perfume still stinging her nose, Jolie might have wondered if she'd seen a ghost.

She hadn't.

Amy was back and she was the woman Randal wanted. Had always wanted.

And worse yet, she was jealous. Jealous. That couldn't be. Yet, that's what the dark anger inside her was, she knew that.

"I'm sorry for the way I sprang that all on you," he said once they were in the car. "I just thought you should know."

He hadn't started the car, was twisted in his seat, facing her. She kept her gaze straight ahead. "I'd like to go home."

Home.

His home. One she'd readily accepted as hers, but it wasn't.

She didn't have a home.

Worse than that, she'd have to return to the home that drove her crazy. What was she doing? Worried about moving home when she'd been tricked. Tricked again by Amy. She'd suspected that in the beginning.

No, she'd known that in the beginning.

She should have remembered that. It explained why he said they'd take it slow, get to know each other. He never planned on her becoming his wife in every way. He just wanted Dad's company. As soon as he found out it wasn't for sale, he must have called Amy to come home.

So many things made sense now.

Except for one.

"Jolie, I—"

"I'd prefer not to talk." She drew a deep breath, but

that didn't help get her jumbled emotions under control. Nothing would. Nothing was under control. But they would be. She just needed time to figure out what she was going to do.

Do about how she'd let herself fall in love with him. That was not supposed to happen. How could it have?

She would not become her mother. Jealous and— Oh, lord. She already *was* becoming her mother.

She didn't wait for him to open her car door when they arrived home, and would have beat him up the stairs, too, if Peter hadn't stopped her at the door to inform her that Danielle had stopped by and picked up some *things* out of her sewing room.

"Thank you," she told him, moving toward the stairs.

"She also asked that I let you know both of your ideas are going to work splendidly," Peter said, sounding confused by what he was repeating.

"Thank you, again, Peter," she replied. "Good night."

Randal was beside her, taking the steps at the same pace. "What ideas?"

Her level of caring what he thought had dropped to nil. He and Amy could have each other. She was not going to turn into her mother for anyone. "Ways for her and James to make enough money that they won't ever have to worry about moving back in here with you." She upped her pace, rushed up the steps and down the hall.

He'd kept pace with her the entire way, but now passed her, opened the bedroom door and held it for her to enter. "I told them not to worry, that I would—"

"No one likes being made a fool." She walked past him, into her sewing room and closed the door, locked it before he could enter behind her.

"Jolie," he said through the wood. "I'd like to talk to you about all this."

There were plenty of things she'd like, too, starting with never having met him. Despite the fact she was shaking so hard her legs didn't want to work, she flipped on the light and moved away from the door.

"Jolie!"

Catching the side of the table with both hands, she used it to remain upright, and gave in to the tears burning her eyes. There were blurring her vision so it was no use trying to hold them back any longer.

"Jolie, please unlock the door."

She closed her eyes, bowed her head and let the pain consume her as she slowly sank to the floor. Time passed, or maybe it stood still. She didn't know or care. Eventually, the pain turned into an ache that left her numb. Her ability to feel had been all used up. There was nothing left inside her.

But she had to find something. Anger. Hatred. Something. Because lying on the floor wasn't an option. Neither was caring so much about one person that nothing else mattered.

She had to figure out what to do about that. Rising to her feet, and once again using the table to keep her upright, she glanced around the room. There had been a time when she'd dreamed of a room like this. Thought she'd have it all then.

She'd been wrong.

Or maybe she just wasn't the same person as she'd been then. Things had changed. She had a way to make money now. There was only one pile left of completed bras, the one for Jane to distribute. Danielle had picked up the ones with her name and Willa's, and she'd left a note, with measurements for more.

Would people still want to buy the bras when she was no longer married to Randal?

Flinching, she folded her arms around her midsection. She'd been wrong. She wasn't numb.

She was just foolish. A fool for being tricked again.

A fool for falling—

No. That wasn't her.

But it was.

She'd told him things she'd never told anyone else. Things about Amy. Their feud had started the first time they'd met in grammar school. There had been mice in her desk, her name put on things she'd never written, lies spread...

But this was by far the worst betrayal, and it hurt so bad to know Randal was a part of it. A part of her didn't want to believe that, but how could she not see the truth? It was all there. He'd told her right from the start that the only reason he was marrying her was for Dad's company.

Her spine stiffened. He wasn't going to have it, and Amy wasn't going to have the last laugh. Not this time.

No.

She was.

She wasn't sure how, but she would come out the winner. There had to be a way, and she had to find it, because she was done. Done being tricked. Done being lied to. Done living a life everyone else dictated instead of the one she wanted.

If a person could fall in love without even realizing it, they could fall out of love, too.

Sewing had always been her escape, so that's what she did now.

Sewed.

Plotted.

And planned.

Chapter Eighteen

The click of the door being unlocked caught Randal's attention. Stiff from being on the floor all night, he wasn't quick enough to leap to his feet before the door opened. His heart, however, was fast enough to leap into his throat at the sight of her.

It also sank when she barely looked at him while stepping over his legs.

He jumped to his feet and reached for her arm. "Jolie."

She eluded his touch and entered the bathroom across the hall without a word.

Stopping himself from taking his frustration out on the door, he spun around and leaned against the wall next to it. She couldn't stay in the bathroom all day.

Then again, he'd thought she wouldn't stay in her sewing room all night, yet she had. The hum of her sewing machine had penetrated through the door deep into the night. When it had finally stopped, he'd thought she'd leave the room.

She hadn't.

He hadn't left his stance outside the door, either.

The long hours of sitting on the floor, leaning against the door, had given him plenty of time to think. He'd expected her to be confused or shocked over Carl giving her his company, but she was beyond shocked and confused.

And he was beyond knowing what to do about that.

As soon as the doorknob turned, he stepped in front of it, blocking her exit. "I'm sorry. I shouldn't have said anything, or maybe I should have told you the night Carl told me. I don't know, but we need to talk about this."

The hollowness of her eyes as she lifted her face and looked at him, nearly gutted him.

Feeling at his utmost lowest, he tried again. "I wanted you to know so you could make a decision, decide what you want."

Never pulling her gaze off him, she blinked several times. "When we entered this agreement, you said that I'd never have to do anything in private that I didn't want to do."

Nodding, he replied. "I did, and that's still true."

"Good, because I don't want to talk to you. I don't want to even see you." She waved a hand. "Step aside, please."

He could be as stubborn as her. "No. We have to—"

"I have things to see to for tonight's party."

"I don't give a rat's ass about tonight's party. Cancel the damn thing."

Her eyes narrowed. "And let you make a fool of me again? I don't think so."

"A fool of you? No. Jolie, that's not—"

"Step. Aside. Please."

Tears were starting to well in her eyes, and disgusted in himself, he stepped away from the doorway.

Careful to not so much as brush against him, she entered the hallway and walked toward the stairway, then down it.

He'd never felt so helpless in his life. Had never felt so empty and incompetent. A disgust-filled growl rumbled in his throat and he slapped the wall. How in the hell had he ended up so damned if he did, damned if he didn't?

This was by far the worst day of his life. He kept his distance from her, but that didn't stop him from hearing her laugh as she helped the housekeeper, aided Mrs. Hoover in the kitchen, directed Peter as to where to set up tables for card games and dominoes, and joked with Grandpa over whether he should wear a suit coat or his blue smoking jacket.

Randal accepted the fact that she was ignoring him on purpose. As the day went on, the craving for a simple smile, a simple touch, from her began to eat away at him, leaving his insides raw. Had he ever really believed this would work? No physical contact whatsoever while in private, yet in public, pretending to be a happy, loving couple? If that was so, he was a bigger fool than he'd ever imagined.

He'd gotten used to her in his life and... No, that wasn't entirely true. She'd made him realize what had been missing from his life. After having a sampling of it, he wanted more. He'd wanted her to want more, too.

How could he not? She was like the missing piece of a puzzle. The one, interconnecting link that made everything work.

If it was up to him, he would cancel the party, but she obviously wanted it to go on as scheduled, so it would. He would put everything inside him aside and make

Lauri Robinson 233

sure it was exactly as she wanted. Copying her persona, he planted a smile on his face and assisted Peter in re-arranging furniture, setting up card tables and doing other tasks he'd never known needed to be completed in order to host a dinner party.

As evening approached, he retreated to their room, bathed and dressed in a clean suit. He took his time in the hope that Jolie would enter the room and they could have a brief private moment. He had things to tell her. Things he now understood.

But she never entered the room, and as guests started arriving, he made his way downstairs. Both of his sisters and their husbands had already arrived, and he pulled Danielle aside after searching and not finding Jolie anywhere.

"She's upstairs getting ready," Danielle replied, as if his question was pointless.

He nodded as if he had known that, and hadn't been harboring fears that she'd somehow left without him knowing it. "So, her ideas are working for you?" he asked, once again pretending he knew all about them.

"Yes." Excitement filled his sister's face. "Roger thought it a great idea and so did the telephone and electrical companies."

"Roger...Wayne?" he asked, searching his mind for any other men he knew named Roger.

"Who else owns a plane and works with telephone and electrical companies?" She slapped his arm. "You don't have to pretend that you didn't know. The companies said pictures of possible routes was a fabulous idea and would help their engineers greatly. James will start accompanying Roger next week. And, since I'm sure Jolie told you about her other idea, too, James has already spoken to the superintendent of schools, who said he'd heard of other schools taking individual pictures of children, in addition to group photos, and would really like to try it this coming school year." Danielle stretched on her tiptoes and kissed his cheek. "Thank you for marrying her. She's the best sister-in-law I could ever have hoped for. I just love her to pieces." Lowering her voice, she added, "And the bras." She giggled. "Everyone loves them."

As he had all day, Randal kept the false smile on his face and nodded, even though he felt completely in the dark. Bras? How had that even entered the conversation?

"Oh, there's your beautiful bride now."

Following Danielle's gaze, he turned toward the staircase, where Jolie slowly made her way down each step. It reminded him of their first date, when he'd watched her come down her mother's stairway. Only this time, he recognized what the sight of her did to him. How it filled him with pride, joy and something else. He didn't want to admit that. Didn't want to go down that road.

Love could break a man. He didn't want to be broken.

A nudge in the back sent him forward to meet her as she approached the bottom of the steps.

She was wearing a long dress, made out of the shimmering blue material that he'd picked out, knowing it would make her eyes look darker, browner, but it was what was wrapped around her waist that made his heart thud harder. His white-and-gold pirate rope. She'd wrapped a long strand around her midsection several times and had it tied in a square knot above one hip. The rope emphasized her breasts, as did the V-shaped neckline, and the sleeves were layers of three triangles that barely covered her shoulders.

He held out a hand, and his insides rejoiced as she took ahold of his fingers. His elation faded as he noted the smile on her face was superficial. For show only. The dimness of her eyes proved that.

"You look stunning," he said.

She stepped off the last step. "I didn't care for the way the waist looked, so I borrowed your rope to cover it up. I hope you don't mind."

"Not at all." He kissed her cheek. "It looks lovely."

"Well, it's homemade." She withdrew her hand from his and stepped around him to greet Danielle, and then the others.

The rest of the guests soon arrived, and as she had all day, Jolie kept her distance. She would grant him a smile when she knew others were watching, but it was little consolation.

Shortly before dinner was to be served, she and Jane disappeared up the stairway.

"Another bra order, I'm sure," David said, standing next to him.

What was up with bras? Why did everyone keep mentioning them? Besides Danielle, and now David, he'd heard others whispering the word.

David slapped his shoulder. "And her siblings are working out great."

Randal shook his head to clear his mind from bras. "Siblings?"

"Yes. Jolie's brother and sister are both working for me, selling tickets at the airport. I should have thought about students. The hours work perfectly for them and for me."

Silas and Chloe were working at the airport? When did they get jobs? Why did they get jobs? He would have given them money.

David chuckled. "Your mind is still on the bras. I know. Jane loves them, and, well, they are..." Slapping his shoulder again, David said, "Well, you know."

No, he didn't know. It appeared as if there were a lot of things he didn't know.

Getting through the evening was far harder than Jolie had thought it would be. The day had been tough, but she'd been able to escape to another room each time Randal had gotten too close. That wasn't possible with a houseful of people who thought she and Randal were a happy married couple.

They weren't.

She wasn't sure if that made her mad, or sad, or just so frustrated she wanted to scream.

Which she couldn't do.

All she could do was keep a smile pasted on her face and not punch Randal in the stomach every time he took her hand, or rested a hand on her back, or draped an arm around her shoulders. This was all his fault. If he wasn't so...so perfect in every way, she could walk away, forget she'd ever known him.

This was not turning out as she'd planned last night, while locked in her sewing room, sewing bras. She'd thought she could simply not care. Simply fall out of love.

That thought had been shattered as soon as she'd opened the door, and realized he'd been in the hallway, in front of her door, all night.

Then, he'd had to help with the preparations for the party tonight. Happily!

Even her dress had fought her plan. The side zipper had gotten snagged on a thread. Rather than take the dress off and snip off the thread, she'd tried to snap it off, and had broken the zipper. His stupid pirate rope was her only option of saving her outfit because people had already started to arrive.

Damn it all! And damn him!

She had to get everything back in focus. Remember that he and Amy had been in on this together. That was a real stickler. How could she win? She couldn't, because Amy would end up with Randal, and that was what she wanted.

She shouldn't, and was trying hard not to.

"Excuse me, big brother," Willa said. "I need to steal your wife for a moment."

Randal tugged her closer to his side and looked down at her rather than at his sister. "Only if you promise to bring her right back."

Jolie chided her heart for defying her by skipping a beat as he kissed her temple.

"I promise," Willa said. "We won't be long." She looped an arm through Jolie's and led her out of the den where they had been watching Gus Albright and Grandpa play dominoes.

Once in the hallway, Willa apologized. "I'm sorry, but Don and I must leave soon. The babysitter can only stay until nine and I have a proposition that I need to talk to you about."

"A proposition?"

"Yes, it's something my mother-in-law and I came up with, and I promised her I'd discuss it with you tonight."

"What is it?"

Music was coming from the front room, where the radio was playing a popular opry show, and the laughter and conversations from the other rooms made the hallway loud. "Could we go upstairs?" Willa asked.

"Sure."

"You know, you did the one thing I never thought possible," Willa said as they walked.

"Oh? What's that?"

"Made my brother happy."

Willa was tall and slender, with sandy blond hair and big blue eyes that were much darker than Randal's, but right now were glowing the same way his often did. Looking at them made Jolie's voice lock up.

"Even as a kid, all he did was work," Willa said. "Because that's what our father expected. Randal never complained. The only time he was defiant was when it came to something to do with me or Danielle, then he'd tell our father to leave us be and he'd take care of whatever it was. I always felt sorry for him, how hard he worked to take care of us, and how little he got in return. He acted as if he didn't want appreciation or love." Willa shrugged. "Because of you, I've seen Randal laugh more, be more relaxed, happier, than I've ever seen him. So thank you."

Jolie cleared her throat. "It's nothing I did."

"Yes, it is. You taught him about that one thing that Osterlunds aren't real good at finding, because it was never really shown to us growing up."

"What's that?"

Willa laughed. "Love."

Jolie stubbed a toe on the top step and grabbed ahold

of the railing. She was the last person to teach anyone what love was about. Furthermore, Randal didn't love her.

"Are you all right?" Willa asked.

"Yes, just, ah, caught the hem of my skirt," Jolie lied while stepping off the stairway.

"Your dress is gorgeous, and I love the silk rope. It's adorable. How did you come up with that idea?"

"To be honest, it was a last-minute repair. My zipper broke."

"Oh, my gosh, I wish I had your ingenuity."

"I wouldn't call it that."

"I would, and that brings me to my proposition. Alice, my mother-in-law, and I both love the bras you make, and as you know, the other people we've told about them love them, too. We are wondering if you would be interested in selling them at the drugstore?" Willa paused and drew in a breath. "We were thinking that you could make half a dozen bras or so, of various sizes, for women to try on in the powder room at the drugstore and then determine if they wanted to order one, or more. Of course, they will want to order, once they try them on. Seriously, what's not to love about them? So…what do you think?"

Jolie thought this was a way she could bring in money regularly, which she would need once she moved back in with her mother. She had thought to stay here, just to thwart Amy and Randal, but she wasn't good enough at pretending for that to work. "Well, um, last night, I couldn't sleep and sewed a few extras. You could take those until I get a chance to sew a few more."

"That would be perfect, can I take them now?"

"Of course." In her sewing room, Jolie wrapped the bras in tissue paper, put them in a bag and gave them to Willa. She and Don left a short time later, and others soon followed suit.

With her nerves dancing, because she wasn't sure what would happen after everyone left, Jolie stood beside Randal. His arm was around her waist, tight enough to let her know escaping wasn't going to be easy. Part of the problem was that she didn't want to escape. She'd tried so hard to be mad at him, but every time he looked at her, smiled at her, she had a hard time believing, or maybe just accepting, that he'd been in on this with Amy right from the start.

But he had been, and that explained why he didn't expect love from their marriage. He was already in love. With Amy. The jealousy inside her peaked again. She hated how she couldn't stop it.

As the last guest left, leaving an invitation to their own dinner party soon, Grandpa closed the door. "That was the best party I ever attended."

"Yes, it was a good party," Randal replied, tightening his hold on her waist even more. "Good night."

She dug her heels into the floor as he turned. "I need to clean—"

"No, you don't." With a solid, steady stare that didn't falter, he continued, "You either walk up those stairs on your own, or I'm carrying you, because we are going to talk. Now."

Short of making a scene in front of Grandpa, and Peter, who was discreetly staying out of sight, other than the toes of his shoes poking around the corner leading into the living room, she had no choice. "Fine."

Randal's hand never left her waist as they crossed the foyer. "Don't even think about escaping. I will not spend the night on the hallway floor again."

"That was your choice."

They started up the stairs, side by side. "And it was your choice to not talk to me all day."

"I didn't have anything to say. Still don't."

"I do. Plenty."

Chapter Nineteen

Now that he had her where he wanted her, Randal wasn't sure where to start with all he wanted to say. There was plenty. He locked the door and dropped the key in his pocket before turning to face her.

She stood near the sofa, arms crossed.

"Would you care to change first?" he asked.

"No."

"Would you care to sit down?"

"No."

One-word answers. Her defenses were up, making broaching the subject all the more unfavorable. He shrugged out of his jacket, tossed it and his tie on a chair, and chose to bring up another subject first. "Your brother and sister are working for David at the airport."

"So?"

"Why?" he asked.

"They needed jobs. Ways to make money."

"That's why you married me, so they would have money. If they need more, all you had to do is tell me."

She pinched her lips together and lifted her chin. "They wanted to earn their own money."

He was trying his best not to be angry, but couldn't do much about the other emotions. That of being hurt that she'd gone to someone else, rather than come to him. "I'm your husband, I could have found jobs for them."

"You'd already done enough."

He rubbed the back of his neck, where tension was building. "And Danielle and James, you took it upon yourself to find jobs for them, too? Taking photos of Roger's routes and schoolchildren?"

"They were just ideas I provided them."

"Why?"

"Because they, too, want to earn their own money."

"You're trying your damnedest to make sure no one needs my help, aren't you?"

She shrugged.

"Why?"

The way she shrugged again got his ire. "Damn it, Jolie, we aren't going to solve this if we don't talk about it."

"Maybe there's nothing to solve."

"Yes, there is. You're my wife, and—"

"Am I? Or am I just means to an end?" She planted her hands on her hips. "Fine, you want to know why I helped them? Because no one should take advantage of someone else." Breathing so fast her breasts rose and fell, she added, "No one should enjoy making a fool out of someone, either."

"You aren't a means to an end and I wasn't trying to make a fool out of anyone."

She let out a false laugh. "Dad's company is why you married me."

The truth stung, and he hated that. "It was, and that's why I thought it was only fair for you to know about

Carl's intent to give you the company before our relationship went any further."

"Fair?"

Her voice grew louder each time she opened her mouth. So did his. "Yes!" He threw his arms out at his sides. "I thought you should have all the facts before deciding if you want to stay married or not."

She spun around, stomped along the length of the sofa. "When we discussed this arrangement, I seem to recall you stating you had no intention of seeking a divorce."

"I don't."

Turning, she glared at him. "You mean didn't, until you found out you can't buy Dad's airplane company."

"No, I mean I don't." He kept his gaze locked on hers. "A divorce will be totally up to you."

She planted her hands on her hips again. "What about infidelity?"

He shook his head, momentarily lost by her question, then a hard knot formed in his stomach. He had said that in the beginning, but there was only one reason for her to bring it up. "Infidelity?"

"Yes, infidelity!" She spun around, walked across the room. "You know. When a man is married to one woman, but in love with another."

His entire body went rock-hard. No wonder she was so willing to marry him. So willing to not want love. "Who is it? Who are you in love with?"

"Spare me!" She pivoted, pointed a finger at herself. "I'm not talking about me! And you know it! Well, I know things, too! I know everything. How you and she set this all up to make me look like the ultimate fool! A wife who can't keep her husband happy, a wife whose husband divorces her for another woman!"

"Stop it!" He grasped her upper arms. "What are you talking about?"

She shoved his arms aside. "The jig is up, Randal. Amy told me everything."

His anger hit a new level, and he let out a curse under his breath. He should have known that as soon as Amy hit town, so would trouble. He'd been so focused on Jolie, on how he'd fallen in love with her, he'd forgotten Amy was back. "Whatever she told you is a lie, Jolie. That's what she does. She lies and she hurts people."

"Did she lie about you meeting her at the airport the morning she arrived?"

He shook his head in disbelief. Amy would have told her that for sure, and made far more out of it than there had been. Damn it. He spun around, paced the floor.

"As soon as Dad told you about the airplane company not being for sale, you came home and called Amy, then met her at the airport the next day. I'm sure the two of you had a good laugh that day!"

"No, I didn't! I didn't come home and call Amy. When Carl told me, all I thought about was you, and how I couldn't force you to stay married to me when you didn't have to. Didn't need to."

She swiped at her cheek. "I suppose you *didn't* meet Amy at the airport, either?"

"I saw her at the airport, but I hadn't gone there to meet her. I'd gone to see Carl, to tell him that I couldn't keep a secret like that from you. That he was going to give you his company. He'd already left his house, so I drove to the airport to see if his plane had left." Could this get more jumbled? Not that he could imagine. He crossed the room, to his dresser. "Amy's flight landed while I was there. She told me I could give her a ride home. I told her no." He opened the drawer. "And I bought these."

She glanced from his face to the tickets in his hand.

He walked closer, holding out the tickets. "They are for our flight to South Dakota, to see Mount Rushmore. It's still a couple weeks away, but it was the earliest a plane was flying up there."

She was looking at him, but her eyes were still full of skepticism. He couldn't blame her. The entire thing was a mess. He should have told her right away. Should have told Carl. Should have done so many things differently.

He tossed the tickets on the table, held up both hands. "Other than that brief encounter at the airport, I haven't seen or talked to Amy since she left town months ago. And I didn't marry you to make a fool out of you!"

"Then how did she know we'd be at the restaurant last night?"

"I don't know!" He was so mad he couldn't think straight, but he was sure he hadn't seen Amy last night.

Shaking her head, she walked away from him, around the edge of the sofa. "She said someone like you would never fall in love with someone like me. She was right."

The coffee table and sofa were between them. Using the table as a launch, he leaped over the sofa, landed in front of her. "She lied!"

"No, she didn't!"

She attempted to sidestep around him, but he moved so she couldn't.

She gave his chest a hard shove. "You said so yourself the night of Dad's party. That you could never love me. I didn't expect you to, and—"

"I lied! I didn't want to fall in love with you!"

"I didn't want to fall in love with you, either!"

They had been yelling loud enough for the entire house to hear, and everyone probably wondered about the silence that filled the house now.

His ears were ringing, wondering if they'd just heard right.

Both breathing heavy, they stared at each other. He took a single step closer, not wanting to frighten her, but needing to be closer. He loved her, and wanted to love her. Wanted her to love him in return more than he'd ever wanted anything. "But I did fall in love. With you."

She pinched her lips together, closed her eyes for a moment, before saying, "And I fell in love with you."

He couldn't take it any longer, had to touch her. Gently, he rubbed her upper arms. "I didn't want to fall in love because I've seen it hurt too many people." His stomach sank. "And now it's hurting you."

Tears trickled from her eyes. "I've seen it hurt people, too. Make them jealous and not care about others."

He pulled her close, hugged her. "I know. After my mother died, my father hated everyone. Everything. Because he'd loved her so much."

Her arms went around his waist. "My mother quit caring about anyone else after my father died, and before he died, she was so jealous he couldn't speak to someone else without her being mad and upset."

He tightened his hold on her, rocked her gently. "You are nothing like your mother."

She buried her face against his shirt. "Yes, I am. I was so jealous at the thought of you and Amy that I—" She let out a little sob.

He tightened his hold even more. "There's nothing to be jealous about." Yet, because he'd experienced a large bout of jealousy only moments ago, he admitted, "The idea of you with someone else makes me jealous, too, because I love you so much. Love you in a way I never thought I could love anyone."

She lifted her head, looked at him with tears in her eyes. "I love you, too, and I can't stop." She shook her head. "What are we going to do?"

He laughed and framed her face with both hands, kissed her lips. "We are going to love each other, for the rest of our lives. We both know what we want and what we don't. It's that simple."

Jolie's heart pounded so hard it hurt to breathe. He loved her, and she loved him, so very much. Would for the rest of her life. Not loving him wasn't an option. She'd tried that, and it hadn't worked. But it couldn't be that simple. Not after all of her fears. "But what if—"

He pressed a thumb against her lips, shook his head. "We'll make it work. No matter what, we'll make it work. I love you, Jolie. That will never change. I'll love you tomorrow, and the next day, and the one after that. Forever."

The tears flowed from her eyes. Tears of joy and happiness. She believed him, wholly, completely, because everything he'd said was reflected in his eyes. Maybe it was that simple.

She laid her hands on his shoulders, those broad, wonderful shoulders that she'd admired since their wedding night when she'd wiped the rice off his back. She already had so many wonderful memories of him, and she wanted more. So many more.

"I'll love you tomorrow, and the next day, and the day after that." Emotions made her voice crack. "I also loved you yesterday, and the day before that, and the one before that. I don't know exactly when it happened, but it did."

She had more to say, more to admit, but his lips stopped her. What happened next was like nothing she'd ever experienced. Something inside her broke open. Like it had been given wings.

Their kisses grew. The air between them became charged, hot and intense. Their arms, their hands, their lips, were frantic, touching, caressing and coming together over and over again.

All the wants, all the desires of becoming his wife in every way, hit with ten times the force as before.

When their lips had to part so they both could gasp for air, his hands were on the sides of her face again, keeping their gazes locked.

"You've made me happy since our first date. Without you, my life means nothing. I know that for a fact, because it's meant nothing for years. Until now. Until you." He pressed his forehead against hers. "You're my pirate's treasure, Jolie."

Nothing he could have said would have meant more. Her heart was still pounding, her body still burning with need. "And you're mine."

He ran his hands over her shoulders, down her arms, and then hooked them inside the rope looped around her waist. "I knew this pirate rope would be lucky."

He was so handsome. So wonderful. She regretted thinking badly of him for even a moment. "I'm sorry for doubting you. I will never do that again. I'm sorry I didn't tell you about Silas's and Chloe's jobs, and the ideas for Danielle and James, and—"

"And the bras?"

Her cheeks heated up. "You know about them, too?"

"I've heard mention, and am curious to know more."

The way he glanced down at her breasts made them tingle and grow heavy. The swirl of heat was elsewhere in her body, and so strong, her toes curled.

His hands slid to the knot in the rope. "If you want to tell me."

Her entire being reacted, pulsated, as he began untying the knot. An eagerness filled her, recalling how others had stated their husbands liked the bras. "I've always sewn my own bras, and so I made one for Jane. She liked it so much she asked me to make some for other people, so did Danielle and Willa after I made them each one, and now Willa wants to sell them at the drugstore."

The knot let go and he began to slowly unwrap the rope from around her waist. "Are they like the one in your sketchbook?"

She'd forgotten all about that sketch, but it excited her that he'd seen it. She tightened her hold on his shoulders against the thrill happening inside her. "Somewhat. That was my first attempt."

He dropped the rope onto the floor. "They've gotten better since then?"

The teasing, the heightened senses between them was so exhilarating, she felt emboldened. She lifted one shoulder in a playful way. "Would you like to see?"

His hands slid upward, brushing the sides of her breasts. "Very much."

With the rope gone, and the zipper broken, her dress was loose. She took a step back, slipped one sleeve and then the other off her shoulders, and held her breath as her dress slowly slid down her body, into a pile around her feet.

She watched his expression, the lift of his brow, the shimmer of his eyes, but the way his smile grew was the best part.

He slowly slid a finger across one cup and then the other, making her nipples grow hard.

"I've never seen anything more..." His eyes met hers. "Enticing. You are a very talented seamstress."

Her breath came out in a gush.

"I already knew that." He took her hand, guided her steps over the gown at her feet. "But now I'm completely convinced."

"Do you like it?"

"I intend to show you how much I like it." He pulled her close, covered her mouth with his.

From that moment on, she was lost, fully absorbed into a world so wonderful, she hoped it would never end. Before long, they were on the bed, naked and glorifying in their open admissions of loving one another. His touch was so loving and gentle, she truly felt as if she was the treasure he'd searched for his entire life.

He was hers. A treasure she hadn't known she'd been searching for, but certainly had discovered. He kissed her, tasted her, touched and teased her, and filled her with a pleasure that was all-consuming. There was no room for her to be self-conscious or worried about what to do next. He guided her, enticed and encouraged her so thoroughly, that when the moment came, when she became his wife in more than name, it was a true coming together. The one thing they both wanted more than all else.

She'd imagined what the moment might be like, but it was so much more. The only thing she had to compare it to was their wedding chase, when they'd been speeding toward the hotel. It was as if they were once again racing to a finish line, the two of them, together. Her heart was pounding, her breathing hard and fast, and exhilaration filled her.

The feel of his bare skin touching hers, of him filling her, of the friction that was taking her on what could only be called an impossible journey filled with indescribable pleasure, left her unable to think. All she could do was feel.

And she felt wonderful!

Amongst all the excitement, a moment hit when she felt her entire body go tense, lock up. She looked at Randal, momentarily stunned. The smile on his face told her there was nothing to fear. That he was here with her. Forever.

Believing him, she let herself go, and embraced the way everything inside her burst into something that was even more pleasurable, more satisfying, than anything she'd ever known. It was as if their bodies had become one, their souls, too, dancing together on some magical waves of blissful love.

As everything slowly faded into pure contentment, her body was so lethargic, she couldn't move, just lie there, breathing and smiling.

Slowly, her mind returned, and the happiness that filled her made her laugh out loud. She flipped onto her side and snuggled close against him. Content, free to not hold anything back, she used the tip of one finger to draw a heart on his chest. "Had I known the outcome I would have shown you one of my bras long before now."

Still basking in the aftermath of their lovemaking that had been so utterly fulfilling he was completely drained, Randal let out a groan, not wanting to think of the past few weeks of tortuous nights of being so close to her, yet so far. "I was at my wits' end as it was. If I'd seen you wearing that bra, my final bits of control would have snapped."

Her fingertip was still roaming across his chest. "You always appeared to be in control."

"I wasn't." He shifted enough to look at her upturned face, and feasted on her beauty as strongly as he had when she'd let her dress fall to the floor. A formfitting, delicate garment made of shimmering white silk, the bra had been pretty, but her wearing it had nearly sent him over the edge. Had he truly considered letting her go? It would never have worked. He'd been too enticed, too smitten, right from the start. From the moment he'd seen her walking down the stairway at her mother's house. He just hadn't wanted to admit it. He'd been too afraid of failure, yet the ultimate failure would have been not falling in love with her.

She stretched, kissed him and sighed sweetly. "I think that's my favorite part."

Confused, he asked, "What is?"

"That I can kiss you whenever I want."

Her honesty made him smile, and touched his heart like nothing ever had. He traced a finger over her lips. "That's one of my favorite things, too." He let his fingertip trail over her chin, down her neck. "Another is touching you, and yet another is looking at you and thinking how lucky I am."

She blushed and bowed her head. "Can I ask you a question?"

"Of course." He lifted her chin so they were again eye to eye. "You can ask me questions whenever you want. I'll tell you anything you want to know."

"Did you ever do what we just did with Amy?"

After the way Amy had treated her, he understood why she'd want to know. "No. I never had any feelings toward Amy. Especially none that would lead to making love to her. Nothing even closely related to what I feel for you."

"Then why did you date her?"

"Because it was safe. Amy guaranteed that I'd never fall in love. She's the complete opposite of you. You're beautiful, smart, caring, and most of all, lovable." He kissed the tip of her nose. "It's impossible not to love you."

"That's how I feel about you."

His body had just known the greatest satisfaction imaginable, but his desires were far from appeased. After one taste, he wanted more, but was also concerned about her. "How are you feeling?"

"Wonderful."

Despite her bravado of dropping her gown, he'd sensed her shyness, and had gone slow introducing her into lovemaking. "Are you sore? Did I hurt you?"

Twisting a leg around one of his, she kissed his chin. "No, in fact, I was wondering... Now that I know what to expect, maybe we should try it all again."

His answer came through in the kiss he gave her. Their first time had been amazing, but with experience came confidence, and his wife was soon a very confident woman.

Chapter Twenty

Familiarity, closeness, grew between them throughout the weekend, to the point Randal was late going into the office on Monday morning, and every other morning that week. Waking up next to Jolie was just too enticing to immediately climb out of bed. Once at work, all he could think about was returning home, of having Jolie in his arms, her perfect body molded and melded with his.

That's where his mind was on Friday morning when his secretary knocked on the door, and then opened it. "Telephone. It's a Mr. Blocker—Carl Jansen's butler."

Randal thanked her and picked up the receiver.

"Good day, sir," the butler said. "Mr. Jansen would like you to know that he will be home this afternoon, and would like to invite you and Mrs. Osterlund to join him for dinner at seven o'clock this evening."

"Thank you, Mr. Blocker," Randal instantly replied. "Mrs. Osterlund and I are honored to accept the invite."

"Very good, sir. Good day to you."

"And to you." Randal hung up, grabbed his jacket and told his secretary he wouldn't be back until Monday morning. He and Jolie had discussed her inheritance several times and he knew how difficult it would be for her to face Carl. Tell him no. That was her decision, and he'd support her in upholding it. Not so long ago, all he'd wanted was Carl's company, but now Jolie's happiness is what he wanted above and beyond all else.

She wasn't expecting him home so soon, because he'd left for work only a couple hours ago, and he found her in her sewing room, head bent over the sewing machine and pumping the treadle with her feet. He stood in the doorway, watching for several minutes, until she must have sensed she was being watched and looked over her shoulder.

The joy on her face stirred the love inside him that just kept growing and growing.

"What are you doing home?" She rose from the stool and met him in the center of the room.

"I missed you."

She lifted her face for him to kiss her.

He obliged.

As the kiss ended, she sighed. "I missed you, too."

She fit into his arms so perfectly, as if she was made just for him to hold. He kept his arms around her as he glanced at the machine behind her. "More bra orders?"

"Yes." Her smile brightened even more. "Willa sold another ten yesterday."

A tinge of guilt struck him at interrupting her sewing. Orders had come in every day this week. "Is there anything I can do to help?"

"No." She frowned slightly. "Maybe."

"What? Just tell me, other than sewing. I've never done that, but I suppose I could learn." He nuzzled the side of her neck. "You could teach me."

She laughed. "I could, but right now, I just need your brain."

He nibbled on her earlobe. "Are you sure that's all you need?"

She let out an encouraging little moan. "You're going to make me forget what I needed help with."

Giving in, he lifted his head. "Okay, what can my brain help you with?"

The smile in her eyes promised what he wanted would come later. "Willa wants a name for the bras, so people can ask about them and not be embarrassed."

He ran his hands up and down her sides. "Your bras aren't embarrassing."

"It is a delicate subject for some women. Jane has been calling them Jolie's dream bras, but that's…" She shrugged. "Not very discreet."

He grinned. "It's a fitting name. I dream of you every night." He cupped her backside with both hands. "Sometimes you aren't wearing anything."

She blushed and gave his chest a playful slap. "I'm trying to be serious about this."

He loved teasing her, but could also tell the name was a real concern for her and grew thoughtful. "What would you like to call them?"

"I don't know. I like Jane's idea, because it proves I am a designer. That I designed them, but it could be embarrassing if word got out and people pointed at me, saying that's Jolie from Jolie's dream bras."

He'd never be embarrassed by her. He was proud of her, but could relate to what she was saying. "So you don't like your name or the word *bra*?"

She nodded, then shook her head. "I don't know."

Taking a shot in the dark, he said, "How would you

feel about JO's Dream Wear? JO as in capital *J*, capital *O*, for Jolie Osterlund, and dream wear instead of dream bra?"

"JO's Dream Wear. JO's Dream Wear." Her smile grew a little each time she repeated it. "I like that, and it would leave it open for me to design other things."

"Yes, it would."

She slid her arms inside his coat, wrapped them around his waist. "You really are a smart man."

He brought their bodies tighter together. "The smartest thing I've ever done is marry you."

With a tiny, sweet moan, she kissed him. Which led to another kiss, and another one, each one more passionate. He'd been ready to take her to bed the moment he'd walked in the room, and with the encouragement she was demonstrating, stating that she wanted the same thing was impossible to ignore.

Pushing him backward, toward the door, she said, "I think we should go to our room."

Thrilled, and more than willing, he walked backward, kissing her the entire time. Unable to dismiss the opportunity to tease her, he waited until his back was up against the door before asking, "What for?"

With a teasing grin, she reached around him and turned the doorknob. "Because I want to show you something."

"Will I like it?" He would, that was a given.

She shrugged, and gave him a slight shove so she could open the door.

Following her out the door, he caught her around the waist as they hurried down the hallway and into their bedroom, laughter floating in their wake.

* * *

Jolie hadn't known she could be so happy, or that her body could respond so quickly to nothing more than the sight of her husband. Her husband! There were times when she sat by herself, sewing, that she'd laugh, so happy that she'd gotten over her fears of loving him. She couldn't even remember why she'd been afraid.

After he locked their bedroom door, she held up a hand. "Stay there."

He frowned slightly, which made her pinch her lips to keep another giggle inside. When she'd put the new bra on this morning, she'd been excited, and thought she'd have to wait until tonight for him to see it. "I said I had something to show you."

Eyes shimmering, he nodded.

She began unbuttoning her dress. It was amazing how confident she'd become, because of him. He made her feel so loved, so beautiful. "You bought some blue silk material when we'd gone shopping." She'd only made white bras, but he'd bought so much blue material, she figured that was his favorite color. "And I used some of it to make a new bra."

"You did?"

"Yes." Biting her bottom lip, she watched for his reaction as she pulled the front of her dress wide for him to see the bra. "What do you think?"

"I like it, but I need to see more." He stepped forward and grasped the bottom of her dress, lifted it over her head. Tossing her dress aside, he ran a finger under one strap. "It's beautiful. Almost as beautiful as you."

Her body knew his touch so well, and that's all it took. One touch, and she was filled with need, with want, that only he could satisfy. Making love with him was far more than she'd ever imagined, far more thrilling and exciting. She'd been so wrong when she'd once thought that liking him, liking each other, would be enough. She'd love him for the rest of her life, and still want him as badly as right now.

He picked her up by the waist. Her shoes fell off her feet and she wrapped her arms around his neck and her legs around his waist. "I want you. Now."

"I want you, too." He laid her on the bed and slid her panties off. "You should make some of these to match your bra."

"Would you like that?"

"Very much." He kissed her bra, the very tip of each cup, making her nipples harden.

Barely holding on to keep from spiraling into the unknown world he took her to every time they coupled, she pushed his jacket off his shoulders. "Then I will, but right now, you have too many clothes on."

He continued to kiss her in sensitive spots, pausing only long enough to remove another article of clothing. When he finally stood naked, she indulged in the glorious sight.

Anticipation spiked as he climbed on the bed, positioned himself, and her eyelids fluttered at the pleasure of him entering her. It was no wonder that she'd fallen so deeply in love with him. There wasn't anything in the world that could have protected her from not falling in love with him. He was such a good man, kind and caring, and loving. Falling in love with him had been so easy, and continuing to love him was even easier. It was as natural as breathing.

There were times when their lovemaking was fast and furious, and other times when it was slow and so sensual it was as if every bone in her body melted. She loved all of it, every minute, and had learned a lot since their first night, and that was empowering.

Wrapping her legs around his, she arched into him and increased the tempo, increased the glorious friction that would soon overtake her ability to think of anything, send her heart racing and cause her breath to become locked in her lungs. Before that happened, she cupped his face with both hands. "I love the way you love me."

"I love loving you. It consumes me day and night."

"Me, too," she admitted, and then let herself go, soak up every nuance of the waves of pleasure that led her to the ultimate peak, where gratification struck with a burst that left her gasping as she sank deep into the softness of the mattress and reveled in just how lucky she was to be married to him. To be loved by him.

A warmth spread across her stomach at the idea of how their actions might someday cause her to become pregnant. She'd cherish that moment. Wholly.

Reality was slowly returning when he touched the center of her bra. "I like the little bow right there."

She was still wearing the bra. He, however, was stripped of all clothes, except his socks, which made her giggle. He was lying on his side, and she flipped onto her side, so they faced each other. "I hoped you would." She had sewn on the tiny silk ribbon bow to make the bra prettier, just for him.

"When did you start sewing bras?"

"For myself, shortly after I started wearing them. The ones my mother bought for me were just flat strips of material that flattened and squished everything. They weren't very comfortable, and there was only one set of hooks, so you couldn't adjust anything. I tried a few designs before finding one I liked. I made some for my sister and a couple of elderly neighbors, but Jane was the first other person."

"Do you like sewing them?"

It was her dream, to be a designer, yet, with him she had to be honest. "Yes, and no. I'd always wanted to be a clothes designer, and I love sewing, but I have to admit, sewing bras all day, every day, can get tedious. It is still exciting to know so many people like what I've designed and want them, though."

"You need to hire people to sew for you."

"Maybe someday. I don't have the money to do that yet."

"I do."

"You need your money for your airline."

He ran a hand up and down her side. "No, I don't. I think we should focus on JO's Dream Wear instead. It has as much potential as an airline."

She forced the smile on her face to not falter. She knew an airline was still his dream, and was going to make sure it came true for him. If it meant giving up her dream of being a designer so he could have his airline, she would do it. Do it in a heartbeat. Leaning forward, she kissed him.

His smile said he was aware of her attempt to avoid his suggestion. "Carl's home. He's invited us for dinner tonight."

Her plan had been to go see Dad as soon as he was back, so tonight was fine with her. She scanned Randal's face, taking in his handsomeness, as well as who he was. A proud man, who had only ever had one goal, that of taking care of his family, financially. That's what had driven him and she loved him for that. For who he was. And she didn't want that to change, because that would change him—the man she'd fallen in love with.

"Okay. What time?"

"Seven."

"Then we have plenty of time."

"For what?"

She scooted closer to him, nuzzled his chin. "Nothing."

"Nothing?"

Shrugging, she trailed a finger along his side. "Unless you can think of something you want to do."

Chapter Twenty-One

"That fish tasted as good as it used to over the campfire," Jolie said as the meal concluded.

"I caught them this morning," Dad answered. "Cleaned them, wrapped them in a wet towel and stuffed them in my tackle box so they'd stay cold all the way home." He laughed. "There were some wrinkled noses on the airplane when people got a sniff of them." Winking at her, he added, "I remember how much you liked eating fish."

"I had forgotten how good they taste when they are fresh caught." She smiled at Randal across the table from her. They'd spent a large portion of the day in bed, and the contentment of that still lived inside her. "I've told Randal all about your cabin."

"It's never locked and you know how to get there," Dad said.

She laughed. "I'm afraid I don't. I was too excited to arrive and never paid attention as to how we got there."

"I've missed having you kids with me, as much as I've missed your father," Dad said. "We'll all have to go down there together someday." He set his napkin on the table. "For now, shall we retire to my den?"

Jolie waited for Randal to arrive at her chair and held his arm as they followed Dad down the hall and into his den.

As soon as they were seated, side by side on a brown leather sofa, Randal patted her knee and said to Dad, "I owe you an apology, Carl."

Seated in his wingback chair, Dad lifted a bushy, gray brow. "Oh? How so?"

"For breaking a promise of silence." Randal took hold of her hand. "My vows to Jolie take precedence over all else and so I told her about your intention of a possible inheritance."

"I see." Dad leaned back in his chair and settled his gaze on her. "So you know I have willed my airplane company to you?"

Her heart softened as she thought of all the years she'd known Dad and how generous he'd been over those years. "Yes, and I'm honored that you think so highly of me, but I hope you will understand when I say that I can't accept a gift like that. You've already been more than generous by paying for the wedding."

"I bought that company with every intention of sharing it with your father," Dad said.

"I understand that." She also understood some of the actions her mother had taken, and why. Her mother had refused to ask Dad for help because she'd felt that would mean Jolie's father had failed his family, and she wasn't willing to let anyone believe that. Jolie would never allow someone to believe that about Randal, either. "And I appreciate your kindness and friendship. It's my greatest wish to maintain that, and I hope we can come to an understanding about this."

Dad sighed. "I do understand. I should have given you the company before now, back when you needed it."

"No, you shouldn't have," she said, "because I wouldn't have been able to accept it then, either. No more than my father would have been able to accept it."

"You certainly are your father's daughter," Dad said.

"Thank you, I consider that a compliment."

"Do you agree with her, Randal?" Dad asked.

"Yes. I will always support every decision she makes." Randal tightened the hold on her hand. "Jolie has created her own clothing design business that is well on its way to being extremely successful. I'm very proud of her, very proud to be her husband."

There had been a point in her life when she'd thought that falling in love would make her vulnerable, change who she was and wanted to be. Now she knew it did just the opposite. Because of him.

Dad cleared his throat, making them both look at him. "Congratulations, I'm not surprised. You always had get-up-and-go. That's why I wanted to give you the company. Once you married Randal, I knew the two of you could turn that company into something I could only dream about."

Jolie smiled to herself as she looked at Dad. This was her chance to make Randal's dream come true. She'd told him she wouldn't accept the company as a gift, but hadn't fully explained why. Randal was a man of principle and would never accept the company as a gift. But he wanted it. Wanted to create an airline, and she wanted to help him in every way she could. "I agree, and though I can't accept the company as a gift, I am interested in knowing if you'd be willing to sell it to us."

Dad frowned. "What about the clothing design company Randal just mentioned?"

Not surprised by his question, she shook her head. "I'm just sewing for friends and family. Randal is the true businessman and will take the plane company to new levels in no time, and I'll be there with him every step of the way."

Dad let out a chuckle. "Oh, Joey-girl. Right now, I know your father is looking down on you, smiling." Leaning back in his chair, he looked at Randal. "I'm not ashamed to admit that I was aware that you were interested in buying my company for some time, and that's why I told you about my plan of willing it to Jolie. I wanted to know how you'd react to that news, because it would prove to me whether or not you had ulterior motives for the marriage. That may not have been any of my business, but I felt I had to look out for Jolie. Thankfully, the two of you have proven that I have nothing to worry about."

"I love Jolie," Randal said. "Her happiness is what is most important to me."

She leaned against his shoulder. "Your airplane business will be our saddle shop, Dad."

Randal wasn't sure what she meant about a saddle shop, but he now understood why she'd been so adamant about not accepting Carl's company. She'd planned on them buying it. Them as in both of them. The idea would have excited him, if he was just thinking of himself. But he hadn't been doing that in weeks now. Her bras were amazing, and he believed in her talent, was prepared to provide whatever support she needed to achieve success. It bothered him that she made it sound like it was nothing by saying she was just sewing for friends and family. It had grown well beyond that. Yet, right now, she was beaming and he couldn't take her joy away from her. In order to buy some time, he suggested to Carl, "Perhaps we could set up a time to meet and discuss this further next week?"

"Of course," Carl answered. "Whatever is convenient for you. I'm interested in hearing what your thoughts are for the company."

"He has it all planned out, Dad, and it's amazing," Jolie said. "Air America will become the largest airline in America, mark my words."

Randal's heart thudded. He loved the way she looked at him, with such pride and confidence. Not very long ago, he'd have been as excited as she was about buying Carl's company, but his focus was different now. His entire life was different now. He still wanted to succeed in business, but he wanted her dream to come true, too. That dream was JO's Dream Wear, not Air America. "I think we've taken up enough of Carl's time tonight."

They left a short time later, and he'd barely started the car when she asked, "Why do I have the feeling you aren't happy about buying Dad's company?"

He countered with, "Why did you belittle your design company?"

"It is little. I'm just sewing for friends and family."

He put the car in gear and drove around the curved driveway. "No, you're not. Your bras are being mailed to women in other states."

"Friends and family of friends and family."

He shook his head. "It's more than that. It has real potential. With salesmen and advertising, you could soon be selling thousands of bras each week. We'll hire workers, find a building and—"

"Selling thousands of bras a week won't compare to an airline," she interrupted.

"Yes, it could, because it won't be just bras. You can design all sorts of women's clothing."

"But an airline is something people need."

"So are women's underclothes."

"Why are you refusing to talk about it? You had the chance to tell Dad all about your ideas and didn't."

His spine stiffened. He didn't want to argue with her, but wasn't going to let her give up her dream of designing clothes. "Why are you refusing to talk about your design company?"

"Because we weren't at Dad's to discuss that. We were there to talk about his company. I thought you'd be happy about buying it. Not argue about it."

"We aren't arguing," he insisted.

She let out a loud *humph*. "Aren't we?"

"No." He turned on the dark, empty road that would take them back to town.

"I say we are. Just like the last time we left his place."

Randal huffed out a sigh. They had argued last time they'd left Carl's, and he didn't want to do that again. "I'm just curious as to why you want us to buy it so badly?"

She was staring out the passenger window and didn't answer.

He shifted the car into a higher gear, still waiting for her to answer. When she didn't, he asked, "Are you going to tell me?"

She sighed again, but this time it sounded different. Sadder.

"Jolie?"

"The truth?" she asked.

"Yes, the truth."

"Because I want you to have it. I want your dream to come true."

"And I want yours to come true."

"I know you do, but mine isn't as important as yours."

"Yes, it is."

"So, that's what we are arguing over?" she asked. "Whose dream is more important?"

He was about to say they weren't arguing, but they were. Why? Last time they'd left Carl's it was because he thought he was giving up his dream, now it's because he didn't want it? He'd thought he'd come to grips with it all, made sense of everything.

Downshifting, he slowed the car and pulled it to the side of the road. "That's a stupid thing to be arguing over."

"Yes, it is."

They sat there, staring at each other for a moment. He knew she wouldn't give up, and reached over, took ahold of her hand. "My entire life, I've been afraid of failure. Even more after I sold the lawn care business. That's why I said no divorce, no infidelity, because that would have been failure. I don't want to fail you, Jolie. Not ever."

She wrapped her other hand around his. "You will never fail me."

"Yes, I would, by not helping you bring JO's Dream Wear to its full potential so that it becomes everything you dreamed it could become."

A tiny smile tugged up the sides of her lips. "You've already made my dream come true."

"And you made my dream come true."

"Maybe it's time we start to focus on a dream we share." She scooted closer to him, kissed him. "The only true failure is not trying at all."

He had to smile at her fortitude. She was not one to give in easily. He never had been, either. "It would be a lot," he said, "building up two businesses at the same time."

"Two?"

"Yes." She was right, giving up was the only true way to fail. Furthermore, he already had all he wanted, so truly didn't have anything to lose. It sure had taken him long enough to figure that out. "We'll buy Carl's company, but JO's Dream Wear will be just as important. It won't be one or the other, it's both."

Smiling, she shook her head and then nodded. "I'll agree to that."

He folded his arms around her, hugged her tight. "But neither will come before you."

"Before us." Lifting her face, she reached up, cupped his jaw. "I love you."

Pure contentment filled him. They could turn both companies into multimillion-dollar enterprises, but they'd never be worth as much as she was to him. She was his everything. His dream come true. "I love you, more than anything."

"So I guess we aren't arguing anymore," she said.

He planted a quick kiss on her lips. "No, we aren't."

She slid her hand inside his jacket and fiddled with the buttons on his shirt. "We probably should completely make up."

He knew what she meant, yet asked, "How would we do that?"

She was still unbuttoning his shirt. "I can think of a way."

He was more than willing to comply, but did have to point out, "You do know we are on the side of the road."

Her hand moved to the waistband of his pants. "Yes, and I know we haven't seen another car since we pulled onto this road."

He was growing harder by the second. "One could come along at any moment."

She undid his pants. "I guess we could wait until we get home." Her hand slid inside his underwear and her fingers wrapped around him. "But it's a long drive."

He found the lever, pushed the seat back, so there would be room for her to straddle his lap. "Too long of a drive."

Jolie felt as if she was floating on air the following week. They'd met with Dad, bought the company, which was exciting, but she was more excited about her and Randal's trip to see Mount Rushmore tomorrow.

She had already packed their suitcases, and just had to deliver the bras she'd made for some of Willa's customers. Evidently, there had been a party where one of the women had been wearing a JO's Dream Wear bra, and the next day, the drugstore had been overrun with women ordering bras. She'd be sewing for a straight month once they got back from their trip.

A hint of chagrin washed over her as she picked the bag off the seat of the car she'd just parked near the drugstore. When she'd discovered who one of those customers was, she'd gotten a glimmer of satisfaction knowing who had made a specific request to have several layers of padding sewn in the bras. Willa had suggested charging the person extra, and extra again to have the order rushed. Jolie could have declined the rushed order, but had agreed, because of the satisfaction it provided, even though she and Willa were the only ones who knew.

A moment later, as Jolie stepped up on the curb, that very customer walked out of the drugstore. Despite all she knew, her stomach sank as it always did upon seeing Amy.

"Well, well, well, look who it is," Amy said. "Little Jolie Cramer."

Jolie wished that Amy couldn't get her goat so easily, but it was hard to break a habit that had been with her for years. "It's Osterlund now, but you know that."

Amy stepped closer. "Not for long."

Telling herself to just walk away, Jolie attempted to step around the other woman.

Amy sidestepped, not letting her pass. "Your *husband* never told you about meeting me at the airport, did he?"

Jolie's spine stiffened.

"Afraid to face the truth?" Amy continued. "That your husband only married you to make me jealous."

Jolie cracked a smile, stared directly in the other's woman's face, but didn't say a word. There was plenty that she could say, but nothing she said would penetrate Amy's thick skull. She'd been a bully too long, had gotten away with too much. Jolie knew the truth, and the truth was, Randal was hers. Would be forever, and knowing that left her with absolutely no reason to be jealous, but a lot to be proud of. She had no doubt of Randal's love for her. Of their love for each other.

"He'll get tired of your cute, sweet little innocent

act sooner or later," Amy sneered. "And want a real woman."

Jolie looked at Amy and was a bit surprised that all she felt was pity. She began to walk away.

"Go ahead, run away," Amy jeered. "But just know, I'm not going anywhere."

Jolie stalled her steps. This wouldn't stop until she put an end to it. She reached into the bag and grasped ahold of one of the special-order bras. "Of course you aren't going anywhere, because you are here, at the drugstore, to pick up the bras you ordered. You know, JO's Dream Wear bras."

"How do you know that?"

Jolie pulled the bra out of the bag. "Because I design and sew them."

Amy's eyes widened and her jaw went slack.

Jolie feigned surprise. "You didn't know the *J O* in JO's Dream Wear stands for Jolie Osterlund? It does. Randal suggested using my initials in the name. He loves everything I design and sew. Loves it even more when I model them for him." She spun the bra by one strap with a finger. "I must admit, yours were the first ones that I've had to sew in several layers of batting, because, well, you know."

"Give me that!" Amy reached out to snatch away the bra, but Jolie was quicker, held it out of her reach.

"You haven't paid for them yet." Jolie dropped the bra back in the bag. "And special orders like this are twice the price, to pay for the extra materials. Padding, so it looks like you have boobs…" She lowered her voice. "We wouldn't want that getting out, now, would we?"

"You…" Amy let out a growl. "You can't go around talking behind people's backs."

"I'm not talking behind your back." Jolie stepped closer. "I'm talking to your face."

Amy's neck and face had turned beet red. "They are terrible bras. I don't want them."

"That's fine. I understand that they might be too expensive for some people." She smiled. "As you know, they've become quite the rage. Everyone is talking about them and I'm sure Willa will be able to sell these to someone else. Of course, she'll let them know that I'll take out the extra padding that you'd ordered."

"You can't do that."

"Yes, I can."

"Those are mine," Amy insisted.

"No, they are mine." Jolie's heart skipped a beat as she noticed a car fly around the corner, hit its brakes and pull up next to the curb. A dark blue Cadillac. "Mine," she repeated. "And so is Randal. I suggest you remember that."

He was already out of the car and arrived at her side within seconds. His arm instantly went around her shoulders and he pulled her up against his side. "Are you okay?"

"I'm fine. Just delivering some bras," Jolie answered, smiling up at him. Then, because she could, she stretched on her toes and held her face near his. He promptly responded to her unspoken request, and she was overjoyed by how he extended the kiss into far more than a simple hello.

"You do know you're not alone," Amy snarled.

"Yes," Randal said as he ended the kiss. "Feel free to leave."

"Oh!" Amy huffed. "You two deserve each other."

Jolie bit back a grin.

"You're right," he answered, but his eyes were on her, not Amy. "We do. That's why we married each other. I knew I couldn't live the rest of my life without her."

"And I couldn't live mine without him," Jolie replied, releasing a smile that was so big her heart doubled in size.

He kissed her again, and when that kiss ended, they were alone. It was a moment before Jolie caught her breath, because his kisses always left her breathless, then she asked, "How did you know I was here?"

His gaze went over her shoulder.

She twisted, saw Willa and Don standing beneath the awning of the drugstore. "They called you?"

"Don did. He knew you were on your way to drop off bras and Amy had been there for half an hour, complaining because her bras hadn't arrived yet."

"And you came to my rescue."

"Yes, and I always will." He rubbed her shoulder. "Are you all right?"

"I've never been better." She kissed his chin. "Except for this morning, and last night, and the night before that, and tomorrow, and the day after that, and—" She let out a sigh of happiness. "Forever."

He laughed, picked her up, spun around and hugged her tight. "Me, too."

Epilogue

Jolie leaned closer to the window and watched as the huge monument disappeared behind a cloud. They were too high up to see much, but having seen it, not once but twice, from the ground level, she knew the carvings were majestic and grand. The changes between the carvings of faces from last year to this year had been inspiring.

She continued to stare out the window. The beauty of sky, the clouds, and of the fact that they were flying high above the ground never failed to amaze her. This trip was even more amazing than last year's because they were flying in an Air America airplane.

The past year had been a whirlwind. A magnificent one. Starting two companies simultaneously had been a challenge at times, but also fun and exciting. There was still a lot to do to bring Air America and JO's Dream Wear to their full potential, but it would happen because they believed it would. She and Randal believed in each other, and in their love.

She turned and looked at him. Unlike many others, Air America planes had two seats, instead of only one, on each side of the center aisle, so traveling companions could sit side by side. Customers liked that, and so did she. The smile Randal bestowed upon her melted her insides, and she had no doubt it would be that way for the rest of her life.

He rested a hand on her stomach. "We don't have to wait a year before coming back."

Covering his hand with both of hers, she said, "This little one will only be a few months old a year from now." The life growing inside her was their greatest accomplishment.

"They'll grow up flying the skyway," he said.

"It's so exciting, isn't it?"

"Yes, it is." He kissed her cheek. "Every day with you is exciting."

"Excuse me."

Jolie glanced past Randal to smile at the stewardess.

"Mother asked me to give you this." Chloe handed her crackers wrapped in waxed paper. "She has more if you need them."

"Tell her I said thank you, but also that I'm fine," Jolie said, taking the crackers. Her bout with morning sickness had ended last month, but her mother had been concerned flying might make it return. "My stomach isn't upset." This was the first flight for Air America, therefore, all members of her and Randal's family, including Dad, were aboard. "What do you think of being a stewardess?"

"I think it's going to be the best job ever," Chloe answered. "I'm not going to want to go back to school in the fall."

"You can work shorter flights around your school

hours," Randal told Chloe. "And your college schedule after graduation."

Chloe rolled her eyes as she replied, "Yes, sir."

Randal shook his head, and looked at Jolie. "I hope our children aren't as impetuous as her."

"Ha, good luck with that," Chloe said. "Look at who you married."

Jolie laughed at both Chloe and Randal, because teasing like this is how they always reacted to one another. "Is the dress comfortable?" she asked her sister. It was navy blue, with red piping, white cuffs and brass buttons. She'd designed them for all the Air America stewardesses and similarly colored suits for the pilots.

"Very, and it makes me feel so official." Chloe straightened and squared her shoulders. "I need to go check on other passengers." She gave Randal's shoulder a playful slug. "Do what I'm getting paid to do."

That was another thing that both of their companies had done, provided jobs. Good jobs, and many of them. Ironically, even for her mother. She was a top salesperson for JO's Dream Wear, and loved it.

"You know, that's a good idea," Randal said.

He was staring at her purse that she'd just picked up and put the crackers in. "What is a good idea?"

"Giving passengers something to snack on," he replied.

Letting the idea settle, she set the purse back on the floor by her feet. "It is. We'll have to look into how we can do that."

Randal winked at her. "Every once in a while your mother has some very good ideas."

She leaned closer to him. "That you instantly go along with."

He kissed her and rubbed her stomach. "Look how well the first one turned out."

She had to agree with him, but also insisted, "I'll never force one of my daughters into a marriage."

Randal would never force one of his children to do anything they didn't want to do, but couldn't not take advantage of the opportunity to tease Jolie. "Even if he's the most wonderful man on earth?"

She hugged his arm. "Even if he's the most wonderful man on earth."

He chuckled. His children would have a very different life than he'd had. They'd grow up knowing they were loved and encouraged to follow their dreams. If one or the other, God willing that he and Jolie had several, would be interested in taking over an airline or a clothing company, they'd be welcomed, but they'd also be welcomed to pursue their own hopes and dreams.

Jolie leaned her head on his shoulder and closed her eyes. He shifted in order to wrap an arm around her so she'd be more comfortable using him as a pillow. She had completed his life in so many ways, and the future of his family was now brighter and broader than he'd ever imagined.

He leaned his head back and let his eyes close as his own drowsiness grew, smiling as he drifted off to sleep, thinking about the little baby Jolie was carrying.

Uncertain what had woken him, he sat up straight, heart pounding. The first place he looked was at Jolie. She was staring at him, eyes wide. "What is it?" he asked.

She pressed a hand to her chest. "I had a dream."

His senses were returning, and noting that every-thing about them was fine, he realized that's what had woken him as well. A dream. "I did, too."

She laid a hand on her stomach the same time his gaze landed there. "It's a girl," she said.

That's what he'd dreamed about, too, but wasn't con-vinced he wanted to share that. Or anything else about what he'd just dreamt about. He laid his hand over the top of Jolie's.

"She'll get married someday, to a man she loves," Jolie said.

His dream had been about that, too, but there had been more. Much more. His spine shivered, yet he wasn't about to cause Jolie any concern. "We have years and years before we need to worry about that."

"Years go by quickly."

He swallowed, hard, and took ahold of her hand. "They do, and we'll be together the entire time."

"Through thick and thin."

Remnants of his dream, of their daughter, pregnant and unwed, flashed in his mind again as he repeated, "Through thick and thin." A resolution formed. He was putting too much into one fleeting dream. Laughing to lighten the mood, he said, "Look at us, the baby isn't even born yet, and we're worrying about things that don't even exist."

She smiled up at him. "You're right."

Turning the conversation even lighter, he said, "If it's a boy, we should name him Joseph, after your father."

Her eyes shone. "Boy or girl, this baby will be named after you."

"A girl named Randal? No. She wouldn't like that."

"I was named after my father. Jolie, for Joseph, and my daughter will be, too. Her name will be Randi, with an *i*."

He laughed, and gave in for now. "If you say so."

"I say so."

He still couldn't say no to her, so kissed her instead.

Twenty-two years later

"Mother, Father."

Randi Osterlund pressed her lips together and forced herself to keep her chin up. She was about to tell her parents something that would cause them to be disappointed in her. Severely disappointed. She wasn't married. Didn't even have any prospects in that direction. Yet here she was. Pregnant. By a man she'd been told to steer clear of for years…

* * * * *

Look out for the next book in Lauri Robinson's
The Osterlund Saga duet, coming soon!

And while you're waiting for the next book, why not
check out her other miniseries Twins of the Twenties

Scandal at the Speakeasy
A Proposal for the Unwed Mother